I'LL WAIT FOR YOU

An Adoption Memoir

EILEEN MARY COYNE RESTA
NÉE: MARIE MONIQUE COMTOIS

CONTENTS

Untethered

Suddenly and for reasons unknown to her she is ripped from her foundation, adrift and looking for the place where she will fit in. She has all she needs for the moment but without a secure base she will not be able to grow from the illusion of normalcy and safety within the four warm, glowing walls to a life of freedom and expansion.

Her beginning seemed secure and filled with promise. A short lifetime of familiar sounds, sights, and smells into which she began to feel the comfort and security of what it is to be "home."

But then a great turmoil began and she felt the shudder of pushing and pulling away from her place of belonging, the place where she fit in perfectly. How will she find that again?

Now she is adrift without the promise of a new "perfect" place. She is without a compass or anchor to guide or secure her. She is powerless to help herself and will have to trust others to find the way for her. When she finally lands she will have to adapt to new and foreign sounds, sights, and smells. It will be up to her to adjust to her new place in the world.

Will the new place be better? Or just different. There will be new and diverse landscapes to be explored, people to embrace, customs to learn and follow. Will the landscape be harsh or mild, the people and customs kind and welcoming or wary of this intruder.

As she floats over the changing vistas she wonders if she has a choice. In her realistic dreams, she hears voices and sees faces as she drifts along waiting to be noticed and secured. Then the sounds change and there is a new excitement in the voices as she becomes aware of everything slowing down. Drifting along with no purpose or end may be over.

As suddenly as she was unanchored and set loose, she is now facing a new attachment in an unknown land. Over time normalcy and safety will be hers along with the freedom to expand her place in the land and grow outward in a new world where she will once again possess the compass and anchor she was missing and feel the comfort and security of a warm and glowing environment where she will again "fit in perfectly."

PART I

THE PHONE CALL

"Hello, Mrs. Coyne?"

I didn't recognize my maiden name because the caller pronounced it with an accent. The date was February 22, 2011. At that time, callers soliciting products or services had started coming in on my cell phone. So I said,

"No, you must have the wrong number." As I was about to hang up, the caller said,

"Wait, Mrs. Resta?"

"Yes, this is Mrs. Resta."

"My name is Nadia. I am calling from the Centre Jeunesse in Sherbrooke, Canada.

I am the social worker who has been assigned to your case. I have your adoption files here with me...I think I can find your mother and she has been looking for you!"

All my life I've known that I was adopted but I never intended to look for my birth mother. Here I was, 61 years of age, and over the last five years my curiosity and desire to find biological information, or even a reunion, kept gnawing at me.

In 2011, my husband Frank Claude (I and the family call him Claude) and I had been married for 40 years and had two children: Eric and Elise. Eric has one son, and Elise and her husband Mike have two sons and a daughter.

So on that day, February 22, 2011, I was off from work for President's week visiting my daughter Elise, my son-in-law Mike, their new daughter Evelyn who was born on February 1, and their sons Jackson and Owen. We were in her living room and she was in her rocking chair nursing Evelyn when my cell phone started ringing. Jackson and Owen were playing with their toy cars in the playroom.

As soon as I heard this I slowly floated to the floor; but as I did I asked her to hold on. In a higher than normal-pitched voice, I exclaimed to my daughter...

"Elise, they think they can find my mother and she has been looking for me!"

Elise and I just stared at each other in disbelief. Tears welled up in our eyes.

I could hardly breathe. I ran upstairs so I could concentrate on what Nadia was saying.

She told me that my birth mother had looked for me several times over the years--in 1949, 1951, 1957, 1986, and 2002. Nadia explained that she has phone numbers from 2002 that she will call to try to locate her. Also in my files was a letter that my birth mother had written long ago asking for help in finding her baby girl who she had to give up for adoption. She said her investigation will take time since the last number she has on file is nine years old. Besides having the phone numbers as leads, she would also get information from the medical card that every Canadian citizen must have.

Nadia shared that my birth mother was 20 years old when she gave birth to me so she would be 81 years old. There was the very real and sad possibility that she had passed away during the last nine years.

"I'd like to ask you some questions. Do you have time now?" she asked.

"Yes!" I was happy to say.

She then interviewed me about my life. She asked me about my height, weight, hair and eye color, education, my parents, my husband, children, and work. When I told her my height, weight, hair, and eye color Nadia said,

"It sounds as if you take after your birth mother because everything is the same except she is a few inches shorter."

This bit of information, revealing the looks of my birth mother, and Nadia's comment gave me a feeling of contentment. Adoptees often wonder if they look like their biological mother, and I wondered also. I never expected to find out.

The American Adoption Congress in a study of American Adopted Adolescents found that:

72% of adoptees want to know why they were given up for adoption,

65% of adoptees want to meet their birth parents, and

94% of adoptees want to know which birth parent they look like.

When I started this search, I was looking for biological information. Now I was faced with the decision, should I actually pursue a reunion? It quickly became an easy decision for me after learning that she had looked for me. I often wished I could write to my birth mother to let her know that I was safe and happy and that I felt I understood her decision to place me in the orphanage. From when I was very young I would feel sad that I couldn't let her know. I never believed a mother could give up a child and not give it another thought. I would think of her on my birthday and hope she was happy.

Nadia said she would follow all leads to find out if my

birth mother was still alive and where she is living. She would be working on my case and would call me as soon as she had any information. She told me,

"I'm so excited about the possibility of finding your birth mother, and because of her age, the search will be accelerated."

"Can you tell me my birth mother's name?" I asked.

"I'm sorry but no," she replied, "first I must find her and obtain permission to disclose any information."

My adoption papers listed my birth name as Marie Monique Comtois but I always wondered if that was truly my birth name.

"However," she said, "I am happy to send you not only a copy of the letter written by your birth mother and translated into English but also the original in French and in her hand-writing."

She added that all the names will be blocked out to protect her identity and the identity of her family.

Still, I will be able to read what she wrote about wanting to find me. I could hardly believe this was happening. Soon I will have something written in my birth mother's handwriting.

So I waited the rest of the day hoping for more news. In retrospect, it was unreasonable to have expected information so soon but I couldn't imagine how I was going to be patient.

This began a 7-week period of emotional ups and downs as Nadia followed a trail of leads attempting to locate my birth mother.

News of Nadia's phone call spread through our family causing excitement and joy for everyone.

Claude and I, Eric and his son Cash, Elise and Mike, and their children, Jackson, Owen, and Evelyn all live in the same town. We see them often and they knew I had started a search for biological information in September, but we didn't talk much about when we might hear back and what information I could hope to receive. The link between biological information and the health implications for future generations was not known in 1949 so perhaps medical information was not requested from my birth mother and therefore is nonexistent.

And not for a minute did I ever think my birth mother was looking for me.

Besides our immediate family, my father-in-law, Frank, and my sisters-in-law Martine and Corinne and their families also live in our town. Claude's mother passed away in 1995. His sister Anne-Marie lives out of state. My brother Brian's children, Brian and Kellianne, also live out of state. We kept everyone up to date from the beginning about my biological search starting when I first thought about going to Montreal, deciding to go through with the application process, and up to now, knowing about my birth mother's search for me.

LUCKY ME

Lucky me! I have been saying that my whole life. I feel that way when I think that in 1949 I was adopted as an infant from an orphanage in Montreal filled with babies needing homes, by a mother and father so happy to have their little girl.

My parents were very open about my adoption from Montreal. I was three months old, born there on June 6, 1949, placed in an orphanage, and adopted by my parents, Mary and Owen Coyne, and brought home to Brooklyn, NY, on September 9, 1949.

Since 2008 I was feeling a strong pull to visit the city of my birth, Montreal. In 1972 Claude and I visited there and I remember loving the vibrant, cosmopolitan city. Unlike the recent, increasing curiosity about my birth there, finding birth information or family was not at all on my mind at 23 years old when I innocently called my mother, Mary Coyne, from Montreal to tell her how we were enjoying the city and I heard silence and a long pause before she asked,

"Are you looking for someone there?"

That question was all I needed to understand how hurt she would have been if I were to look for my birth family, and made me realize the fear she may have felt about the possibility of my finding them.

I never intended to look for my birth family. Most adoptees are encouraged to believe that their birth mothers, after giving birth and giving their baby up for adoption, kept their pregnancy and baby a secret. She may have married, and had more children, and to suddenly appear in her life could be very disruptive to her and her family. You may not be met with the kind of acceptance and joy that you would seek.

I didn't want to cause trouble; neither for my birth mother nor my parents, who adopted me and raised me with love and care. I also did not want to think of how it would feel to be rejected by my birth mother. These thoughts became my beliefs, and I would come to the same conclusion every time; that it just isn't worth it.

1972 was the last time Claude and I were in Montreal until July 2010. There were many more thoughts about my birth there than I admitted to myself. Even though my mother shared as much information as she knew, I was still curious and had more questions.

So although in 2010 I believed I was going there just to experience Montreal, in retrospect, I think I was unconsciously looking for something to connect me to my birth.

Why, at 61 years old, did I suddenly feel the need to pursue this search for more information? I can't explain it but it started long ago with the wish to let my birth mother know I was happy and having a good life, and that wish never went away.

My father Owen Coyne passed away in 1964, my mother Mary Coyne in 1992, and my brother Brian Coyne in 2004. That was my family. Those who may have been hurt by my seeking information about my birth family had passed. It would not be hurtful to anyone should I pursue this. So there were really no more obstacles preventing me from searching for biological information, and perhaps even a birth family reunion. There was no excuse now for me to ignore what I was feeling.

When we visited Montreal in July of 2010, we stayed at the Hyatt Hotel in the heart of the city. Just outside the hotel, there was a summer street festival and for two days we enjoyed everything it had to offer: food, music, dancing and street performers.

I looked out the window of our 18th-floor hotel room, saw all the beautiful old buildings, and wondered aloud,

"Wouldn't it be fun to find the building from where my parents adopted me?" Finally, I was acknowledging my curiosity and longing for more experiences related to my birth.

THE SEARCH IS ON

After deciding to go forward with this search, initially only for biological information, everything fell into place with nothing but help coming from every agency and person we met. At first, we didn't know where to start. Which agency would be able to give us the answers to our questions? At the hotel, Claude and I went online to see if we could find out where we should begin our search while in Montreal.

The online sites directed us to the information desk in the National Library and Archives of Quebec. We left the hotel and headed over to the Library, located only about three-quarters of a mile from the Hyatt. We entered through the revolving door and saw the information desk to our left which spanned the entire outer wall. The ceiling looked to be about three stories high. In front of us was a very long escalator leading up to the next floor.

There were several people behind the information counter and after saying,

"Good Morning", followed by "Bonjour", it was time for

me to state my purpose. This was my first official step and I blurted out,

"I was adopted in 1949 in Montreal, and I would like to find the building that was the orphanage at the time."

They all stopped what they were doing, accepted my request, and went off in different directions, returning with many books. They were all written in French, but they were happy to translate for us.

They photocopied all the buildings that would be possibilities. From there we ruled out some of the places because of the age of the children who would be in the orphanage. Some were for children from 0-2 years or 3-5 years, etc. So we narrowed it down by age knowing I was adopted at 3 months old.

We drove to one building that was outside the city, but soon realized that could not be it since my mother, Mary, told me she was in the city of Montreal when she adopted me. After driving to two other possibilities, we decided on one in particular because of its location in Montreal and the outside structure of the building.

When my mother told the story of arriving at the orphanage to adopt a baby, she described the broad steps leading up to the large wooden double doors of a three-story brick building. She also talked about the nuns, most of whom only spoke French, who were caring for the infants. Over the doors, etched in glass, was the name, Soeurs de la Miséricorde. This particular orphanage in Montreal was run by the Catholic sisters. Although the name over the doors wasn't part of my mother's story, we would come to learn about it and know for sure this was the building.

Eileen on the steps of Soeurs de la Miséricorde Orphanage
July 2010

At the library, we were told to go to the Centre d'Archives de Montreal for more information, which we did, but the person there gave us the number of Centres de la Jeunesse (Batshaw) where we could request forms that were needed for us to obtain birth information and/or forms to try and find my birth mother. I left there unsure of whether I would take the next step.

On the walk back to the hotel we were deep in thought and barely noticed the festivities going on in the streets.

At the hotel, as we were preparing to go to dinner, Claude went online and found a website for the Soeurs de la Miséricorde. The foundress of this mission was Rosalie Cadron-Jette and it dated back to the 1800s. The mission of the Sisters was to take in unmarried, pregnant women who were rejected by their families and society, and care for them with compassion and love. These young women of the 19th Century were treated as outcasts, and their babies would face the same harsh judgment, so the young mothers were given no choice but to relinquish their child for adoption.

Although there are no longer any active orphanages, there was the Soeurs de la Miséricorde Convent and Museum listed online with pictures depicting a typical orphanage in 1949. Seeing the pictures was overwhelming because it was exactly how my mother had described it to me. She told me that the orphanage had three floors of cribs, each crib containing a baby. On each of the three floors, the white cribs were lined up in rows. She said it was like shopping for a baby. It's an analogy that conjures up a picture in my mind of people milling about the cribs, assessing each baby, and either rejecting or accepting the child.

When I called the phone number listed for the Soeurs de la Miséricorde to ask about seeing the museum, I was directed to Sr. Jeannette, who spoke English. She said that she was unavailable until one o'clock the next day, but that she would love for us to come and view the museum. She had been in the orphanages in Montreal and other Canadian cities since 1948. Sr. Jeannette said she was working in the orphanage in Montreal at the time. Was she there in the orphanage when I was adopted in 1949? It was unbelievable that I would be connected to someone who was working in the orphanage while I was there. We were very happy about the prospect of getting a first-hand account of what it was like then.

4

"EVERY ONE OF YOU COUNTED"

We were up early, mapped out our route to the museum, and planned the trip to arrive at 1 p.m. to meet Sister Jeannette. Montreal is an island and the museum is located to the west of Montreal on the Prairie River. For the past three days, we enjoyed the location of the Hyatt Hotel in Montreal because it is just a short walk to the St. Lawrence River. These two rivers surround Montreal. We drove out of the city of Montreal and into the suburbs.

On the way, we found a small florist where I bought a bouquet of flowers for Sr. Jeannette.

We found the museum and convent easily and pulled into the circular driveway. There are two buildings to the left and right of the circular driveway. The first is the museum which is round and modern looking. The second is the convent which is a stately, multistoried brick building where we would meet Sr. Jeannette.

We entered the large reception area, and as we were telling the receptionist about our appointment, Sr. Jeannette arrived in the lobby. I would describe her as petite, energetic, and happy to meet us. Her life has been one of service to others, caring first for young mothers and their infants, and now caring for the elderly Sisters of the convent.

When we spoke the day before, I told her about my adoption in 1949, and how the pictures I saw online look exactly as my mother described the orphanage when she adopted me. She said that many others have come to the museum also seeking history and information about their adoption.

Sr. Jeannette told us that the sister who usually conducts the tour of the museum was on vacation and that she was filling in for her. Ironically, the other sister doesn't speak English! We were so lucky to have come when Sr. Jeannette was there. Not only because of the language, but also because she is a warm, loving, beautiful person and we are fortunate to know her. She explained the mission of the sisters through the years, and as she guided us through the museum we were touched by the love these sisters gave to young women who were ostracized and disowned by their families, pregnant and without emotional or financial support.

The museum is a detailed replica of the rooms in the orphanage so clearly described by my mother. There are wax figures of the Sisters tending to the children, sleeping babies in identical white cribs, and toddlers playing with blocks and toys on the floor. It is reminiscent of a day care center with the Sisters overseeing the welfare of the young children. Sister Jeannette shared many stories with us about her experiences caring for pregnant young women and their babies. It was the way unwanted pregnancies were handled at the time, but it caused so much pain to those separated from their child and to the child separated from knowing who they are. It was all done with the best intentions, and no one foresaw the depth of the loss to mother and child.

Sr. Jeannette shared the history of the order of the Soeurs de Miséricorde—their mission was one of mercy for unmarried pregnant women who were homeless and had no resources to care for themselves or their unborn baby. When it was started in the 1800s, even the Pope and the Catholic Church would not support their mission. They believed, at the time, that by supporting these young women through their pregnancy, they would be encouraging promiscuity and sin. Some of the circumstances of the young women becoming pregnant were frightening--rape and incest. There was one bishop, Bishop Bourget (1799-1885), who believed in the mission, and because of him, they were able to continue.

These missions provided shelter and food for young women who were destitute, rejected by their families and society. During their stay with the sisters, they were taught skills they could use to find employment after they gave birth. Still, they had to relinquish their babies at birth, knowing the stigma both mother and child would face in society.

We were in the elevator during our tour when I offhandedly commented to Sister Jeannette,

"I never thought there would be records about me and my birth after 61 years."

She stopped me, turned me toward her, took me by the shoulders, looked straight in my eyes, and said,

"Every one of you counted!"

We were all in tears. It was a comment that has resonated with me since that day. I think many adoptees may feel as if they didn't count, knowing that the occasion of their birth was not one for celebration but more likely,

"Let's move on and make this better!"

A rebirth of sorts to an unrelated family, but one in which you will be chosen, celebrated, and welcomed.

I told Sister Jeannette I would not want to disturb my

birth mother at this point in life if in fact, she was even still alive. She said that might be a wise choice. She shared with us some stories of adoptees that have come to the museum and convent seeking information about their biological family and a possible reunion. Many of them experienced rejection by their birth mothers who did not wish to reunite with their birth child. Since I was feeling hesitant about a reunion, she reminded me that I could just apply for biological information and not ask for a reunion.

She gave me a number to call to request the forms to apply.

She guided us to a large room off the lobby of the convent where the crypt of the revered foundress of Soeurs de la Miséricorde, Rosalie Cadron-Jette, is located. There she placed the flowers we brought and we all said a brief prayer.

Eileen and Sister Jeannette

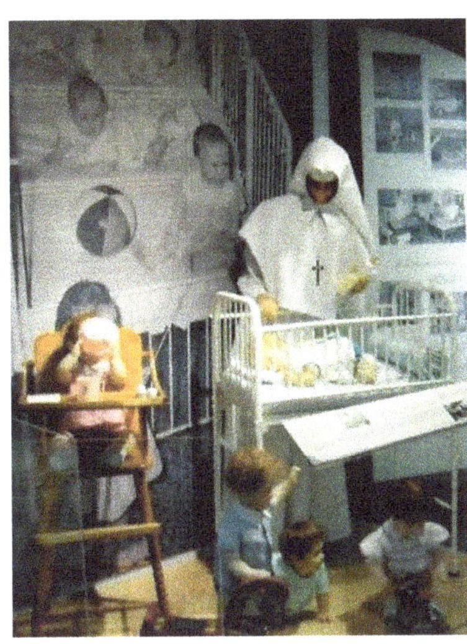

Museum Soeurs de la Miséricorde

5

APPLICATION RECEIVED

In September of 2010, prior to Nadia's phone call in February 2011, I sent in the application to Centre Jeunesse requesting information about my birth family. On the form, it asked if I wanted them to try to find my birth mother. I indicated on the application that I would like to write to her.

Shortly after sending the application, I received a reply in the mail from the social worker, Nadia, letting me know she would be working on my case. I could expect it to take 6-8 weeks for them to find information. In fact, it took 5 months! There were no files for me in Montreal, Canada. They were in Sherbrooke, Canada and they would transfer my request there.

Periodically I would try to find information about my birth family, but they were half-hearted attempts. Most of the time I denied wanting to find information. In the 90's I found a website (which no longer exists) where you could register that you were looking for your birth family and families could register that they were looking for their child. They listed girl or boy and the date of birth. Periodically I checked that site looking for myself.

Claude and I were looking at my baptismal certificate which is from St. Patrick's Church in Sherbrooke, Canada. (Adoptees are not given their birth certificate.) We decided to call and ask if the priest whose name is on the certificate was still there, but no one knew him.

At the time I didn't know that I could contact the Centre Jeunesse in Montreal and obtain an application seeking information or a reunion. Even when I was given the phone number in Montreal to call for an application, I didn't think I would call. It was finding Sister Jeannette and the Museum for the Soeurs de la Miséricorde that finally gave me the courage to pursue my birth family.

Claude was always supportive and encouraging. Without him, I don't think I would have pursued my birth history. He has been with me throughout this search, not just with his encouragement, but taking time to help me research. He is the one who found the museum. He always believes in the power of love and is not afraid to take a risk. He doesn't think of everything that could go wrong, he thinks of everything that will go right!

Eileen in Montreal - July 2010

Claude in Montreal - July 2010

❧ 6 ❧

THE LETTER

When Nadia called in February 2011 she told me that my birth mother had looked for me many times over the years and had written a letter requesting information about my adoption. Nadia said she would send two copies of the letter; one translated into English and typed by the Social Services Department and one in my mother's handwriting.

When the letter arrived, Claude and I were overwhelmed with emotion as we read it. The most startling revelation was when she wrote,

"If I could just see my little Monique before I die and know that she is well." I looked at Claude and said,

"She named me!"

What a feeling. Now I was overwhelmed again with a sense of urgency. We had to find her as soon as possible and I could only pray I'm not too late.

The letter was translated from French by the Centre de Jeunesse.

10-4-86

Hi Mr. Dube,

Following calls and researches everywhere trying to find my little daughter that I have to give up for adoption. I was young and poor at this time, my father had passed away and my mother was working hard. We were four kids.

Later, I got married and I tried everything I know to find my daughter but without any success. I read about reunion with biological family and I finally learned from the Social Services Centre in Montreal that my daughter was transferred to the Social Services in Sherbrooke for adoption.

I live in hope to know if my daughter is fine and if she is happy. I would like to know if she would like to know who her biological mother is. For me, it would be the most beautiful dream to know if she is happy before I die and to see her because every time I see a girl who is about her age, I am wondering if she could be her, my little Monique that I dream of hearing from her.

She was born on Ayrd Street, a private little clinic in Montreal East. It was a real nightmare. We were treated like criminals. I would like to tell her how much I love her, how much I miss her through the years and that I have tried everything I could to find her. I wish God will help me in my search.

I beg you to try to find her so I can know, at least, she is doing fine and she is not unhappy as I am right now.

Thank you.

I trust you even without knowing you. I am waiting to hear from you soon with a lot of hope. Thanks again.

Was my birth mother still alive? We were all wondering and praying that she was.

The following is the original handwritten letter in my birth mother's handwriting.

Châteauguay   10-4-86

Bonjour Monsieur Dub[...]

Suite aux appels téléphoniques et de recherche un peu partout pour retrouver ma petite fille que j'ai due laisser en adoption j'étais jeune fille je n'avait pas de moyen à ce moment étant célibataire de fille ma mère travaillait nous étions quatre enfants nous vivions très modestement Plus tard je me suis marier et j'ai essayer tout les moyens que je pouvais pour la retrouver sans jamais avoir aucune réponse. J'ai lue dans certaine revue au sujet de retrouvaille j'ai essayer partout pour enfin recevoir une réponse du Centre Services Sociaux de Montréal Métropolitain me disant qu'elle avait été   transférée au Centre des Services Sociaux de l'Estrie

pour Adopté i Je ne vie que d'en
l'espoir de savoir si elle va bien
et heureuse et si de son coté
peut être aimerais savoir qui est
sa Mère Naturelle pour moi ce serait
le plus beau rêve avant de mourir
de savoir si elle va bien et de la revoir
puisque quant Je vois une fille a peu
près de son âge Je me demande
toujours si ce ne serait pas Elle
ma petite Monique dont Je rêve
d'avoir des nouvelles puisqu'aujourd'hui
presque tout est possible).
    Mon Nom
    Mde Mireille Comtois nom de fille
elle est née sur la rue Aird petit clinique
privée dans l'est de Montréal un vrai
cauchemar nous étions traité comme
des criminels J'aimerais tellement
pouvoir Lui dire combien Je l'aime
qu'elle m'a toujours manquée et que
j'ai essayer surtout faire pour la retrouver
et j'espère bien que Dieu m'accordera
ce grand désir que j'attend depuis si

long temps.

Je vous supplie d'essayer de la retrouver pour que je sois au moins rassurer qu'elle va bien et qu'elle n'est pas aussi malheureuse que moi

merci à Garance

89 rue Marguerette apt 104
Chateauguay P.Q
J6J-5L8

Téléphone 514-693-9548

J'ai une grande confiance en Vous sans vous connaitre

J'attend des nouvelles avec un grand espoir.

merci encore

7

CHOOSING THEIR DAUGHTER

The word was out in the Flatbush section of Brooklyn in 1949 that there were babies available for adoption in Montreal, Canada.

My mother and Father were friends with Teddy and Virginia who were interested in adopting a child. My parents shared their experience of adopting my brother from the New York Foundling in 1945, however, they knew there weren't many babies available for adoption in the United States anymore, and the wait for a baby could take years.

Together the two couples decided to send the necessary application to La Societe de Rehabilitation Inc. in Canada. It wasn't long before they heard back, and they were able to plan a "road trip" to Montreal to adopt their babies. The friends drove their own car, but my parents and they planned to "caravan" together throughout the trip and to the orphanage.

My parents took the trip from Brooklyn, New York to Montreal, Canada looking for their baby girl to complete their family. When my mother Mary told a story, it was like being transported in time.

They arrived at the orphanage, a three-story brick building with double entry doors. Inside they saw the Sisters of Miséricorde walking up and down the rows and rows of white cribs checking on the babies. My mother, father, and Brian walked along looking in at the babies, some sleeping and others awake. As my mother Mary tells it, she stopped at my crib and a feeling came over her that I was the one. I was sleeping at the time so my eyes were closed. My father and brother were lagging behind, but she had already decided. When my father came to her side and looked in, my mother said to him,

"I wish her eyes were open so I could see the color."

She was hoping they were blue or green since my father and brother had blue eyes and hers were green. She thought it was best if we all looked somewhat similar. So they waited with anticipation for me to wake and open my eyes.

"Brown eyes!" my mother said. She looked at my father and said,

"Oh well, your father had brown eyes!"

So, hearing this particular story, I clearly imagine the three of them at the foot of my crib, peering in and deciding that I was the one even with the wrong eye color.

Many times I have thought about this scene and wondered why.

"Why me?"

"What made her stop at my crib and decide I was to be her daughter?"

When I asked her that question as a child she said I had a "cute button nose." As I grew I would tease her that choosing me for my nose didn't work out for her since I have anything but a "button nose." She would laugh and tell me she loves me AND my nose!

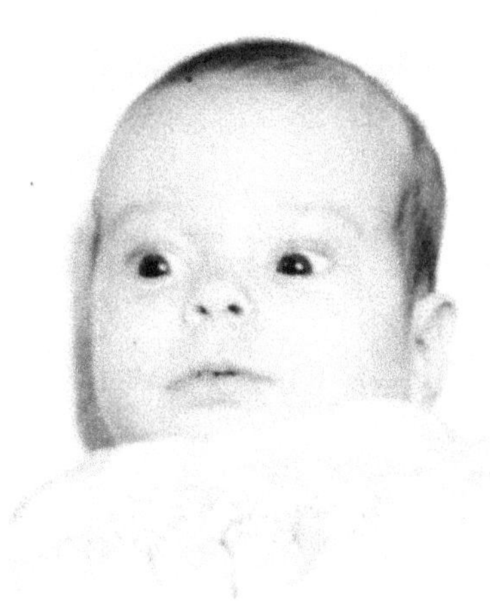

Eileen in the orphanage at 3 months

Their friends, Teddy and Virginia also found their baby that day, a boy they named Alex. Recently I was going through some old letters and photos and I found a letter written by Alex's mother to me after my mother died in 1992. It was a heartfelt letter in which she shared her memories about my mother's kindness, thoughtfulness, and sense of adventure, but I was very interested in seeing the last name on the return address. I remember visiting them at their house and meeting Alex when we were about 11 years old. They still lived in Brooklyn at that time. After finding the letter, I used google to search for Alex. He had passed away about five years before and was living in Florida at the time of his death. There was an extensive obituary and it was heart-warming to know that he had an excellent and very successful professional and family life. He had a sister, two years younger who I met on one of our visits to their house. His parents went back to Canada two years after they adopted Alex and adopted his sister. I wasn't sure Alex knew he was adopted so I wouldn't have contacted him. It was my curiosity that made me look him up. I would think about him through the years. He was with me in the same orphanage and adopted on the same day. I didn't expect to find that he was gone.

My father holding me and my mother holding Alex March 1950

From <u>Orphan Train</u> by Christina Baker Kline, "Your life begins when you are chosen." The beginning of my life as an adopted baby was a good one. I was only three months old and had not suffered any neglect. We know how the first year of life can impact a person's ability to love and cope with problems as they grow. I was off to a good start.

They brought me home from Montreal to their apartment in Brooklyn, NY. My father was an NYC Detective and my mother was at home with my brother, Brian. Everyone was so happy and my brother was very proud of his new sister. After they took me home, my brother was still in charge. When someone would come to see me, his new sister, they would have to ask his permission. He would go to my room, tiptoe in and look into my crib.

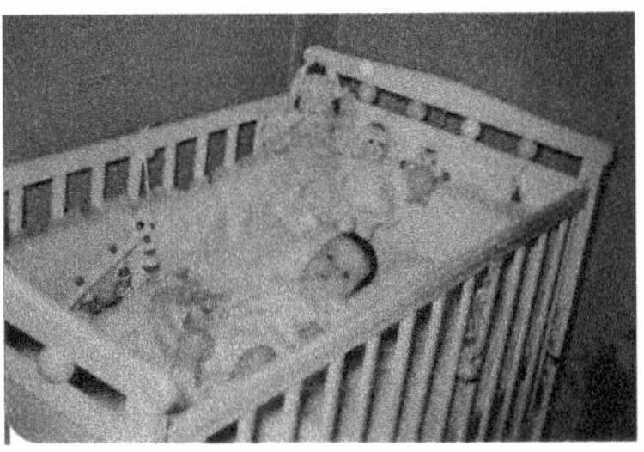

Eileen at home in Brooklyn September 1949

Then he would run back out to the door of the apartment and tell them if I was awake or asleep. He was my first protector. As an adult, he used to say,

"Hey, watch your language. I have my little sister's picture in my wallet!"

So began a beautiful time for my parents. Their family was now complete and the one they had imagined. My mother was the supreme homemaker and would tell me how she would iron my dresses and hang each one, perfectly done, on a line across the dining room. I am sure I wore more than one dress in a day. I love to look back at pictures of us posing on the streets of Brooklyn on our way to a daily adventure. We looked as if we were going somewhere—not just shopping. From what my mother told me, this was the social scene. Everyone would take the children out in the afternoon "on the avenue."

My mother Mary with me at 11 months and Brian at 6 years old "On the Avenue"

Eileen at 11 months and Brian at 6 years old

My favorite picture is of my mother and father, my brother and me sitting on my Aunt Mae's couch. Aunt Mae was my father's oldest sibling. It must have been one of our Sunday visits. I just arrived in the family, maybe a couple of months, and it's such a happy family picture. My mother did not have a secure, loving childhood and her dream was to create one for her family, providing for her children what she didn't have. Her contentment is plain to see in the photo. My father was one of nine children. He was the second oldest and had a lot of experience with young children. He truly loved children.

Owen, Brian, Eileen, and Mary Coyne 1950

8

MY BROTHER BRIAN "ONE DAY AT A TIME"

When I got on my brother Brian's nerves, as only a little sister can, he would say,

"I should have closed the drawer!"

My brother was with our parents, Mary and Owen, when they went to Montreal to adopt me. He was five and a half years old when they told him,

"We're going to adopt your sister and you are going to pick her out."

Although our parents weren't educated in child psychology or the products of sensitive upbringings, they somehow knew how to make us feel secure about being adopted.

In 1949, after my parents and brother chose me in the Montreal orphanage from a roomful of babies in cribs, they brought me to a hotel room where we would spend the night. Hotels didn't accommodate babies back then so the dresser drawer was my crib for the night. Brian would tell me that he remembered that night and seeing me in the drawer. It became the funny link to us starting out as brother and sister.

My adoption story is one that had a good beginning. I was only three months old when I was adopted and had only spent two days in the orphanage. My birth mother had kept me with her for the first three months of my life so I was nurtured and loved.

My brother's adoption story was very different from mine and the circumstances of his birth and subsequent neglect adversely affected his life. In 1945, after applying to the New York Foundling for a baby to adopt, Mary and Owen finally received the call they had been waiting for. There was a baby boy for them to meet!

A few days later, excited and hopeful, they arrived at the orphanage and the social worker brought them my brother Brian, a 13-month-old toddler. They were expecting a baby boy but told us,

"As soon as we laid eyes on him we knew he would be ours."

He had been in foster care since he was born on March 17, 1944, and this was now April 9, 1945. His opportunity for an earlier adoption was delayed because his birth mother didn't want to give him up for adoption and was desperately trying to find a way to keep her son. Women had little choice in the '40s and '50s and fathers were not held responsible for care or support of the children. He had been severely neglected and hadn't met some milestones that would be expected in a 13-month-old. He could not sit up steadily and was kept indoors in a crib for most of his life with little stimulation or loving contact.

My father was holding Brian and talking to him. When he had to hand him back to the social worker, Brian held on to his lapel.

"Well, it looks like he chose us!"

Brian still holding on to our father Owen 2 years after his
adoption – Brooklyn May 1947

In preparation for the day when our parents would take Brian home, they had to consult with an eye doctor for special glasses before they could bring him outside. His eyes were extremely sensitive to light but in time he would adjust.

They say the first year of a baby's life is most important. A solid loving beginning can set you up for an emotionally stable life. An insecure beginning can forever impact your ability to love and be loved.

Our parents brought him back to their apartment in Brooklyn and with the care and advice of many doctors, he did really well. Our mother would tell us how he loved to play with his cars and trucks and was such a happy and good boy.

Kindergarten was the beginning of life being difficult for him. He didn't like being away from home and was very unhappy. It was impossible for them to get him on the bus. He was just too frightened. Our parents would drive him to school but when they arrived, he would try to hide in the back of the car. When they moved from Brooklyn to Queens they hoped he would be happier there in St. Kevin's School. When I look at pictures of my brother through the years in

Queens, when he was 7 until 14, I can see when he was about 10 he started hiding his emotions, forming a sort of protective mask. School must have been a hard place for him, one where he never felt successful and there was no help. When he was only ten he started getting into trouble in spite of our parents trying to help him. They took him to a psychiatrist who labeled him "an all-American boy." He had serious issues that were never recognized or addressed. After I became a teacher and experienced first-hand all the help and interventions that are available to students today, I wished my brother could have had that help. Back then school was more about discipline and less about emotional health.

Eileen (age 5), Brian (age 10), and Ricky (Foster child)

Eventually, my brother was introduced to alcohol. My parents didn't drink alcohol but my brother discovered it with friends in the neighborhood. Alcoholism wasn't widely understood back then. Most people thought, if you can hold a job and function, you were in control. In fact, it governed his life and affected him and those who loved him. He married for the second time in 1974 and had his two children, Brian and Kellianne.

At 37 years old, after he and his wife divorced, he went to his first AA meeting. He told us later that it was his daughter Kellianne at 5 years old looking up at him and saying,

"Daddy, why are you drinking beer?"

That innocent comment gave him the courage to go to his first meeting. AA was the forum he needed to stop drinking.

"One day at a time," he would tell us.

Brian and Kellianne were very close to us during those trying family times and Claude and I, Eric, and Elise loved having them spend time with us at our house. Weekends were fun when they would all play together and we loved watching them grow.

Because my mother, their Nana, only came to New York infrequently, and she wanted to see them more often, she paid for her four grandchildren's plane tickets and the six of us went to Florida for Thanksgiving to visit her and enjoy a Disney trip while we were there.

Brian and Kellianne are wonderful, loving adults with beautiful children of their own, and we feel so fortunate to have them in our lives.

Through his life Brian never drank at home; he always went to his favorite bars where he would see his old friends. It appeared that the AA meetings replaced the bar setting and became the safe place for him to go whenever he needed to connect with friends who would accept and befriend him.

Brian embraced the 12 step program and sought forgiveness from those he may have hurt during his drinking years.

He was working toward redeeming himself, and we were all so happy to see him rebuilding relationships.

One addiction he was not able to overcome was smoking. On September 25, 2004, he died at 60 years old due to COPD and emphysema. My children were 28 and 26 years old at the time, and Brian's children were 30 and 27. My children and his children were very close cousins throughout their childhoods spending many weekends and vacations with us.

Brian died on our 33rd wedding anniversary at 3 p.m. This was extraordinary and memorable because every year on our anniversary, my brother would send us a beautiful floral arrangement to mark the occasion and then in his inevitably irreverent way, a funny card expressing his sympathy to us for having to endure many years of a married life.

Brian was living in Florida since the late '70s and his children eventually moved there to be near him. Claude and I and Eric and Elise went to Florida for the funeral, and although my children were close to their uncle, they didn't know the extent of his involvement in the AA chapter where he lived in Florida. I told them how he mentored new members of AA and was on call for them whenever they needed him. We would often have our phone conversations interrupted by callers beeping in needing to talk to my brother, their mentor.

There was a service for my brother at the AA meeting room, and the place was packed. When we arrived, we saw a man in the parking lot changing into a Jets Football uniform. Brian was a diehard Jets fan and actually had a "Jets room" in his house filled with memorabilia.

We were all seated and this man in the Jets Football uniform went up to the podium and exclaimed,

"Brian saved my life!"

He went on to give an account of my brother Brian's life-changing deeds and his friendship that helped him stay sober and would continue to guide him going forward. He counted on my brother's on-call availability day or night to stay on the phone with him or meet him somewhere and talk him through his crisis. He told us,

"I would only put this uniform on out of respect for Brian. As you all know, I'm not a Jets fan!"

The room erupted in sounds of agreement. Brian and he had a friendly football rivalry.

So began a stream of one person after the other speaking about my brother Brian and how he saved them. My children and we were crying as we heard of how their uncle, my brother, had helped change and impact so many lives, helping them to live "one day at a time."

He sought forgiveness and redemption and we know he found it.

Brian and Eileen 1985

❧ *9* ❧

FAMILY LIFE IN BAYSIDE, NY
1951-1958

My father worked shifts as a New York City Detective in the Homicide Division of the 90 Precinct in Brooklyn so he was home at times when many other fathers were at work. There are many pictures of me with him during that time in Bayside. My mother was always busy with the house—I never remember her playing with us at that time of our lives. She was the one who was always planning for our future. She worked from home to make money. In those days there was a job for women at home stringing beads. I can't imagine what that was all about, but I remember her telling me how she helped make the payments on the house.

We also had foster children who lived with us. I only remember one. Her name was Ricky and she had very long hair that my mother would braid for her. I don't remember very much about her stay with us except that I was happy because I had someone to play with. Did I understand what it meant to be a foster child rather than an adopted one? I really don't know. Maybe not consciously but probably on some level I suspected I was the lucky one.

Mary, Owen, Ricky and Eileen – Easter 1955

We also had a girl around my age who was not a foster child stay with us during the week and her mother would take her home on the weekends. She never wanted her mother to leave.

One Sunday evening I remember her mother said,

"I promise I will not leave you here overnight. Look I'm leaving my shoes here on the floor by the bed. I'm just going downstairs for a little while."

My bedroom had twin beds and the little girl, who I don't remember other than from this memory, was sitting on one bed and I was in my bed looking at her crying and begging her mother not to leave. I kept looking from my mother to the little girl to her mother trying to understand what would happen. I remember thinking,

"Is this ok? Why doesn't she just take her home with her?"

We both finally settled down and went to sleep but I woke

to the little girl crying again because the shoes and her mother were gone. Both the little girl and I really believed her mother but how would she ever believe her mother again?

When I asked my mother why her mother lied to her she said she had to go to work and had no one at home to care for her. She was a single mother and knew she would be safe with us until she came back to bring her home for the weekend.

My family was very proud of their Irish heritage. My parents had parties in the backyard in the summer, and it seemed as if all my relatives played a musical instrument. I'm sure it was just a few but it sounded like more since everyone sang too. My father played the violin; he called it the fiddle. I was so young but I remember going to sleep to the sounds of Irish music. I'm sure everyone was dancing the jig out there in the yard. My father was always dancing and I was usually dancing with him, standing on his shoes as he led me around. My bloodline may be French, but my soul delights in Irish music.

My parents had a very progressive marriage for the times. When my parents were dating, she worked at the New York Life Insurance Company. In those days (1937), once a woman married, she had to leave her job. My mother was not happy with that, but she married and dedicated herself to setting up her first home as a married woman. Once she had everything just so, and no baby was coming, she decided to get a job. Although many men at the time would not allow their wife to work after they were married, my father did not restrict her.

One job she told me about was in a restaurant at or near Ebbets Field, the historic baseball park where the Brooklyn Dodgers played. One day she made a mistake on the bill for one of the customers. Her boss started yelling at her, but the man she had waited on intervened. He said,

"She made a mistake! That's why erasers were put on pencils!"

Then he left her a very generous tip. She never forgot the kindness of that stranger.

During World War II, help was needed in the war office. A Gallup poll in 1936 reported that 82 percent of the respondents believed that wives with employed husbands should not work outside the home, and three-fourths of the women polled agreed. However, one in every ten married women entered the work force during the war. My mother worked there for a few years and I remember her telling me how much she loved it. Not only the work part and feeling useful, but she made many friends there as well.

My mother took care of all the finances at home, but they shared many of the household chores. My brother and I never thought it unusual when we would find my father vacuuming or cooking. When my brother and I were older, my mother worked outside the home. They seemed to have it worked out very well. My mother was ambitious and wanted to continue to make a better life for us all.

She told us that when she was a little girl there was a doctor and his wife who lived in a house near them. My mother and aunt were fascinated with this big, stately doctor's house and would walk there for a visit. The woman didn't have children and sometimes she would invite them in to see the house. She would show them her jewelry and my mother said she vowed that she would have pretty things when she grew up. And she wasn't afraid to work for it. She wanted to give my brother and me what she didn't have. She was fearless and had faith. She didn't wait for someone to make her life better—she depended on herself to make life better. When she found she could not have children, she knew she would adopt. She told me my father said,

"Don't worry, Mary. I grew up the second oldest of nine children, if it's just you and me, that's ok."

Owen Coyne with his mother and sister Circa 1930

No, she would not be happy without children and she knew he wouldn't either.

She had a hard childhood, as many did during the years from her birth in 1913 until she married my father in 1937. She was two years older than her sister Catherine, and as with many siblings, the sisters had different personalities. My mother was a tomboy and a self-declared "fighter." My aunt was compliant and the model of decorum. They lived in a "cold water flat" apartment in a tenement building which was typical housing for the immigrant population of the city.

When she was eight years old a neighbor offered my mother 5 cents to climb up the laundry line pole to reconnect her clothesline that had broken away. Imagine walking among the tenement buildings in the 1920s and as you looked up between the buildings, hanging over the stark cement court-yards; you would see and hear the lines and lines of laundry extending from windows to poles, waving and flapping in the breeze. This neighbor lived on the third floor of the apartment building and her clothes line, when connected, stretched across the cement courtyard. My mother, always the entrepreneur, agreed to take the job. She saved any money she could earn, usually from collecting bottle caps, so she could go to the movies.

Just as she was completing her job, her father was walking home from work and saw her three stories high, her long strawberry blond hair blowing free, straddling the upright pole which held all the laundry lines for the tenement apartments, reaching to connect the line.

Rather than panic and yell at her, he very calmly called out,

"Hello, Mary. Come down. Be careful and take your time."

She could hear her father gently coaxing her and he was not angry. She was an adventurous nine-year-old girl who was not afraid and rather brave. When she told me this story it was clear how she could still recall the look on his face, filled with concern for her safety.

Then as he exhaled in relief he said,

"Please do not do that again. It is dangerous and I don't want you to be hurt. If anyone offers you 5 cents to climb like that again, I will give you 10 cents not to take the job."

This memory was one that lasted a lifetime for my mother because in that moment she felt his love for her and her importance to him.

Their mother, my grandmother, favored my Aunt Catherine because she was more passive and easygoing than my mother. My mother and aunt were very close sisters and their closeness lasted a lifetime. As children they had to share a pair of roller skates, but my aunt was younger and even though she didn't want to skate, she didn't want to give up what belonged to her.

"Would you like me to get you a piece of bread and butter as a trade for the skate?"

Lucky for my mother who loved to skate, my aunt always agreed to the trade. My aunt, now with bread and butter in hand, had strict instructions to wait there on the stoop until my mother returned. She skated away just in time to catch a passing delivery truck as it careened down the city street. Grabbing hold of the back corner of the truck she got the free ride she loved.

"Your mother was a daredevil and I was afraid of everything," my aunt told me when I was old enough to understand.

My brother and I were skeptical when our mother would tell us her daring skating stories. One time when we lived on Francis Lewis Boulevard in Bayside, my mother, Brian, and I were all in the finished basement of our colonial-style house. My brother was ten years old and I was five. The flooring was green, square linoleum tiles, and I had just been skating around and into every corner of the basement. She was tired of our disbelief of her skating talent so she put on skates and scooped us up, one in each arm, and skated all over the basement with us in her arms. We were laughing and screaming. It was not such a big basement so there were many turns and spins. It was rare to see our mother play like this and Brian and I just kept looking at each other with wide eyes and open mouths.

When my mother was nine years old and her sister was seven, they received the worst possible news. Their father had drowned at work. What a terrible blow to them all. He worked for the city on the garbage barge, and they were told he fell off and was lost in the ocean. When my mother and aunt were old enough to understand, their mother told them he was having a problem with one of the other men on the barge and she thinks he was pushed off. What a horror to think about. He was only 30 and their mother was widowed at 29.

There was no social security or support for widows back then so their mother took in laundry, cleaned apartment buildings, and took in borders newly arrived from Ireland. When their mother cleaned the apartment buildings, my mother remembers sitting with Catherine on the steps of the buildings waiting for their mother to finish her work.

We had just moved to Bayside, NY, when my father became very ill and almost died from two different illnesses. I don't know which illness came first. He had spinal meningitis and was in the hospital with a raging fever. My mother told me that the doctors had to "pack him in ice" in the hopes they could bring his fever down. They told her to go home; they didn't expect him to live. My poor mother went home to wait for a phone call and be with my brother and me. Brian was seven years old and I was two. She told the story that she couldn't sleep so she went outside to walk around the house saying the rosary over and over. She startled the milkman as she came around the front of the house at 5 am. When she went back into the house, the hospital called to say that his fever broke and he was out of danger.

But the peace of that happy news didn't last for long. He had a second brush with death when they discovered he had a benign brain tumor on the pituitary gland and it was inoperable. Luckily, they were able to give him radiation to shrink the tumor and again he recovered well.

We lived in that house from when I was 2 until I was 7.

10

AGE OF REASON

They call it the "age of reason." It was May of 1957, and I was seven years old. I was living in the United States from the age of three months but I was not yet a citizen of the United States.

"It's time for you to become a naturalized citizen." My mother announced one day.

"What does that mean?" I asked.

There was preparation to be done although I only remember making sure I could say the Pledge of Allegiance without any mistakes. Of course, I knew the Pledge of Allegiance. I said it every day in school, but now I would have to recite it in a court of law in front of a judge.

What if I made a mistake? Would they send me back to Canada? Deem me unworthy to be a United States citizen? I remember having these scary thoughts so becoming a citizen was not something to be excited about but rather an important performance. I could not disappoint my parents and I could feel my mother's apprehension.

The day was here. We drove in our 1949 green Plymouth sedan to the courthouse. I loved that car. No such thing as seatbelts; I rode in the back seat in the middle, with my arms on the back of the front seats, and my head sticking through. In my mind, I pretended that I was driving, looking at the road and reading all the signs.

We walked into the big city courthouse and I remember the inside more than the outside. It had a large, cavernous lobby that echoed your footsteps when you walked. It was a very hectic place, but everyone walked with such certainty and appeared to know exactly where they were going. I hoped my parents knew where we were going! It was very imposing I would say now, just frightening I would have said then.

We entered the courtroom from the lobby and through the back door of the courtroom. There were seats on either side of an aisle and at the end of the aisle was a huge, wooden, looming structure. At first, to my young eyes, it looked like it could be a wall but it stopped short of the ceiling by a great distance. On top of this structure, I could see a man's head and his arms stretched out on the top. It was something like a desk I thought, but way up there. I knew I was only a small child, but I felt invisible standing there in front of the judge.

But then I realized I was not invisible because he spoke to me. He said,

"Good Morning."

His hair was gray, wispy, and sticking out at different angles. He looked very serious as he looked over his half-glasses to observe me looking up at him. I have a picture of myself from that day and my hair was sticking out all over too —maybe it was a windy day.

As soon as he said good morning to me I began as if on cue, to recite the Pledge of Allegiance. As I began, he put one hand out and said,

"Oh not yet, you will say that later."

And everyone, including the judge, chuckled that chuckle adults do when children make a mistake and they think it's so cute. It wasn't cute to me. It was my first mistake and I wondered how many more would be allowed.

After the amusement settled down, he became very serious again. He began to shuffle the paperwork before him and again looked over his glasses, his eyes resting on mine. He proceeded to guide me through the rest of the ceremony. Repeating after him, I recited the "Oath of Allegiance" where I renounced allegiance to any other country. Then, finally, it was time and I recited the Pledge of Allegiance without hesitation or error.

After completing these requirements I was taken with my parents to another room where my picture was taken and my official papers were presented to us. The importance of these papers was not clear to me at the time, but I learned their importance as I grew and applied for my passport and marriage license. The papers were proof of my belonging.

Every time I have needed to present this paper and I have to look at myself as a seven-year-old, my mind brings me back to that distressing ceremony. My picture is a picture of fear and anxiety. I do smile at it now though.

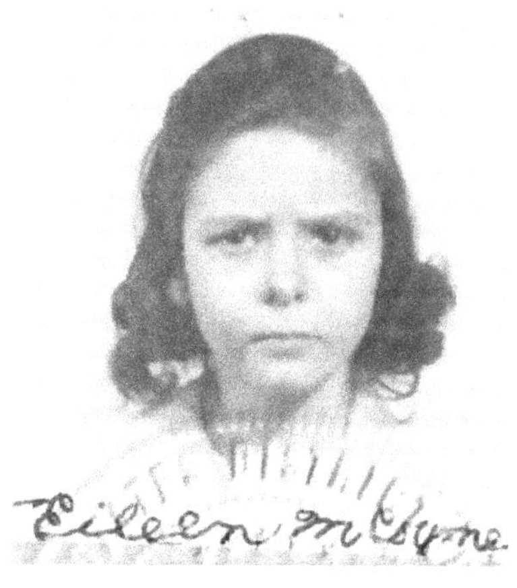

Certificate of Naturalization Picture

When I taught first grade, I had a student in my class who had been adopted from Russia. His mother was my class mother and that year was his year to become naturalized. He had a date for the ceremony and subsequent celebration in the spring. Of course, things had changed dramatically since 1957. The ceremony was child-centered and shared with many other children who were being naturalized that day. There were balloons, music, and food. It was like a birthday party. In the days leading up to his celebration, we shared books and information about what it meant to become a United States citizen and his classmates were very interested. We all wished him well and afterward his mother brought in pictures from the celebration that she shared with us during a celebratory snack time in class.

I do wonder to this day where the judge was in my student's ceremony on Long Island. Was he mingling about with the new citizens? I don't believe there was a traditional judge's bench. They were not in a formal room at a courthouse, so perhaps he stood at a podium with a microphone and addressed the room from a level standpoint.

I hold nothing against my serious, slightly disheveled judge. Things were not as child-centered then as they are now. I am thankful he did his job well and I became a United States citizen.

BAYSIDE, NEW YORK TO
GREENLAWN, NEW YORK

My father drove the 1949 green Plymouth from our house in Bayside to his job at the precinct in Brooklyn. The 1949 Plymouth was his "baby." He loved that car and I remember it so well. He would push a button on the dashboard to start the engine while he would pump the gas pedal. He would talk to the car, pleading with "her" to start so he could go to work. Even after the front driver seat collapsed back into a permanently reclining position, my father took an old milk crate and propped it up behind the seat. That was fine with him but not for my mother who knew it wasn't a safe repair. Soon after, they must have gone car shopping while I was at school and when I came home there was a new Plymouth in the driveway. It had to happen eventually, but now the car was just transportation. The old Plymouth was a relationship.

He loved his job and was nicknamed "the confessor" because of his quiet, calm way of questioning the suspects. Back then "roughing up" the suspects was the norm, but he did not believe in that approach. He subscribed to the Boys'

Town philosophy of Father Flanagan, founder of Boys' Town of the 1940s.

"There's no such thing as a bad boy. There is a bad environment, bad training, bad example, or bad thinking."

My father's approach, when possible, was more like that of a counselor.

My father was happy living in Bayside, Queens; it was an easy commute for him from there to Brooklyn. However, my mother was always looking to move up. At that time, the growing suburbs on Long Island were booming. It was 1957 and there was new construction everywhere. She had heard about Huntington, Long Island, and decided to look for a new house for us out there. My father was concerned because, as a city employee, he was required to live within the city limits. Nevertheless, he agreed to consider moving. This was very hard for him because he would have to use his sister's address in Howard Beach as his residence for work. He was the most honest person I have ever known so I'm sure he was never comfortable with this arrangement, but he would do anything to make my mother happy.

They found a house in Greenlawn in a new development named Fountainvale Estates. My mother wanted to live in Huntington, but the house she loved was in Greenlawn which is part of the Township of Huntington. I was 8 at the time and Brian was 13 so moving to a brand new big house was an awesome adventure for us. My parents, Brian, and I would hop in the car and head East on Long Island to see the model homes and find the right one for us. Then after they purchased the house, we would take Sunday drives to Greenlawn to watch the construction. I loved that part. I remember seeing the foundation completed and the framing go up. We would drive on 25A East from Francis Lewis Boulevard to

Huntington and then take Park Avenue South to our new development.

Just before Cold Spring Harbor, on a big curve on 25A, there was a drive-up snack stand with benches and tables outside. We would always stop there for a hot dog and maybe something else but I only remember the hot dog. We never ate out so this was a big deal for me and Brian.

Finally, in early Spring 1958, we moved in. I don't know the date but I do remember I was just 8 years old. My brother was 13. All the streets in our development were named after colleges, and we lived on Duquesne Drive for the next seven years.

Whenever my father worked nights, I would sleep in his bed in my parents' room. They had twin beds which, as we saw from many shows in the '50s, was not uncommon. Whenever he would go to the barber, there was a certain after-shave or hair product that would emanate from his pillow and I loved it! It made me feel close to him when he wasn't there. My father was a gentle, loving man who knew how to relate to children. He was often home in the morning and would wake me up joking and then make me breakfast. There was almost always music playing.

Eileen and her daddy

Eileen and her daddy

There was little opportunity to ride my bike when we lived in Bayside since our house was on a major four-lane road. It wasn't until we moved to our new housing development in Greenlawn that I could ride from one wide street to another, some flat and some hilly, without ever going onto a main road. My bike that we brought with us from Bayside was not only too small but had tires that deflated after only one ride around the block. I rode that bike every day; it was my favorite pastime. As I rounded the corner with my house in sight and tires hissing, there was my father at the end of the driveway ready to pump up my tires so I could have another go around.

He was all about his love for his family, and this was just one illustration of many where he taught me that actions speak louder than words. Finally, that Christmas, my mother, and father presented (surprised!) me with a new, beautiful Ross bike. And it was exactly the right size for me. Maybe I should not have been surprised by this gift, but I was for two reasons.

First, it was winter and we used to get a lot of snow which was not conducive for bike riding.

Second, my birthday is in June, so I reasoned with myself

that most likely a new bike would be mine for my birthday which would guarantee very nice bike riding weather.

Christmas morning all our presents were opened so I was not expecting anything. Then they sent me to the garage on a bogus but believable errand, and there it was with a big bow on it. It was a beautiful metallic blue with a headlight, and a small metal rack on the back fender to transport anything I needed. After all of my father's dedicated, tire-inflating afternoons, I think it was a gift he appreciated almost as much as I did.

12

MY FRIEND CLARE

Clare and I recently talked about when and how we met. At first, our memories differed, but after hearing and thinking about the timeline of dancing school classes, I realized her version was correct. I thought we met in dancing school, but she reminded me of meeting on our bikes one day when she was visiting another friend, Nancy. It was before I was enrolled in dancing school.

It was a usual non-school day for me; get up, get dressed, have a quick breakfast, and head out on my bike to see what friends I would find riding and playing that day. Our neighborhood was filled with young families so there were usually many kids around. As I turned the corner of my street onto Nancy's street, Hofstra Drive, I could see Nancy at the end of her driveway talking to a girl on her bike. Since this development of houses was built on farmland, there were no mature trees, just little saplings planted by the builder. We had unobstructed views that stretched the length of every block. This added to the safety of our bike riding since we could see a car pulling out of its driveway in plenty of time for us to stop. As

I approached, Nancy waved and I stopped to say hello. She introduced me to Clare and we all decided to go riding together. That was the beginning of our friendship. Although we remained friends with Nancy, Clare and I quickly became "besties." Clare and Nancy were 10 and I was 12.

Our mothers became friends too and we would freely bike or walk back and forth between our houses during the days we played together. She remembers coming to my house the first time and meeting my mother and father. I discovered through the years how much my friends liked talking to my mother. I don't know if it was her stories or that she showed interest in them by asking them questions about themselves, probably a little of both. My parents were quirky. My mother was a Lucille Ball-type, a little flamboyant, and my father loved to tease and sing to everyone. Because of my father's rotating work hours, he was often home during the day and that was unusual for fathers in the early 1960s. When my friends came over they would be surprised to see him home.

One day my mother and Clare's mother had a conversation, and the happy result of it was that my mother learned about the dance studio where Clare was taking class every week. When we lived in Bayside, NY I was enrolled in dancing school and took ballet classes once a week. I was only six years old, but I really did love it. After we moved to Greenlawn, I didn't dance for a few years. It probably wasn't in the budget since my parents just bought a new house and car. After speaking with Clare's mother about the dancing school and witnessing all my improv dancing around the house, my mother asked me,

"Would you like to take dancing lessons again?"

"Absolutely yes!" I said as I danced away.

My father took our only car to work and as a detective, his work schedule differed from week to week so we couldn't count on having the car. Clare's parents had two cars so they were available and agreed to drive when needed. Because of that, my parents were able to enroll me in class with Clare. After a few months of the larger class, Clare and I started taking semi-private lessons and we really loved that. Sometimes our giggles got out of hand but Miss Roberts, our teacher, was patient with us.

The dance studio's name was Andre and Bonnie's of Huntington. The owners, Mr. and Mrs. Andre, and their partner Bonnie, ran the school and also taught the classes. Mr. Andre was French with his beautiful accent and Mrs. Andre was American. My friend Clare and I thought they were exquisite and as young girls, they reminded us of movie stars. He was handsome, she was beautiful, and they were both sweet and kind. They walked as if they were always dancing; very straight posture and very light on their feet.

The building was a charming, two-story house with a large addition on the front of the house for the studio. The building is now an architect's office. The house is still charming and well-maintained, and the office occupies the same square footage as the studio but it is updated with a new tasteful brick façade.

Inside, the studio was spacious and very professional with floor-to-ceiling mirrors that caught the dancers' reflections as they pirouetted across the highly polished oak floors. At the end of the room was a balcony with seats that were graduated stadium-style and from there the audience wouldn't miss a single grand jete.

The Andre's would put on a show twice a year for the parents and friends of their students. The shows were varied and exciting with many different genres of music and dance. One of the teachers, Miss Sandy, had been a choreographer for the Radio City Rockettes during her career. I loved being one of the dancers in a show that was choreographed by Miss Sandy and included many of the stunning elements of a Rockettes routine. It had a well-timed kick line and a finale that made the audience cheer.

Eileen third from left, bottom row – Andre's "Rockette" Show

Clare could not be in this show with me because it was going to be an evening show for adults. Mr. and Mrs. Andre would also be performing and only students 16 or older would be included. I was 16 but Clare was only 14. It would have been so much fun to have her with me, and I knew how disappointed she was. The day of the show her mother brought her to the show to see me anyway, and I felt so happy to have them in the audience.

There was to be another show that Clare and her mother, Jean, would be there for me.

In 1963 I was 14 years old and a sophomore in Our Lady of Mercy Academy when Sister Mary Denis approached me after music class, and again after our glee club practice, to tell me that she would like me to perform in the upcoming yearly talent show. She knew I had been studying dance for many years and she was looking for students to join in and support her effort to make it a full and varied show.

"Oh, no!" I replied, "I could never get up on stage in front of everyone."

She looked at me, not too kindly, and said,

"Eileen, your parents have paid for and supported your love of dance; don't you think you owe them the joy of seeing you perform?"

Oh boy. There it was—the persuasion by guilt approach. I could never stand up to that. Besides, she was right. It would be a joy for my parents to see me. So in my smallest voice, I meekly said,

"Ok."

Without another glance in her direction, I set off down the hall seeming to run from that decision while my mind raced with thoughts of how I would prepare for this and have the courage to perform. I had performed at my dance studio with a group of dancers but I had never had a solo performance.

The preparation for my high school talent show began with first choosing the music and then choreographing the dance for my solo performance. I chose *Waltz of the Flowers* from The Nutcracker by Tchaikovsky and began choreographing by listening to the music over and over as I visualized the steps and combinations I would use. The three performances were scheduled for Thursday, Friday, and Saturday nights. Since my father was working on Thursday night, my parents decided to attend the show on Friday night. I was so happy that my friend Clare and her mother were in the audience to see me on Thursday night.

My memory of that performance is as clear today as it was that night. Such a memory engages all the senses and lives forever in my mind. Standing backstage, I watched as the previous performer took her bows to the cheers and clapping of the packed, standing-room-only auditorium. Up to that last minute, I think I was denying the reality that I would be out there alone on the stage.

As she left the stage, the curtains closed and I quickly walked to center stage in preparation for my dance. Kneeling and bent over on the floor, I was a flower bud not yet opened. On the other side of those curtains, I could hear murmuring and laughing from the audience enjoying their evening. Then the metallic sound of the track of the curtains opening as the audience became silent in anticipation. The music started and I began to perform the dance I had choreographed and practiced for two months, at home and at my dance studio. In my mind, I blocked out the audience and imagined I was dancing alone in my living room. As I completed my performance, the clapping and cheering from the audience brought me back. Oh, the feeling of relief as I curtsied and the curtains closed.

In the end, I was thankful to Sister Mary Denis and her encouragement because that performance provided a much-needed boost to my self-esteem. At the end of that school year, a picture of me on stage appeared in the yearbook with the caption, "Best Dancer." It validated the memory of my first and last solo performance and was the only picture of me from that night. When I think of all the videos, selfies, and pictures taken at children's and other events today, it seems unbelievable that not one other picture was taken but at least I had that one to share with my parents.

Eileen's one and only solo performance, Waltz of the Flowers
- November 1963

The Thursday night show was a great success and in school on Friday I received compliments on my dancing from other students and my teachers. It was a special day until after lunch when, as we were all in our classes, we heard the static from the PA system and a long pause before the principal came on to say she had terrible news to share. Our president, John F. Kennedy had been shot and we would all pray aloud for him. We were 500 students in my high school and every one of our voices could be heard in unison through the hallways and over the PA. It wasn't long after that we received the horrible news that our president had died. Replacing the sound of prayers was crying and overwhelming sadness. I don't remember the rest of the day at all. The news was devastating. Of course, the remaining two talent shows were canceled and my parents never got to see my performance. I had mustered the courage to go through with the performance, only to have the two people I most wanted to see me, never see the show.

This thought was quickly forgotten though as my family

and our nation mourned the sudden violent death of our President.

⚜

Dancing and bike riding were favorite pastimes for me and my childhood friend Clare. We loved our bikes and would venture out early in the morning, come home for lunch and then head right back out for the afternoon. To this day whenever Clare visits we drive around our old neighborhood and marvel at our good fortune to have grown up in such a great development. Even though we went to different schools, we were (and still are) best friends. I remember us having the freedom to ride our bikes from street to street, and to the playground at the local elementary school. There were some high hills in our development, and over and over we would race up and down them. And when we weren't racing, we were performing. Since we were both in dancing school together, we would do our arabesques down the hills, no hands. We were athletic, but really lucky too, because we never fell and no one wore helmets then. Our daily rides demonstrated, "practice makes perfect."

Recently I asked Clare when she remembered me telling her I was adopted. She said that one day in my room, under the watchful eyes of my many dolls, I told her.

She had to bring up the dolls again in this remembrance because she always found them creepy, the way they would just sit there on the shelves looking down. Whenever we would have a sleepover, after I fell asleep she would get up and turn them all to face the wall.

When we moved to Greenlawn my brother and I were told not to tell anyone we were adopted. I was able to keep my secret until after Clare and I became friends, and I knew she was someone I could trust with the truth. We were prob-ably 11 and 13 years old then. She says at first she didn't believe me. Then she said,

"Oh, that's why you look so different from your family."

I remember feeling relieved that I could share such an important part of who I was with my best friend and find that it was no big deal.

Most adoptions during those years of the "baby scoop era-1945-1972" involved secrecy, shame, and lies. The young unwed mothers were often lied to as they were promised care but not always told that the "payment" for the care would be giving up their baby. Adoptees were told that their birth mothers were happy to move on and know their baby would be in a good home. Studies have proven that to be false and in fact, most birth mothers mourn the loss of their baby, often for life. Some adoptive parents posed as the child's biological family and enlisted the help of extended family and friends to maintain the deception. This backfired on families when a member of their "close" confidantes would decide to reveal the truth to the child, causing the child to discover that their whole life was based on the most fundamental untruth since birth.

Our parents believed in truth and transparency regarding our adoption and only asked us for secrecy when they knew from experience that it would protect Brian and me from those who had no understanding of adoption.

After my revelation to Clare, it wasn't on our minds except we would marvel at how she resembled my mother and I resembled hers. When the four of us went out together we would pretend (and our mothers would play along) her mother was mine and mine was hers.

My mother and Clare's mother both loved classical music. There was always music on in my house; show tunes, sad Irish ballads as well as jigs and beautiful classical. Huntington High School had a concert series, and they decided that the four of us should be members. Clare and I loved to get dressed up as if we were going to Lincoln Center instead of the local high school, but we felt so grown-up and appreciated the beauty of it all. Of course, we were young so we were given to fits of giggling during the performance which prompted our mothers to give us those killer looks. We both remember one time when a particular piece was becoming so quiet as to be fading away when suddenly the cymbals clashed and Clare and I looked at each other as we shot up and flew off our seats. We were in a heap, laughing uncontrollably and trying to swallow the sound of our laughter. Luckily the music was rising to a crescendo as our mothers were trying to help us get ourselves under control, but they could hardly control themselves either after watching us.

We had an excellent childhood when we lived in Greenlawn until Clare and I both experienced serious family trouble. The events of her mother and father divorcing and my father dying happened within a year of each other. As a result, she and I had to move away from each other and our muchloved Greenlawn neighborhood and homes. I stayed on Long Island and she moved to Hempstead, a town about 30 minutes from Greenlawn. Two years later she and her mother moved to Manhattan, but we were always close in heart. Her mother Jean, who I loved as another mother, passed away when Clare was only 19. Clare was not on the road with her dancing career yet, and I was working in Manhattan at the time, so we had a lot of time together especially through her mother's last days.

Clare went on to become a professional dancer and as dance captain for Shirley MacLaine, she traveled and danced all over the world. It was an exciting career and we easily maintained our friendship through the years even though our lives were so different. Whenever she was home in her Manhattan apartment, she would travel to Huntington to see me and my family. Eric and Elise still remember visiting her in the city when they were very young. Everyone loves it when Aunt Clare visits, especially me after almost 60 years as my trusted friend.

Eileen and Clare

13

ELEMENTARY AND HIGH SCHOOL

My Grandmother, who Brian and I called Nana, was my mother Mary's mother, and our only living grandparent. She lived in the St. George Hotel in Brooklyn Heights for many years. In the 1950's the hotel was failing and welcomed the elderly as residents. It was once the largest hotel in New York City. My parents had their wedding reception at this hotel in 1937 so it was already a part of their history.

While my grandmother lived there she would occasionally visit us in Bayside. My father would pick her up after work and bring her to us for a day or so. She would bring us the hotel soaps, and I loved those soaps because they were small and fit my hand so well.

About two months after we moved into our house in Greenlawn, my mother received a phone call from the hotel manager concerning my grandmother. He and some staff were noticing behaviors that led him to believe she was no longer capable of living there alone. My parents didn't hesitate and brought her to live with us.

After seeing the doctor, she was diagnosed with dementia;

they called it "hardening of the arteries." She was only with us for about a year before my parents knew they could no longer care for her safely at home. She kept leaving the house at all hours and wandering the streets. As much as we tried to make sure she didn't leave the house, sometimes it was late at night so we weren't always successful. Fortunately, the neighbors knew about my grandmother and would call us if they saw her.

On a few occasions, she called me to her room to look out the bedroom window with her.

"Eileen, come here. See that white house over there? My mother lives there and I'm going to visit her this afternoon."

At eight years old, I believed her and later told my mother what Nana said.

"No, Eileen. She is remembering when she was young and close to her mother."

When she wandered away from our house we discovered that she invariably walked to that white house. She was looking, and probably longing for, her mother. Our Nana was from Ireland and came to the United States as a young 18-year-old woman. That was probably the last time she saw her mother and now she wished to see her again.

After my mother found our house in Greenlawn, which is in the township of Huntington, she told me an interesting story. We were driving into Huntington to do some errands when she said,

"My mother came to the United States from Ireland when she was eighteen years old and worked as a housemaid for a doctor and his family on High Street, in walking distance to the town of Huntington."

"Really? Is that why you wanted to move here?"

"No," she said, "it just happens to be where the new

affordable houses are being built right now. I never thought I would live in Huntington."

Then she went on to share a story her mother told her about working for this family.

My grandmother told her that she was sent into town to pick up some groceries that would be waiting for her at a particular shop. She arrived at the shop, paid for the packages, and was on her way back to the house when she smelled the most horrible smell emanating from one of the bags. She stopped by a bench and began to remove some items from the bag when she discovered the source of the odor. It was a hunk of cheese that was the problem and thinking it was rotten, she threw it in the "gutter." Upon arriving back at the house she entered through the kitchen door and gave the two packages to her employer who quickly looked through and said,

"They forgot to give us the cheese."

My grandmother answered,

"Oh no, the cheese was in there but it smelled horrible so I threw it away on the way home."

Her employer was very unhappy to hear that and explained to her that the cheese she threw away was Limburger and it was supposed to smell that way.

My mother thought that was such a funny story and she loved to tell it, especially because she happened to like Limburger cheese.

I didn't know my Grandmother very well. She rarely visited us and I don't remember her being at any holidays at our house. Later on, when I was older my mother explained that she and her mother were never close and her mother favored her younger sister. My grandmother spent all the holidays with my aunt and her family rather than with us. My mother and grandmother had a contentious relationship and after my grandfather died when my mother was nine, things only got worse. My mother was the scapegoat and was blamed for everything.

The most shocking story to me was about the day my father went with my mother to my grandmother to ask for her permission to marry and she told him,

"You're marrying the wrong sister."

He replied,

"Oh no, I'm marrying the best sister."

In the days leading up to the wedding, my grandmother told my mother she would not be at the wedding.

"Up until I walked down the aisle and saw her sitting in the front pew I did not know she would be there. I didn't expect her and was surprised to see she changed her mind."

There were many other hard times growing up with an unloving mother but my mother and father were happy with their lives and their choices so she didn't dwell on the past.

Then so many years later, when my grandmother needed a place to live my parents didn't hesitate to take her in. My aunt and uncle, the recipients of all my grandmother's love and goodwill, didn't even consider it.

Surprisingly it did not affect the relationship between my mother and her younger sister. She was protective and loving to her throughout their lives.

My mother never wanted to admit her mother into a nursing home, but realizing she was becoming a danger to herself knew it was the safest choice. My parents researched and found a reputable one very close to our home. We were able to visit her often and be sure she was well cared for. A short time after my grandmother arrived at the nursing home, she was diagnosed with leukemia, and she passed away within six months. She was the only grandparent my brother and I knew and we had very few memories of her except for when she lived with us. Later when I was an adult my mother revealed to me that she had never been supportive of adopting children. Perhaps that's why we didn't see much of her over the years, but we know the troubles between my mother and grandmother began long before that.

As a young woman of eighteen, she left her family in Ireland and found employment in Huntington, Long Island where she started her new life in America and lived there until she married and moved to Brooklyn, New York. She raised her family and worked there until she had to return to Huntington at 75 years old to live in our care until her death at 76. Quite an unforeseen circumstance that she ended up where she began in this country, but comforting to think she died peacefully and not alone in a hotel room.

My mother, Mary Clancy Coyne, with her mother - 1940

Brian and I had to keep another secret besides being adopted when we moved to Greenlawn.

We could not tell anyone that my father worked for the city. I hoped no one would ever ask me, but if anyone asked what my father did for a living, I was told I had to say I didn't know. One time, a friend in the neighborhood did ask me. When I said I didn't know, she looked at me a little dumbfounded.

It was very important to my mother that my brother and I go to catholic school. Our parish was St. Hugh's in Huntington Station, New York but they had no room for us at that school. So she looked for another catholic school. She visited St. Patrick's School in Huntington, New York and asked for us to be enrolled there. Brian was in eighth grade and I was in fourth grade. I don't remember the bus transportation that first school year, but after Brian graduated from eighth grade, I had to travel without him. The school was out of my home school district so it required some maneuvering on the part of the bus company to get me to school. One year I took two buses to school and two buses home from school. Each way took an hour.

The first bus would take me from my house in Greenlawn and drop me on the side of the road in Centerport, about a 30-minute trip. From the dirt pull-off where I stood on that road, I could see a gas station across the street and behind me was Centerport harbor. There was nothing else on that stretch of road. I would wait there for about 10 minutes for the second bus to pick me up and take me the rest of the way to school. I was only 11 years old, and I was alone in that "drop off" area in all kinds of weather. It really wasn't a safe situation. Someone must have intervened on my behalf because that bus arrangement didn't last long.

When I was enrolled in St. Patrick's, I was supposed to be in third grade but in Queens, each grade had an A or B session. Because I had already completed grade 3 A, they skipped me to grade 4 rather than back to 3. That was very unfortunate for me since I was a very good student up until then. I don't feel I'm exaggerating when I say that it impacted my entire education and my self-confidence through twelfth grade. It took me until sixth grade to catch up by attending after-school help and summer school. I worked hard, passed the Catholic high school entrance exams in eighth grade, and was accepted to a private Catholic school, Our Lady of Mercy Academy, in Syosset. Still, I was very young and immature. I was sixteen years old in my senior year of high school when most of my classmates were 18. I turned 17 just six days before my high school graduation.

My mother was very proud of me for persevering and being accepted to this competitive high school after all my difficulties in elementary school. This high school was an academic, college prep high school.

My mother told me that our next-door neighbor, who had a daughter in my grade, always felt superior to us. They knew about our family struggles and my initial school difficulties. The day the acceptance letters were delivered to our mailboxes, my mother ran out to see if I had been accepted. She opened the letter and must have jumped for joy! The neighbor was also at her mailbox getting the letter for her daughter, opened it, and read that she was not accepted. She kept saying to my mother that there must have been some mistake. She was saying,

"How could Eileen have made it into the school and not my daughter!"

I had no idea of this rivalry, I think my mother probably didn't want to give me additional pressure about the testing, but I am happy that I was able to make my mother proud.

❧ 14 ☙

MY DADDY

The years on Duquesne Drive when my father was healthy were the best for me. Since he was often home in the morning he would make sure I was ready for school and he would wave from the front door as I drove off on the bus. He was always joking with me. I could be silly with him, and he made me feel important. I went to school happy. My mother would always say he was spoiling me, and he was, with love and affection. She also spoiled me but in a different way. She didn't think my father was strict enough so she would say,

"Someone has to be the disciplinarian around here!"

When I was fourteen years old, my father became ill again. It was the end of my second year at Our Lady of Mercy Academy when he started having symptoms. At first, Brian and I were not aware of his difficulties, and it was my cousin Phil who noticed and alerted us all to his declining health.

My father was a strong swimmer and he loved the water and boating. When he met my mother, he owned a boat and they would go out with friends whenever they could. It was a short-lived pleasure though because my mother would be seasick every time they went out. When she told me about their early dates and her aversion to boating, I couldn't help but think about how she lost her father to drowning when she was only nine years old. Perhaps she was seasick, but maybe also terrified of the water to the point of sickness. Eventually, she had to forgo these trips, and as their relationship grew serious, he decided to sell his boat.

Owen, his sisters, and brothers-in-law and my mother facing backward - probably seasick

My mother and father on the boat at dock

My father's sister Anna, who we saw often, had a son Phil. He was about eight years older than I. My Aunt Anna and Phil lived alone. He had no father in his life. I remember as a child asking my mother about my Cousin Phil's father, but the question went unanswered and the look on my mother's face made it clear I should be quiet. As a child, I had a lot of questions and they weren't always appreciated.

"Stop asking so many questions!" I would hear over and over. When I was a teenager and I would ask my brother questions, his answer was,

"What, are you writing a book? Well, leave this chapter out and call it a mystery!"

My mother and brother were of the same mindset.

My father, I realized later, was Phil's father figure. My father would visit them often in Howard Beach on his way home from work in Brooklyn. Other times we would go there to visit on the weekend as a family. My brother and I loved going there. My Aunt Anna was like a female version of my father. She was happy, funny, and kind. They even looked alike.

Aunt Anna with Eileen on her communion day, 1956

When we lived in Greenlawn my cousin Phil was married and lived not too far from us on Long Island. Phil loved boating and fishing, just like my father. He loved my father and enjoyed taking him out on his boat for a day of fishing. After a day on the water, my father would come home sunburnt and happy.

After one of these trips, Phil called my mother to tell her he thought something was wrong with my father. He explained that he was falling asleep on the boat and appeared to be unsteady on his feet. He was worried about him.

My mother found doctors in Huntington to consult about his condition, but after seeing several local doctors, she decided to go back to Queens to see the specialists there. In June of 1964, he was admitted to Queens General Hospital. The brain tumor that had been dormant for twelve years was growing again. He could not have any more radiation, and surgery was not possible because of the location of the tumor on the pituitary gland. It was a long, sad summer.

My sophomore year in Our Lady of Mercy high school was very demanding. The required classes added up to 9 periods a day. I was taking not just one foreign language but two: French and Latin. Pile on the English Language Arts, geometry, world history, science, and religion (the study of the New/Old Testament), and there it is—I was struggling throughout the school year. I didn't even mention PE, Art, and Music. Those were the relief classes.

The two subjects I couldn't pass were geometry and world history. My grades came very close to passing, but I had to go to summer school for those two subjects that summer. My mother and father dropped me off at my first day of summer school. That was the last time I saw my father standing. I watched from the sidewalk outside the school as they drove away to Queens General Hospital.

Every afternoon after summer school, my mother would pick me up, and we would drive to Queens to visit my father. My mother and I would go in to visit him for a little while then she would take me back to the car and lock me in. I would stay in the locked car in front of Queens General Hospital and do my homework until she returned to the car and we would go home. One time I couldn't get my homework done, and in class the next day the teacher didn't believe my excuse of visiting my father in the hospital. I can't blame the teacher. Probably most of the 15-year-olds without their completed homework would make up any excuse. Still, I remember being very angry with this teacher for not believing me. Later I realized that my anger was displaced. I was so angry that my father was sick.

I don't know how it was possible, but I didn't think he was going to die. Brian was more realistic about it, but I don't remember talking to him at all at this time. He was just always out with his friends. His way of dealing with every-thing we were experiencing was to be absent. We were not close at that time.

Then one night, I overheard my mother and her friend having a conversation in our kitchen. My mother was saying she didn't want to tell me the news about my father's prog-nosis and her friend was insisting that she must tell me.

"She's 15 years old and she needs to know what is going to happen."

I was very grateful for that friend's advice to my mother because I could try to prepare myself. By then my father had been transferred to Huntington Hospital and we were with him every day. He was in a coma most of the time and didn't appear to hear us, but he would come out of it occasionally and talk to us.

My brother was having a very hard time with our father's

illness. He was 20 years old and felt guilty that he had caused my father sadness and embarrassment over the previous five years. My father always believed my brother would find his way, and stayed calm in the face of all incidents. My brother loved him very much and was very sorry for his behavior. He had the chance to apologize and make amends with him before he died. My father told him,

"I forgive you, Brian. I love you, you are my son."

My father was a very devout Catholic and even had an altar with a statue of the Sacred Heart of Jesus in our home that he prayed to every day. I had some very sweet moments with him before he died and he gave me the instruction to always carry my rosary beads with me. I am no longer a practicing Catholic, but I carry in my purse the same rosary beads I had with me that day in 1964.

The anniversary of his mother's death was August 20. He was very close to her, and according to his siblings, favored by her because he helped her care for his younger siblings after his father died. During one of my visits the day before he died, he opened his eyes, looked straight ahead at the hospital closet doors, stretched out his hand, and said to me,

"Eileen, open the door and let the lady in."

He died the next day, August 21, 1964, and it brings us comfort to think that his mother came for him. He was 54 years old. I was lost without him.

After he died I had a recurring dream. In the dream, I was walking in the streets around my neighborhood, and I couldn't find my house. I kept knocking on doors and asking if anyone knew where I lived. No one knew me. Then I saw my house and ran up to the door, but strangers answered, said they didn't know me and closed the door. My father was my home, and he was gone.

We got through the wake of three days and nights (inhumane) and then the funeral and burial. After the burial, I was sitting on the front steps with my brother and best friend, Clare. We heard loud noises and people yelling. Then we thought we saw white doves flying over our heads but after another look, we saw it was just paper and debris. There was a tornado that touched down in our neighborhood two blocks over from my house. No one was home and no one was hurt in the house that was hit by the tornado. I know this sounds crazy but my brother, Clare, and I like to think my daddy was saying goodbye!

✿ 15 ✿

THE MEDIUM

The definition of a Medium is different than that of a Psychic. A medium will be able to communicate with the dead. A psychic also communicates with the spiritual world but predicts the future.

I never had occasion to engage with either a medium or a psychic regarding my loved ones who had passed or to get information about my future. I have friends and family who would regularly see a psychic, and I would say,

"Please don't share with me anything the psychic may have predicted about my life and family."

I prefer my life to unfold day to day and not anticipate a prediction that I may or may not be happy about.

So I was very surprised and overwhelmed when my father Owen, who passed in 1964, found a way to say hello to me in 2018 through a medium. My son-in-law's sister Danielle is studying to become a medium. As part of her studies, she asks friends and family to allow her to give them a session and see what happens. So my daughter Elise gladly volunteered.

During the session, only one man came forward. Danielle reported to Elise that she was seeing a man walking along a sidewalk next to a busy road. He had a group of happy, laughing children with him and there was something about candy.

There were many happy memories from living in Bayside with my brother and parents on busy Francis Lewis Boulevard, but Danielle's vision brought back an especially memorable one.

I always loved candy and milkshakes. I was introduced to them by my father at the corner candy store in Queens on Francis Lewis Boulevard. The candy store was also a soda fountain/diner-type place with stools—a typical 1950's luncheonette. It was our neighborhood place, and we were known by the owner who knew I liked a little ice cream left at the bottom of the milkshake after it had gone through the blender. He would make it special for me, and I would eat that little dollop of ice cream with a long spoon. Once a week, when I was about six or seven years old, my father would walk me to the candy store two blocks down from our house. But he didn't just bring me. Along the way, we would stop at all the houses with children I usually played with, and one by one they would join our parade to the candy store. Only one 5 cent candy per child, and we were all happy with that. Except maybe me who always begged for just one more.

When Elise told me what happened several days later, I was stunned. And a new believer. I was not there that day and even more incredible, Elise never knew this story about my father and me.

Even though my father died when I was 15 years old, I have always felt as if he never left me. I remember telling my mother-in-law that something good always happens in my life around the date of his death. So it was 54 years later that Danielle was able to let me know that we are still connected.

I don't understand it, but it gives me such joy that I will not doubt it.

Several months later, I saw Danielle at a family celebration. I told her how surprised and happy I was at the outcome of her session with Elise, and how meaningful it was to me. We talked about her work as a medium, and I commented that it must be exhausting to be receiving messages from those who have passed. She explained that it usually only happens when she is physically with whomever the deceased person wishes to communicate. Then she said,

"Wait, he is showing me a hat. Do you remember something about a hat?"

"Wherever I hang my hat is home."

This was one of my father's favorite sayings. Wondering where that cliché may have come from, I found a song that was introduced in 1946 in a musical. The music is by Harold Arlen and lyrics by Johnny Mercer. It's called, "Any Place I Hang My Hat is Home." It dealt with the feeling of peace you experience when you get home and hang up your hat, literally and figuratively. My father and I would often walk together on city streets, either in our Queens neighborhood by the IGA or in Brooklyn near the precinct where he worked as a detective. During these walks, I would see him tip his hat to passersby as a sign of respect or as a greeting.

I have happy memories of running to the door to greet him when he would arrive home. The first thing he would do is put his hat and service weapon on the top shelf of the closet. Then he was ready to be home with his family.

"Yes Danielle, showing you a hat was a perfect way for him to get my attention!"

The deep connection between my father and me, though not biological, was rooted in love, trust and mutual respect. Not everyone, whether an adopted or birth child, may enjoy this kind of relationship with a parent, but when they do it may be a result of careful nurturing and not biology.

16

MOVING TO DIX HILLS

My mother was devastated after my father's death. You know how they say you should postpone any big decisions for a year after you lose your loved one? She didn't do that. She told me,

"When I come down the stairs in the morning, I see him sitting in the chair. When I hear the front door, I think he is coming home from work. The memories are too much for me to bear. I am going to find another house for us."

Although I found comfort in the memories and would have been happy to stay in that house, I did not need the house to keep the loving memories. I also wanted her to have a distraction and this project gave us both a reason to get up every day and plan our future. It gave us a mutual goal and kept us close. Whatever life threw at her, she didn't wait for someone else to solve a problem or make her happy; she pushed forward and made the best of everything.

She found a beautiful new house about 10 minutes south of where we lived. I was still able to get a bus to my high school; it was just a 10-minute longer ride which I didn't mind. It was a small bus with one other student a grade behind me, and we would help each other study for exams on our way to school.

Everyone wondered how my mother could afford to move and she would tell me it was no one's business. What I learned was that my parents had decided, after my father's first two life-threatening illnesses, to take out house insurance, in addition to life insurance. So when my father passed away, the house was completely paid for.

Still, there were expenses and my mother needed some additional support, not just financial but emotional. She had a friend named Ada, a longtime friend from when she and my father lived in Brooklyn. She was about 8 years older than my mother and was a widow with no children. She was born in England and worked as the chef for one of the royal families before moving to the United States. She had a lovely British accent that we all tried to imitate. She would entertain us with her rockette style kicks and whip up a soufflé that, much to her distress, my brother and I would not eat. We all loved Ada and her one to two-week visits were one of the highlights of our growing years.

"How did you become friends with Ada?" I asked my mother.

I could see in her eyes how quickly that question sent her back to fond memories from Brooklyn when she was a young wife and mother.

"When we lived in the apartment building in Brooklyn we became friends." Then she explained further.

"Ada would invite Brian and me to tea in her apartment one flight up from ours. Brian loved to visit and whenever we would leave our apartment he would look up the stairwell and say in his little four-year-old voice, 'Ada, can we come up for tea?'"

During that time my mother became ill and unable to care

for my brother full time. Ada was the logical choice and loved caring for him until my mother was well again. That began their long friendship.

After my father died, my mother asked her if she would come and live with us. She moved in and helped us move from the house in Greenlawn to our new house in Dix Hills. In the weeks leading up to our move-in date, we were happy and comforted when Ada agreed to move in with us permanently. It was a big change for her to leave her Brooklyn apartment with its familiar surroundings and conveniences to help our family through these changes.

Our moving date was June 12, 1965, and my brother Brian was getting married on June 20. He and his wife were only 21 years old, and the marriage lasted less than a year, but it was a mutually desired break-up. They both realized their motivations for marrying did not support a good beginning for a strong marriage. He wanted to get away after my father died, and she wanted to move out because she didn't get along with her parents. It was really two kids running away from home.

One of the first nights in my new house in Dix Hills I had a dream. But was it a dream? It felt like a visitation. I was awakened by my father sitting on the edge of my bed.

"Daddy, what are you doing here?"

"I've come to see the house. Will you show me around?"

I jumped with joy right out of my bed and took his hand.

"Yes, I will."

Then he said,

"There's one thing though. You know I will have to leave again, and I didn't come to upset you but to let you know I am still with you even in this new house. Promise me you won't be upset and just be content that we had this time together."

I agreed and when the tour was complete he tucked me in

and we said goodbye. A feeling of great contentment washed over me and when I woke in the morning I was at peace.

From our moving date of June 12 until June 19 I was still in school but I remember everyone working hard to complete the move and settle into our new home. My mother was especially short-tempered and unnerved at the time and Ada was working to help in every way she could. When I look back I wonder why we had to be so driven to have everything perfect before the wedding. It wasn't even going to be at our house.

Throughout all the jobs in all the rooms: hanging curtains, cleaning windows, organizing cabinets, none of us stopped to connect or check in with each other. We were completely oblivious to the depth of Ada's despair. She had a room of her own next to mine and none of us suspected her unhappiness. What I didn't know was that Ada had been taking sleeping pills every night for many, many years. Later, my mother told me she knew Ada was taking sleeping pills but didn't know about the effect they can have on a person's mental health.

The evening of June 19, 1965, the night before my brother's wedding, my mother discovered Ada in her bed, unresponsive. On the nightstand, she saw the empty pill bottle lying on its side. She called 911 as she called out to me. In my room, over the music from my turntable, I heard my mother yelling for me from Ada's room. I ran to her, both of us in our nightgowns and hair rollers.

"Hurry! Get dressed. I called 911. They have to take Ada to the hospital and we will follow."

The paramedics arrived in what seemed like minutes, and my mother and I made sure we were ready to follow the ambulance in our car to Huntington Hospital. Just like that, we went from preparing for my brother's wedding the next day to driving behind the ambulance, blinded by its lights and deafened by its sirens, as it sped to the hospital ignoring traffic lights and weaving around traffic.

Ada was admitted and they were able to save her. My mother and I loved her so much and had no idea she was suffering. It was shocking for us but we had no time to think about it or understand what had happened. We spent many hours at the hospital and once we knew she was stable, we left her there and went home to catch as much sleep as we could before the wedding the next day. When you see a picture of the wedding, no one would ever know by looking at my mother and me what had happened the night before. We must have been in shock because we didn't talk about it. We just carried on and the wedding went off as planned.

My cousin Kevin, me, Brian and Mickey

Brian, our mother Mary and Mickey

After Brian's wedding, my mother and I were now on our own in the new house. We visited Ada at the hospital, but after a short time, she recovered physically and moved home to England to be with her family. We kept in touch by letter, but eventually, the number of letters slowed and then stopped.

After my father's death, selling one house and buying another, planning my brother's wedding, and Ada's near-death in her new home, my mother gave in to her grief and went to bed. I didn't realize it at the time, but later I understood that she was depressed. She still cared for me. She made sure there was food in the house and we would eat together, but she wouldn't go out or drive me anywhere. It was a long and lonely summer for us, but I was able to find a purpose.

All along the north shore of Long Island, there were "gold coast" mansions built from the 1890s through the 1930s. It is reported that more than 1,200 were built during that time and less than a third now remain. One, in particular, has great meaning to me.

Burrwood in Lloyd Harbor was built in 1899 for Walter

Jennings, a director of Standard Oil Company, president of the National Fuel Gas Company, and nephew to John D. Rockefeller. After he died, the house and 32 and a half acres of land was inherited by his son who ultimately sold it to the Industrial Home for the Blind. They occupied the house from 1951 until it was sold for development and the original mansion was demolished in 1994. From the veranda of the stately mansion, one could see the sparkling waters of Cold Spring Harbor and walk down to the beach through beautiful gardens, one named for Helen Keller.

There were about 50 permanent residents, blind or deaf-blind. Throughout the week many non-resident blind persons would visit the home to take part in craft activities, lectures, and music concerts. It was a positive, thriving community and one in which the residents enjoyed their lives. Burrwood had the help of many volunteers including those affiliated with the Lions Club organization.

In June of 1965, I was 16 years old, and feeling the effects of a series of sad family events which left me depressed with no direction and too much time to think. The bright spot at this time was that I passed my driver's test and had access to my mother's car so I wasn't trapped at home where I would have no diversion from my melancholy. On nice days I drove to my friend Jane's house and together we would pick up a simple lunch and drive to the Lloyd Harbor causeway. One side of the causeway was lined with large boulders at the water's edge and there we would sit eating our lunch and watching the boats sail or motor by. Jane and I shared our tales of teenage angst and we were good listeners, but we didn't seem to be solving any problems.

I was a practicing Catholic at that time and decided that perhaps I could get advice from someone in the clergy about recovering from the overall sadness I was feeling every day.

On our many drives to Lloyd Harbor, Jane and I would see The Seminary on West Neck Road and comment on its beauty. Unknown to Jane, one day I decided to call and ask if they provided counseling. I purposely didn't go to my parish because my mother and I were known there, and I didn't want her to be embarrassed or alarmed by my reaching out for help. I needed to be anonymous even though I had nothing life-shattering or dramatic to discuss. I was able to make an appointment with a priest at the seminary and during our talk, he encouraged me to find somewhere to volunteer my time to help others. He suggested several places but Burrwood Industrial Home for the Blind caught my interest and I decided I would investigate that opportunity. Jane and I drove by Burrwood often and marveled at the elaborate and stately iron gates that flanked the entrance to the former estate. The priest knew Burrwood welcomed volunteers and gave me enough information to assure me that I could comfortably begin the process of volunteering my time.

I decided to call for more information, and after a brief phone interview the director outlined ways I could be of help to the residents, and we set a date and time for me to begin.

The residents enjoyed a walk outside on nice days, and after introductions, he or she would take my arm as we walked out of the building. One of my very important instructions was to always stay next to the steel pipe railings that lined all the paths around the building and down through the gardens which the resident would hold during our walk. This would give him or her peace of mind to know we were on the approved paths of the estate.

During these walks, they would strike up a conversation with me. They were very interested in me as a 16-year-old and wanted to hear about my school life and plans for the future. It was like spending time with grandparents who showed interest in me and then shared stories about their youth and life in the early 1900s. They talked with pride about their families and also about their life at the home and its fulfilling events and activities.

One of my favorite activities was to read to the residents whenever they received a letter from a friend or loved one. Often they would ask me to read it several times and I loved to see the smile on their faces as they relished the latest news from home. If they were ready to answer the letter, I would be their scribe.

My time and sight were a gift from me to the residents, but their gift to me was an experience that enriched my life, gave me purpose, and helped me through challenging times. Although my time there was only for the summer, the impact of it has never left me.

I still drive by those gates periodically on my way to Cold Spring Harbor, but since 1994 it's a private development of large homes without public access. To jog my memory I look at pictures online and remember walking through the Helen Keller garden and standing on the veranda overlooking the water.

At the end of that summer of 1965, I was a senior at Our Lady of Mercy Academy and my mother encouraged me to find a college to attend. Since I was so frightened at the prospect of leaving home for college, I opted to attend a secretarial school not too far from home. Although there were many local colleges I could have attended, I was looking for schooling that would get me out into the workforce as soon as possible. Shortly after I graduated from that school, all secretarial schools became two-year business schools.

My mother (partial), me, and Brian – Graduation from Our
Lady of Mercy Academy July 1966

At secretarial school in September 1965, I met my friend Alida. She had a car and wanted someone to drive with and share gas expenses. Even though by this time I had my own car, the school was in the next county and my junior license didn't permit me to drive out of my county until I was 18. I agreed to ride with her and it was the beginning of a 60-year friendship. We lived near each other and hit it off right away. We had things in common and couldn't believe some of the similarities—she and her brother are adopted, and her brother's name is Brian also. However, she and her brother Brian are blood brother and sister both given up by their birth mother. Their adoptive mother is French Canadian and grew up in Canada. Silly, I know, but I used to imagine that her mother was really my birth mother but she couldn't tell me.

It was only a one-year program, and that was my choice,

but soon after I began the school year, I would say to Alida or anyone who would listen,

"I should have gone to college."

I said and felt this so often and I took some college courses before I had Eric and Elise, but it wasn't until I was 37 and my children were 10 and 8 years old that I finally went back to school in earnest.

After I completed the secretarial course of study, I began working full time at 18 but first came the interviews. In 1967, the secretarial schools required that their students wear skirt suits, white gloves, and a hat. In the business world then, women were not allowed to wear pants. I'll never forget my first interview after graduating. I turned 18 years old in June and it was July.

It was so embarrassing, but I was too nervous and without a shred of confidence to even care.

It was at an attorney's office. I walked in and there were two secretaries at their side-by-side desks facing the door. I approached one of them and told them my name and that I was there for an interview. Of course, being the good student that I was, I was wearing my hat and gloves even though I was out of sight of my teachers and could have left them home. I think I just trusted that our teachers were guiding us correctly. Maybe it was correct for Manhattan, but certainly not for suburban Deer Park, Long Island, New York. Well, the poor secretaries could not contain themselves. They were laughing so hard that they kept going under their desks as if they had dropped something. I must have been a very funny sight. I was so nervous at the interview with the attorney; I was hardly able to speak, never mind taking shorthand and reading it back. He was a very kind man but there was no place for me there. I had little confidence before that inter-view, so after that experience, I took the easy way out and went to a very large aeronautical company as a clerk typist (no shorthand.) It was a very nice job with a great group of people. I was rather sheltered and obviously young, and this place helped me to gain confidence and look for new opportunities.

17

SMALL FAMILY

Growing up my nuclear family was small; my father, my mother, and my brother. My mother had one sister, my Aunt Catherine, her husband, my Uncle Pat, and their son, Kevin who visited us often for as long as I can remember. We would also see my father's siblings, but those aunts and uncles became less and less a part of our lives as I got older. After my father died, we didn't have contact with many of them except for his brother, Uncle Will, and his wife, Aunt Rita, and sister, Aunt Anna. Uncle Will and Aunt Rita came to my wedding which was seven years after my father passed away, and my Uncle Will danced with me in my father's place.

Other than Aunt Catherine and Uncle Pat, my mother didn't seek out other family members to visit us very often. That may have been the norm for the times. Most people were working hard and therefore didn't have the time or the money for entertaining others. I was very happy when I heard that my aunt and uncle were coming to visit for the weekend. It made life more interesting, and they always treated me special. There was a bakery in Brooklyn called Ebinger's. I would run to open the door when they arrived, and all I would see was a stack of bakery boxes tied with string with my Aunt peeking out from the side. They bought everyone's favorite cake or pie. Mine was chocolate cream pie. We did love our cake.

Since Ada left us, my mother and I were alone at the house in Dix Hills, and her depression became apparent. My mother, being close to her sister who was living in Brooklyn with her husband Pat, asked them to move in with us. My Uncle Pat had a stroke many years before and my aunt was his primary caretaker. My mother thought it would be nice for her and her sister to be together for company and support. This was a happy time for both of them and it pulled my mother out of her depression.

They were with us for two years when my mother decided to remarry. This was a big surprise to everyone and my aunt and uncle were very unhappy to have to move again. We wanted to find a place near us for them to live, but they decided to move back to Brooklyn and their familiar neighborhood.

She married Patrick Martin (we all called him Paddy) whom she knew when she was a ten-year-old girl in 1923 in Brooklyn. At that time, my Grandmother was recently widowed, and upon Paddy's arrival in the United States, he was one of the first of her boarders from Ireland who rented a room in their apartment. He was able to gain entry into the United States because he already had his job as a police officer in the Bronx, and began work immediately. Paddy was in their apartment for just a short time before he was able to settle into his own apartment. He was nine years older than my mother.

When they married, my mother was 55 and he was 64. He moved in with us, and I have very fond memories of him. He was a very good, kind man. My father was an NYC detective in Brooklyn and my stepfather was an NYC Police Officer in the Bronx. His wife died the same year as my father and I think both he and my mother were very lonely. They had a mutual cousin who called each of them for over a year to encourage them to see each other. He was the matchmaker.

Many people wondered how I felt living with another father figure after knowing how much I missed and loved my father, but I never saw Paddy as a replacement. I didn't need a replacement. My father had already taught me lessons that would carry me through even in his absence. Paddy never tried to assume a father role, but let me know that he was there if there was anything I needed. He was easy to love and our relationship grew as the years went by.

When my mother told me they would marry, I looked at her and knew that she was lonely and would enjoy his company. I felt happy that she would have someone to be with day to day and they would be able to travel together. Although they had very different personalities, they had a lot in common, especially from their city backgrounds. My mother was somewhat flamboyant and Paddy would sit in his armchair and watch her fly around the house talking and working on house projects. We used to say he looked like he was watching her on TV. He was a man of few words. One time when I was 19, I was talking while we were outside on our patio and a moth flew in my mouth and I proceeded to cough and choke for a minute or more. All he said when he saw I was alright was,

"A closed mouth catches no flies."

Then I could not stop laughing. He didn't say much but when he did it was memorable.

Paddy had four children; one boy and three girls. They were all older than I, but they were only in their 20s and a lot of fun to be around. We would visit them in the Bronx where they lived and they would make incredible dinners for us. Two of Paddy's daughters married into Italian families and they embraced the Italian cooking, much to my delight.

When my mother married Paddy, I was still working at the local aeronautics company. I was working there for two years when my mother and Paddy told me that they were going to take a trip to Ireland to visit Paddy's family. He had a sister and one nephew with a young family living on the farm that Paddy grew up on. They invited me and Paddy's daughter, Mary, and her husband Ron to join them. We would be going at the end of May, and I would celebrate my 20th birthday in Ireland on June 6, 1969. It was a three-week trip. I saved my money and quit my job with enough money to go on the trip and then have a month off from working when I returned home. When talk of this trip came up, I had been thinking about changing jobs so it was perfect timing for me to be able to say yes to this.

When I returned from Ireland, I decided that I would like to work in Manhattan and commute on the Long Island Railroad. My friend Clare was living in Manhattan with her mother Jeanne, and they said they would help me learn my way around the city using the subways and buses. Clare took me to several job placement services that I had found, and then she escorted me to the interviews.

One interview resulted in employment as a secretary for a family brokerage firm in the Financial District on Wall Street. Klara and her son George ran the business since Klara's husband, George's father, had passed away a short time before. It was very sad for them, and I could empathize, having lost my father just five years before. Klara and my mother were the same age. George's sister, Debbie, only nine years old when I started working there, was a sweet, smart little girl. It was a small firm and they treated me like a family member rather than an employee. My life experience outside of my protected, suburban childhood environment was limited, so working in Manhattan was a huge learning curve for me. Initially, the office was downtown in the financial district, but in less than a year we moved from there to 59th Street and Lexington Avenue, then to 55th Street and Fifth Avenue.

At my previous job and in school, I was always with co-workers and we would have lunch and breaks together. In this new job, I was alone during my lunch time. It took me a while to get used to this because I missed the camaraderie of the co-workers. At the time, in 1969, there was a Child's Restaurant named for its founders Samuel and William Childs. This restaurant chain, one of the first national dining chains, was founded in 1907. I would go to lunch there, eat quickly at the counter, (I remember their mashed potatoes and gravy), and then sit in the historic Trinity Church on Trinity Place. It was peaceful and helped my transition.

I became very familiar with the financial district on my own during my lunch hour, and also because part of my job was delivering paperwork to other companies in the area. During the time I worked downtown, they were building the World Trade Center twin towers. It was a very exciting time to be working there.

We moved to our new office on the 34th floor of a brand new building at 59th Street and Lexington Avenue. It was state of the art with a large marble lobby and elevator banks dedicated to specific floors. As you opened the door to our office we looked straight ahead to a wall of floor-to-ceiling windows with a spectacular view of Manhattan. It took some time before I could walk close to those windows and look down 34 stories.

Now at lunch time I would browse in Bloomingdale's and other fine stores. Bloomingdale's was a new experience for me. There was a particular perfume they were promoting at the time, it was called Paco Rabanne, and when you walked into the store the scent was intoxicating. If I were able to experience that scent today, I would close my eyes and be transported back to feeling 20 years old again.

18

7:07 A.M

The "7:07" Long Island Railroad train leaving from Huntington Station to Penn Station, New York was my morning train to work. When I told my friend Jane, who I had known since fourth grade at St. Patrick's School in Huntington, that I wanted to work in Manhattan she agreed to join me in this adventure of breaking out of suburbia. We both found jobs in Manhattan, and in the first week of September 1969, the two of us started riding the "7:07" every morning.

When we started commuting, we went to the "coffee car" where we began to meet other riders looking to enjoy a cup of coffee and pass the time with others on the hour-long ride into Manhattan. A long bar extended the length of this train car with a narrow counter on the opposite side where you could have your coffee and look out the window. Some coffee/bar cars had a shorter bar so it could accommodate a few bench seats and small round tables with a pole in the middle to grab when the train lurched or braked. Coffee cars no longer exist on the Long Island Railroad but it is from an era when some people enjoyed socializing on their way to and from work. Not everyone of course; most people wanted to sleep or read the paper in their seats in one of the other cars. On the evening trains home the coffee car became the bar car. My hours at my office ended at 4:00 pm so I was able to catch the early train home and the bar car with friends was not part of my evening commuting experience.

The first person I remember meeting in the morning coffee car was Jim. He was an outgoing person who worked in sales and made friends with everyone. One morning he was showing us a picture of his girlfriend and I realized that I had gone to dancing school with her for many years during my ballet days from 11-18 years of age. That was a nice connection and I considered the fun we could have talking about that time in our lives.

After we had been riding the "7:07" for about three weeks, Jane and I arrived at the station at exactly the same time. As we were walking from our cars to the platform, I saw a young man who looked familiar to me. I knew we had met before, but I could not remember his name. I took a guess and said, "Hi Bob." Jane quickly corrected me and said, "Hi Frank." Oh well, I tried. So this was my future husband, Frank Claude Resta, and after all these years he still reminds me that I called him Bob! He joined our growing coffee car group every morning. This was in October 1969. We were both 20 years old. Our coffee car group grew to 14. Eventually, four couples got married from that group, and we were one of them. We were friends on the train until February 1970 when we began dating, and it was Jim, our fun-loving, outgoing salesman, who got us together.

"When are you two going to start dating?" he said to us one morning on the train.

Claude and I just looked at each other.

"Let's go on a double date!" Jim suggested.

So we all agreed, but when the date night came, Jim and his girlfriend canceled at the last minute. Sneaky Jim. We should have known. It was not a problem though for us to venture out on this date alone, since we were already good friends. We had a great time and were engaged in February 1971 and married in September 1971. Remember I said I knew I had met him before?

When we were 16 we both went to a church dance in Huntington with friends. I was with Jane then too. Jane and I wanted to leave the church dance and go to a house party in town, and she saw a boy she knew at the dance, and he had a car. She asked him to drive us to the party and Claude was with him. So that was our official first meeting. After we got to the party we did not see each other again; we all stayed with our own friends.

At eighteen and nineteen years old we went to the same dance clubs and bars around Huntington and would see each other in passing. That was only for a couple of years though, because Claude went into the Marine Corp after college and had just finished boot camp when I met him in 1969. He was in the Reserves then and did not go overseas. It wasn't until we met on the train that we actually talked and got to know each other.

Since we met in September and began dating the following February, our early dating days were not during boating season so I didn't know he was a boater. Early one Saturday morning in May I was surprised and delighted when he called to ask if I was available to go out on the boat with him and a couple of mutual friends. The boat belonged to his father but he was always happy to share it with us. It worked out really well because his father would take the boat out to fish very early in the morning. We would have a later start on weekends and take the boat to go water skiing.

We had many weekends out on the boat with friends: water skiing and swimming. The boat was a 19' wood Penn Yan with a 75 hp Evinrude outboard engine, pull start. Good thing he had the strength from his marine corps training to get that engine going. The outside hull was a lapstrake design which meant it was built with planks of wood that were overlapping. This design gave it a graceful look as it would glide through the water. It was a beautiful sight to see a freshly painted lapstrake boat underway. Inside you could see the wooden ribs of the hull. It had a very short bow and a windshield. There were two seats up front and a wooden bench seat at the back directly in front of the engine.

One time we went out and took his two younger sisters, Martine and Corinne with us. They were little girls, ages 14 and 13. Claude was piloting the boat, and I was standing next to him at the windshield. When I looked back at Martine and Corinne, they were sitting on the bench seat in the stern of the boat. The engine was very loud so we could not hear them talking. They were "tete a tete" whispering to each other and looking me up and down, deciding if I was right for their brother.

The boat was kept on a trailer on the side of Claude's family house in Halesite, a little hamlet near the harbor. Claude would hook it up to the hitch on the car and we would drive down the block to the ramp and launch the boat. I would stay on the dock, holding the boat with the line on the cleat until Claude parked the car. The first time I drove over to his house to go on the boat I met his mother, Simone, and his father, Francesco (called Frank). They were very welcoming and happy to see us enjoying ourselves and the boat. I saw them often that summer and after a day of boating was usually invited to join them for dinner. What better way for them to get to know the person their son was dating, and for me to experience his family. I loved them right away and I think it was mutual.

"A table!"

We would all be called to the dining room table to find our seats and be prepared to eat. In their very French household food must be served and eaten hot, no excuses, so we all sat in anticipation as Claude's father brought the food to the table. Dad (as I later called him) would place the large French stew pot in front of him and, as each of us would hand him our dish, he would fill it just so. When a roast of some kind was being served Dad would carve it tableside. Then much to my delight, at one of the dinners, he cut off the crispy end of the roast and said,

"Here, Eileen, this is the best part!"

This became a common gesture to me until others at the table started complaining that they wanted "the best part too!"

Dad's favorite cocktail was a Negroni. This is an Italian martini usually served with an orange twist, but Dad preferred a lemon twist. Only on special holidays or occasions would there be Negroni served and Dad was the only one who liked them. However, on one occasion when I was visiting for dinner Dad said,

"Here Eileen, try this drink."

He gave a little chuckle as he handed it to me. It's a bitter cocktail and he didn't expect me to like it. Well, I did like it and to this day it's my drink of choice. He loved sharing what he enjoyed, and if you enjoyed it too it just added to his joy. In the last seven years, a Negroni has become a very popular cocktail and is easily found in many restaurants. I remember going out to dinner with Dad and the family, and when he asked the server for a Negroni, he saw the blank look and said,

"It's ok; I'll go talk to the bartender."

Dad was a surrogate dad to many. My mother-in-law Simone one time commented that all four of her children married someone whose father had passed away. He became a dad to us all, and he was up to the task. He was another man like my father who loved children, even the adult ones.

It seemed as if Claude's mother Simone was never at a loss for meal ideas to serve her family. She grew up in her family's French restaurant in Paris, and after moving to the United States, prepared traditional French specialties on a daily basis for her husband Francesco, Claude, and his sisters Anne-Marie, Martine, and Corinne. Claude would sit at the head of their beautiful, hand-carved, country French dining table and eat with such gusto, being sure not to miss one bit of the gravy as he sopped it up with fresh bread. She would chuckle to see him enjoy the meal and tease him about the chances of someday finding a wife who cooks.

Even though she worked outside the home as a French and English teacher, his mother cooked every night as if it was a Sunday dinner. This must have been the result of careful planning and preparation learned from her restaurant days. Claude's sisters said that when they were young, before they had experience eating at friend's houses, they thought everyone ate the way they did every night. They soon realized that was not so.

Their mother, my sweet mother-in-law, was the first person I knew who studied nutrition and supplements. It was in the early '70s when many vitamin shops were opening, and we had Jane Fonda, Jackie Sorensen Aerobic Dancing, Jack LaLanne, and others promoting the fitness craze. So not only were the dinners delicious, they were nutritious too as the more she learned the more she applied what she knew to her menus.

I was always interested in food and enjoyed the little cooking I did at home before I was married. My desk was filled with recipes cut from newspapers and magazines. My mother did not enjoy cooking but the meals she put on the table, as I looked back as an adult, were simple and nutritious. Our food was roasted, broiled or boiled. At twenty years old I wanted to branch out into other cuisines and Claude's family meals were the beginning of that for me.

"You better marry a French girl if you want to have good food."

How shocking is that remark in 2020? It was still the prevailing expectation in 1970 that the woman in the marriage would do the cooking. The French part of that statement merely shows the view of French cuisine as being superior. When Claude learned that I am French Canadian he laughed and couldn't wait to tell his mother that he found a French girl.

My mother-in-law was actually very modern in her thinking about women and she raised independent strong daughters; she just loved creating artful meals for the people she loved. My father-in-law was also a good cook and they would often be in the kitchen together, with Claude's mother the executive chef and his father the sous chef.

Feminism was just beginning to seep into my conscious-ness at twenty years old. Today my personal experience is that my daughter does not enjoy cooking as much as her husband does, and my son calls me for old family recipes. We have come a long way from those earlier stereotypes.

Claude's father's cousins owned a restaurant in Richmond Hill, Queens. We only knew it as a family restaurant, but in 1990 while watching Goodfellas imagine our surprise when the camera panned the red awning over the sidewalk and the name Salerno's.

When we were dating for about eight months, we went to dinner there. We went with his parents and sisters, Martine and Corinne. Their sister Anne-Marie was married and living about three hours away with her husband so she was not with us. The experience of being surrounded by so many loving family members was exciting, and going to the restaurant was like going to a family home. The cousins were waiting at the door for us to arrive, and there was much hugging and exclamations of joy as the cousins greeted each other.

The interior of the restaurant looked like a scene from a godfather-type movie. The walls were covered in red and black wallpaper in a raised brocade design. The windows were covered in heavy red drapes and the paintings on the walls were traditional scenes from several towns in Italy where many of the family were born and lived before coming to the United States.

Claude's father's Aunt Angelina, his mother Anna's sister, was in her 90's at the time and lived over the restaurant with her son (one of Dad's first cousins). She loved to see Dad and his family, and in particular, Corinne whose strong resemblance to her sister Anna, brought her great joy. She would take Corinne's hands and have her sit in front of her so she could study her face and shower her with hugs and kisses. (Aunt Angelina lived to be 105.) Corinne was born after her grandmother Anna passed away so she never met her but loved being able to bring back sweet memories to her aunt.

It was rare to see Dad and Mom so relaxed and happy, but that's what happens when you are surrounded by family sharing memories and food from their childhood. The cousins brought out their best wines and then course after course of every possible food group, all their freshest specialties. Menus were not necessary.

That night on the way home in the car I sat in the back

seat with Corinne and Martine. They both fell asleep leaning on my shoulders and I remember feeling such contentment. I never forgot that feeling and it brought back memories of my father, who often said,

"Wherever I hang my hat is home."

This always meant to me that he only needed his family to know he was home. When I experienced their family love that night, it just felt like home to me.

19

CARS

Cars have been an interest of mine since I was very young. When my brother got his license at 16, we were living in Greenlawn. My parents would lend him the car and sometimes he would take me with him when he went to town. At that time our family car was a 1957 Plymouth Fury. Town was only 5-10 minutes away, but we took Pulaski Road, the longest stretch of the ride. My brother turned 16 in 1960 and the excitement about cars was all around us.

Looking at that Plymouth Fury, which was the first car my parents bought after the 1949 Plymouth, it was clear that car design had entered a new era. In fact, the Golden Age of American Car Design years were 1948-1973. Our 1949 Plymouth, although well-loved, was very practical looking, all one color and not at all aerodynamic. In contrast, our 1957 Plymouth was two-toned green, had shiny flat hubcaps, and very large fins with taillights that ran vertically up the fins. Looking at it from the side it looked as if it was taking off, the slope of the headlights and windshield adding to that vision. It was a sight to see and I remember the first time my father drove away from our house in that car on his way to work, my mother and I stood at the front door of our house and admired it until he turned the corner. It was a big deal. Looking back, we were living in a time when more of the masses were able to afford cars with style and luxury that previously were available only to the very rich.

My brother Brian loved cars and when I would drive around town with him he would test me on the make, model, and year of the cars we would see on the road. My brother and I would cruise down Pulaski Road in the Plymouth Fury feeling very cool, especially me at only 12 years old, playing "Name that Car." To this day I am always trying to recognize and name cars but it isn't much fun now since most are SUVs and they look very much alike. Whenever Claude and I see a vintage car on the road or parked in town we reminisce and try to guess the year.

The "Name that Car" game got me in a little trouble, but it was not deserved as you will see. In 1958, the summer after fourth grade, I had to go to summer school at St. Patrick's School in Huntington to make up for their decision to have me skip third grade when I first arrived in Huntington. So although this was my only summer school experience in elementary school, it took me until sixth grade to catch up on my learning gaps, but I did catch up.

The other summer school students had left and I was waiting on the front steps of the school with the priest. I don't remember if he was the teacher or just assigned to wait with students whose parents hadn't come yet. While we stood there overlooking a busy Main Street, I started naming the make, model, and years of the cars. The priest didn't say too much, but I was having fun. Maybe I was feeling badly about summer school and wanted to show him there was something I was good at. Helping students develop confidence or highlighting their strengths was not part of the Catholic school educators' priorities then. It was the opposite. Most students were called out and embarrassed on an almost daily basis.

The next day when I came home from school, my mother asked me about naming cars with the priest the previous day. He told her I was showing off and should learn humility. It helps for me to think I intimidated him. There's always a lesson to be learned, and I learned to be quiet in school. The other lesson was that in my house anything a priest or nun said was considered an inarguable truth so there was no defending myself.

In 1964, after my father died and we moved to Dix Hills, my mother purchased a 1964 teal-colored Pontiac Bonneville. It was a huge boat of a car with an eight-cylinder engine that was very responsive. My nickname, given to me by my brother Brian when I learned to drive at sixteen years old, was "lead foot." You could see me racing into Huntington village trying to make all the traffic lights (which were synchronized to turn red and green at the same time) as I drove to my friend's house on the other side of town. At the time I didn't think about what a weapon it was. Fortunately, it was so long ago we didn't have the traffic we have today, and we probably didn't have as many traffic lights in the Village either.

I was the first of my friends to have access to a car so I would pick up my friends and take them wherever they wanted to go. I just loved to drive fast. I felt free and independent. Everyone would chip in whatever coins they had to help with gas. In those days fifty cents went a long way.

Learning to drive improved my life immeasurably and I did slow down. My mother was happy to share her car with me. She was very generous, and not just with me but with everyone. In my opinion, she was the person for whom the expression, "She would give you the shirt off her back" was coined.

When I turned 17 she said she thought I should have my own car. I couldn't imagine how I would financially manage that, but she always found a way to accomplish what she dreamed should happen. We went looking for a used car and we found two Chevy II Novas. One was a green hardtop sedan and the other was a blue convertible. The green was less expensive than the blue, but a sedan is never as exciting as a convertible, especially to a teenager. We left the used car lot undecided and went home. The next morning, my mother and I walked out of our bedrooms across the hall from each other and simultaneously said,

"I think you should get the ___________ one."

She said the blue convertible and I said the green one, looking to be practical.

She said that she thought I should have the best one and she would give me the money for it. I think it was $800, and I would be responsible for the insurance and any other expenses that come with owning a car. I had two part-time jobs while I was in secretarial school so I was able to afford the insurance and have a little spending money too. I loved cars and now I was driving a 1963 Chevy II Nova, blue, convertible all over town. I could be seen washing and polishing it every Saturday in my driveway. I loved that car.

20

WORLD WAR II

Claude's mother and father met in Paris in July 1944 just after D-day. His father Francesco was working as a diesel mechanic in the rail yard for the US Army. As the story is told by his mother Simone, his father came into the restaurant during lunchtime, and her mother, Marie Dujany said,

"Look at that young soldier, he looks hungry." And so it began.

Shortly before she met Francesco, her father passed away so Simone, an only child, and her mother were running the restaurant on their own. As their relationship developed he became part of their family and helped them when needed at the restaurant.

They did not have a long courtship. They shared a love of family and food and this was the foundation of their life together.

My mother-in-law, Simone, told us the story about their wedding, or two weddings actually. In France, a couple had to be married in a civil ceremony first, and then they would be allowed to marry in the church. The civil ceremony was on

September 25, 1945. After the ceremony, my father-in-law expected to go home with his bride, but Marie Dujany, now his mother-in-law, waved her finger at him while saying,

"No, no, not until the church ceremony tomorrow."

So he went home alone that night, and they had the church ceremony the next day on September 26, 1945. They celebrated their anniversaries through the years on September 26. After our engagement, Claude and I unknowingly picked the date of their civil ceremony, September 25, for our wedding day. It was 26 years after their civil wedding in Paris.

Simone Dujany and Francesco Resta Wedding September 26, 1945

Not long after they married Dad had to leave Paris with the U.S. Army ahead of his new bride. Once home in the United States, he was able to send for her. She told me about coming over to the United States on a "war bride" ship. She was so nervous about the trip, but there were many other young women making the journey with her and they were able to support one another. She told me her biggest fear was that she would not recognize him out of uniform. She had no language issues to worry about. She was fluent in English and later in life, she taught English and French at the high schools in the Huntington, NY townships.

She arrived in Brooklyn and her fears of not recognizing him did not materialize. Dad was already living with his family and that is where she joined him. He was from a big family of eight children, and my mother-in-law was an only child. Some of Dad's siblings were still living at home with his parents when she arrived. They were very wary of the French girl and in the beginning did not always treat her with respect. I have heard there was a prejudice against young French women who fell in love with a soldier and then came home with them to the United States.

She told me a few stories about living with her in-laws after arriving in Brooklyn. Everyone in the family had chores, and she was assigned to clean the bathroom. She said she would finish the job, and then one or two of the sisters would go in and clean it all over again.

She also wanted to learn how to make some of the recipes that her mother-in-law would make for the family and Francesco liked, but instead of including her in the cooking, her mother-in-law would start and finish the meal preparation while she wasn't home.

The most hurtful and shocking comment her mother-in-law made was when Francesco and Simone's first child was born in Brooklyn. They had their daughter, Anne-Marie in 1947 and when her mother-in-law saw Anne-Marie she said,

"It's a good thing she looks like Francesco."

In later years, Claude's father's family came to accept, love and know Simone as the kind, generous person she was. She didn't hold a grudge and put family first.

While Claude's parents were here in the United States, Simone's mother was in Paris operating the restaurant with no family members to help. She had employees but all the responsibility of the business rested on her. It was very hard for mother and daughter to be separated, so in June of 1948 Simone, Francesco, and their 16-month-old daughter Anne-Marie decided to go back to Paris for a six-week vacation.

21

SIX-WEEK VACATION

When I think about Simone and her mother being separated for so long, it must have been a very painful time for them both. Many letters went back and forth with pictures but they longed to be together again. Although this was supposed to be a six-week vacation, the family thinks there may have been a plan to have them stay in Paris. Who could blame them? After all, Marie Dujany had only one sister and brother-in-law in Paris, and Francesco's parents were surrounded by not only their children but extended family as well.

Simone was so happy to be reunited with her mother and for her mother to experience in person the joy of being a grandmother.

During the six weeks, Simone's mother had many conversations with her son-in-law. She was hoping he would love life in Paris, and she was determined to help that love take root and grow before they were scheduled to return to New York.

"What do you do for work in the states?" she asked him.

"Well, I have a job as a machinist in a company in Brooklyn."

"Is it a job that you enjoy?"

"Not especially," he answered.

"There could be an opportunity for you here in Paris," she said.

"You've seen the apartment here off the courtyard behind the restaurant. You and Simone and the baby could live there rent-free."

She could see he was mulling it over but not saying anything. She could not read his face to know what he was thinking. Maybe he needed more persuasion, so she went on with more reasons why Paris could be a choice he would love.

"Did you know we have a house in the French countryside where we go for periodic vacations, as well as every August when the business closes down?"

"I will buy you and Simone a car, a deux-chevaux, so you can have the freedom to explore the outskirts of Paris whenever you like. And since it is not as easy to get around Paris in a car as it is on a Vespa, I will make sure you have one of those as well."

Francesco still did not answer. It seems she forgot to tell him perhaps the most important part of this offer.

"Oh! And you will have a job at the restaurant. I especially would like to see you as our bartender. You would be a welcome addition to the business and our patrons would enjoy your company."

Francesco Resta behind bar in Paris - 1948

Claude Resta behind bar in Paris - 1999

At this point, who would say no to this generous and exciting offer? So the answer was a resounding,

"Yes."

I'm sure my father-in-law would have stayed in Paris even without all of those enticements. He was happy there, and especially happy to see Simone so content at home with her mother.

My father-in-law was such a people person, as is Claude, and I am sure he was very good for business. Claude was born there in 1949, and at a very young age, he was working at the cash register in the restaurant, taking customers' payment and giving change. That is probably where his love of all things financial began.

Dad was not fluent in French when he moved there. He did know some Italian from growing up in his Italian family and neighborhood. I would ask him how he learned French well enough to not only serve as the bartender but converse with the patrons, which I knew he did well. He told me that he went to a school that used the Berlitz Method of teaching French fluency, a natural approach that immersed a student in the new language. For weeks he went to class after class where only French could be heard and spoken. At one point he was becoming very discouraged and thought he would never understand. Then one day, he said he went to class and understood everything.

Living in Paris was an especially happy seven years for them until, sadly and at too young an age, Claude's grandmother, Marie Dujany, passed away. Claude was seven years old and Anne-Marie was nine years old. Their mother and father did not want to run the restaurant without her so they made plans to sell the restaurant and move back to the United States. Dad still had his big family there and Mom agreed they should go and be with the family.

They did not move back to Brooklyn but to Huntington, New York which is about an hour from Brooklyn. Dad's brother Vinnie and his wife Nancy were living in Huntington at the time and they moved in with them until they found their house nearby.

Claude remembers living with his Aunt and Uncle and their children, his first cousins. It was only for the summer and they moved into their new house in time for school to start in September. This was 1956.

❧   22   ❧

FAMILY VISIT TO PARIS

In 1999, Claude and I and our daughter Elise took a trip to Paris with Dad, Claude's sister Corinne and her daughter Justine, his sister Martine, Anthony, and their daughter Emilie. Our son Eric was not able to join us. My dear mother-in-law, Simone, had passed away in 1995 so she was not with us. Dad had not been back to Paris since he left to go back to the United States with Simone, Anne-Marie, and Claude in 1956.

Simone went back to Paris to visit friends and her aunt and uncle a few times and in 1965 and 1971 she went with Martine and Corinne. Anne-Marie was also with them on one of the trips and it had an important purpose. Anne-Marie was soon to be married and her wedding gown was to be a beautiful French creation.

We arrived at the hotel, very early morning and jet-lagged. As soon as we brought our luggage to our rooms Dad said,

"Leave the suitcases and follow me."

With that, he bolted out of our rooms, downstairs,

through the hotel lobby, and out onto the street with all of us half running to keep up.

"Where are we going?" we asked.

"To find the restaurant," he replied.

We didn't expect that to be his immediate plan for our arrival in Paris. Braced against the wind and rain and leaving the umbrellas to us, he led us on a long walk through Paris to find the restaurant that was such an important and happy part of his life. Finally, he would be able to relive and share his memories of that time in Paris. We were thrilled to share this reunion of sorts with him.

We knew from Mom that on her visits to Paris, she went to the site of the restaurant and found that it had become a bicycle shop. We did not know what we would find that day. To our happy surprise, it was a restaurant again. It was named La Marmitte and it was in the same space as their restaurant forty years ago.

There we were, the eight of us, all standing under our umbrellas outside the large window speaking excitedly with Dad. The restaurant was not yet opened for the day. After about 10 minutes of this, the owner and an employee of the restaurant came to the door to ask if they could help us. We must have been a strange sight through the window, a group of very excited, rain-soaked Americans, all talking at once as we examined every part of the outside of the building. Dad remembered his French even though he hadn't spoken it in many years. He quickly explained his story. We could see they were touched to think they were occupying a space that he owned and worked in back in the '40s. They invited us in, out of the rain, and then Dad began his reminiscing, all in French.

La Marmitte Restaurant, Paris, France - 1999

The layout of the restaurant was exactly as it had been. The bar on the right, the wood/coal burning stove in the middle, and the kitchen downstairs. Dad told the story of how they were short on wood and coal during the war, so he brought kerosene to burn for heat in the restaurant. He said he almost blew up the place, and his mother-in-law almost threw him out.

He went on to tell them that he lived with Mom, Anne-Marie, Claude, and his mother-in-law in an apartment just across the courtyard.

The owner said,

"That is my apartment. Would you like to see it?"

She called her friend who was at the apartment to tell him we would all be coming over. This was very emotional for all of us. I had heard so many stories from Dad and Mom about their time in France, but also from Claude who was seven when they left France. He remembered the courtyard where he played as being so large. Now in reality it was not large at all. Don't we all have a surprise when we return to a place of our youth to see how much smaller it is than we remembered? I stood outside the apartment doorway, behind the family, as Dad and Claude recounted their memories. It was a beautiful and emotional journey for them. They were the only two who had memories of the place.

"My mother used to feed me in that window," Claude said.

It was so touching to see him relive those happy child-hood days. My tears were flowing for the whole family to think that this trip didn't happen while my mother-in-law was still alive.

Eileen, Martine, Corinne, Francesco, Justine, Claude, Emilie, Elise In front of the bar at La Marmitte, Paris, France 1999

23

ENGAGED

Shortly after Claude and I started dating in 1970 I decided it was time for me to buy a new car. The Chevy II Nova was still somewhat reliable, but not always. The paint was fading and peeling and it often needed repairs. I was bringing in a good salary from my job in the city and since I lived at home, my expenses were low. I did contribute to the household, but it wasn't near as much as a monthly apartment rent would be. I wanted a sports car and Claude and I started looking on weekends for the right used car. We looked at and test drove a few, but a Chevy Camaro and a Pontiac Trans Am are the only two I remember. One broke down on the test drive. That started me thinking about buying a new rather than used car.

A Triumph sports car caught my eye out on the road, and I decided to check it out at a dealership. It was a Triumph Spitfire that I fell in love with on the showroom floor. The salesman told me he had a leftover that he wanted to sell to make room for new models, and it was the only one left on Long Island in the color I wanted. It was Valencia Blue with a Saddle interior. It was beautiful.

Eileen in her Spitfire summer of 1971

I was planning on getting a loan from the bank, but my mother wanted to lend me the money and I would pay her instead of a bank. It was $2000, a lot of money. I didn't have a car payment with my Nova so this was an added expense, but one I knew I could afford.

Again, I was in love with a car. There was a big problem though. I never drove a stick shift before, only automatic. Claude said,

"That's no problem, I'll teach you."

He drove a very large 1960 Oldsmobile '98 to the train every day. Now that would be my car while he gave me lessons on my car after work and on the weekends, and he would take my Spitfire home every night. After about two weeks of practice, I told him,

"I think I'm ready."

He said, "I'm not sure."

I said, "I am sure."

With that, he gave me a big smile and agreed. He was just hoping for a little more time with my awesome car.

In February 1971, Claude and I became engaged. We were both 21 years old and would turn 22 in March and June.

Our engagement was one year from when we started dating, although we had been riding the train together for one year and four months. We arranged a meeting with Claude and my mother so he could ask her permission to marry me. She was delighted to give us her blessing. She told us she could see how happy we were, and she wished us a lifetime of happiness.

When we announced our engagement to Claude's family, his mother Simone said,

"We've been waiting for your engagement, now don't make it a long engagement, why wait?"

Claude wanted me to pick out my engagement ring. He didn't have a particular jeweler in mind so my mother was happy to share her story of the jeweler she recommended.

In 1938 when my father Owen Coyne was a patrol cop walking the streets of Brooklyn, there were many street vendors selling their goods. It was common then that some did not have licenses to be selling on the street, and when they saw him or any of his fellow officers coming they would quickly pack up and run. There was one jeweler who respected and appreciated my father. He would say,

"Someday I will have my own store and I will be happy to see you there for all your jewelry needs."

He accomplished his goal and opened his store in the "diamond district" in New York City. Through the years my father and mother would go to his store and they knew they could trust him and that he would give them a fair price.

We chose a day to go to the city and choose my ring. My mother asked if she could come with us, and we were very happy to have her there. My mother knew that the store was still owned by the same family and at the same address. When we arrived at the store we met the son of the original owner. My mother briefly told him she knew his father without elaborating on the very early days of the business. She introduced Claude and me and told him that she was so happy to be bringing her daughter there for such an important purchase.

We planned our wedding for September 25, 1971, only 7 months after our engagement. That would be unusual now. Today a two-year engagement is the norm.

Soon after our engagement, my mother announced,

"Paddy and I are going to move to Florida in October."

"What? Why so soon?" I asked

I knew they were looking at places in Florida and made two trips there over the past six months, but I didn't expect this to happen so quickly. I also thought maybe they would be "snowbirds" and only live in Florida to escape the cold winters in New York and then come home for the summer. But they found a house near Ft. Lauderdale in Florida and were moving there full time in October.

This was very hard for me to accept and I was feeling surprised, angry, sad, and abandoned. I had been completely preoccupied with my engagement, upcoming wedding, and apartment hunting not realizing that my mother would leave three weeks after my wedding. I took it for granted that she would be there as I started my life as a married woman.

We decided to live in Flushing, New York after we were married because we both still worked in Manhattan. Instead of commuting on the Long Island Railroad, we were able to take the subway to work saving us time and money. Also, this meant we only needed one car so we sold the Spitfire. On the pot-holed city streets of Flushing, the car would not have survived. Owning that car was short-lived but we enjoyed many road trips during that time. When I sold it I was able to pay my mother in full and I think the timing couldn't have been better because, generous as always, she used that money to pay for our wedding.

Our wedding was perfect for us. My stepfather, Patrick

Martin, walked me down the aisle, my brother was an usher, and Claude's sisters Martine and Corinne were junior bridesmaids. My mother was very proud, and we were both missing my father that day. She told me I was always his princess, and he was with us that day. I felt that too. She made sure everything was perfect. She gave me a diamond bracelet to wear that my father had given her when they were first together. It made me feel close to her and to my father to wear that bracelet. The wedding was at the Marcpiere, a restaurant in Melville, NY. We had ninety guests. It was a lovely place decorated in a regal way with velvet drapes and a vestibule with fresh flowers and an arched doorway. The food was not wedding venue food, because it was not exclusively a wedding venue, but a popular local restaurant. The food served at our wedding was what we would have ordered from the menu as a restaurant patron. I was the only bride there. The restaurant was closed to the public specifically for our wedding.

Claude, Eileen, Mary, Paddy, and Brian

My friend Clare and brother Brian

We honeymooned in St. Thomas and Puerto Rico. We have been back to St. Thomas but just to pass through on our way to St. John or as a stop on a cruise ship. We looked to find the hotel where we stayed for our honeymoon but it was gone. Even the buildings were gone. It was called the Lime Tree Hotel and it was brand new when we went there in 1971. All the towels were lime-colored and the hotel was directly on the beach. We always remember the lounge chairs on the beach with the little flags that we would put up when we wanted a drink. That is more common now but back then I'm not sure it was or maybe just that we were inexperienced travelers. The Lime Tree restaurant jutted out on stilts over the water. Every evening we would dine on fresh seafood and watch the spectacular Caribbean sunset.

We loved Puerto Rico also but it was not as memorable since it was so much more commercial. Still, we enjoyed the casinos and the dancing late into the night. We had the quiet of St. Thomas for four days and then the excitement of Puerto Rico for four more days.

After our honeymoon in St. Thomas and Puerto Rico, we came home to our little apartment in Flushing, New York. Claude found the apartment about two months before our wedding. It was a very small space in a private home on a block of the same houses. When you walked in the front door, you could either walk up the stairs to the second level or straight ahead through our door and into the apartment. It was very affordable, in a good neighborhood close to public transportation, and in excellent condition with beautiful wood floors throughout.

Initially, it seemed like a good plan, but we only lived in the apartment for about a year before we moved back to Huntington. We found ourselves driving out to Huntington every weekend and staying overnight with Claude's mom and dad so we could see our friends.

Since my mother had moved to Florida, she wasn't around for us to stay with her. My sadness and disappointment at not having my mother close that first year was acute, but I embraced Claude's family as my own. During that first year of marriage, Claude and I flew to visit my mother and Paddy for Christmas and they flew up for my birthday in June, but I was missing impromptu visits and events that would bring my mother and me closer together. In those early years Claude's family provided emotional stability for me, but some days I would become aware that I didn't have any family locally to see or visit. I can still recall that lonely feeling.

It was in September, one year after our wedding, that we found a house to rent in Centerport, a hamlet in the township of Huntington. It was perfect timing because Dad sold us his boat and now we had a yard to keep it in. We lived there through the winter and we were very content. When spring arrived we were happy to get outside in our yard and we began to work on getting the boat ready for the water.

We decided that he would sand and paint the outside of the hull and I would strip the wood inside the boat hull. Armed with a spray chemical to remove the old stain, and a putty knife, I went to work. It was tedious but I could see progress and knew there would be a beautiful finish on the wood when the job was complete. It was a labor of love for both of us, and we were proud of the restoration we accomplished. One day, we were stopped at a light in our 1967 Ford Mustang pulling the Penn Yan on the trailer behind us, when the man in the car next to us, shouted out,

"Beautiful boat!" We felt like proud parents.

19' Penn Yan

The location of the house we rented was around the block from a small boat ramp which was only for the use of the residents in this community. It was the "President's Street" community with every street named after a president. We lived on Buchanan Street.

We would return from work during the week at around 6 PM, hitch the boat trailer to the car and drive down to the boat ramp. By 6:30 we were out on the water with our sandwiches and beer watching a beautiful sunset. We loved the extreme of coming from hot city subways to drifting in Centerport Bay until dark.

24

OUR FIRST HOME

When my mother married Paddy, they both had money to invest, and she wasted no time before she shared her latest idea with Paddy.

"Let's buy a house as an investment and rent it out."

That was my mother with her business planning again.

They found two houses in the South Huntington area and they were in good condition. They wouldn't have to do much to them to make them ready for a renter. One of these houses was a two-bedroom, one-bathroom L-shaped ranch style and it had a one-bedroom attached apartment. The main house, which was the original house, was a simple rectangular-shaped structure with a brick patio in the front and the back. At some point, one of the owners built an apartment on one end of the house which formed the L shape.

When the tenant in the largest part of the house gave notice that they were leaving, my mother offered to rent it to us with the option to buy. It was a wonderful opportunity for us and we moved in in 1973.

The house was on a rolling 1.1-acre lot filled with old, tall stately trees. The picture window in the living room looked out at the largest stretch of this land because the house was set back toward one end of the property. It was a stunning view and I remember us looking out and appreciating all four seasons. It was like being in our own park; a party for our senses. Every year of the seven years in that house we enjoyed sledding in our perfectly sloped front yard, seeing the buds forming in the spring while hearing the birds singing, smelling the flowers, and tasting the fresh strawberries every summer while finding relief in the shade of the huge trees, and after enjoying the beautiful colors of the fall leaves as they rained down onto the lawn, raking and bagging more than one hundred bags of leaves.

The area was zoned one-acre minimum so it was very private in terms of neighbors. The house across the street was on two acres, and the house next door was on four acres and was just a summer home at the time. Those neighbors lived in Brooklyn full time and coming to this property for them was coming out to the "country."

After a few months of living in this house, we decided we would like to buy it from my mother and Paddy. They were very pleased. The tenant in the attached apartment wanted to continue to rent from us, and we realized that this would be good for us to have a rent income to help with the mortgage and expenses.

My mother and Paddy had built up some equity in the house but instead of keeping the equity, they gave it to us for a down payment. That really set us up for success. Because of that generosity, we were able to easily afford the house and start our family there.

We still had the Penn Yan when we moved to our South Huntington house on Beverly Road; however, a big change in our boating experience occurred while we lived there, a wonderful one.

Claude's Dad belonged to a boat club in Huntington Harbor called The Harbor Boating Club. He became a member in 1972, and it was a big part of his recreational and social life. It was started in 1949 as strictly a fishing club, not a recreational one. Dad loved to fish and had many friends in the club. Since 1949 the club became more social, and the families of the fishermen joined in on the boating and fishing. There were also several social gatherings throughout the year in the clubhouse.

This boat club was different from others in Huntington Harbor because the members, 100 of them, formed committees to do all the necessary work and maintenance of the clubhouse, the bulkhead, the docks, and the property. The work is well distributed, with everyone doing their share measured by hours served. Because the members do the work, the dues and slip fees are low. The slip fees are one-fifth the cost of neighboring boat clubs that hire outside contractors to do all their work. Our clubhouse is a beautiful, old house on a hill that overlooks the mouth of the harbor. It is an exceptionally beautiful location.

Claude's Dad approached us and recommended we join the club. There was an opening for a new member which was fortunate for us since this club was in high demand and usually had a waiting list of those wishing to join. This was a great opportunity for us and we quickly said yes.

There was an initiation fee in the form of a bond which would be returned to us with interest whenever we left the club in the future. As of 2020, we are still members and number one in seniority. In addition to that fee, we had to pay annual dues for the year and a per foot cost associated with a slip for our 19' Penn Yan.

Luckily we were both still working full time, and we had the rent income to help pay for our mortgage, so we had the money to become a member. That was in 1974.

That summer, whenever we walked the dock from our boat slip up to the bulkhead and to the parking lot, we had our eyes on another boat, a 24' Seabird that we loved. At the end of the summer, much to our delight, it had a for-sale sign on it. Claude called the number and the owner offered to take us for a ride. It was the perfect boat for us. We bought the boat in 1975 and enjoyed many years of family boating.

24" Seabird

Eric, Elise, Kellianne, Brian

After our son Eric was born in 1976, I didn't go back to work. Two years later, our daughter Elise was born. Losing my income after having the children was not a problem since we had the rent income to help with our bills. I would have liked to work, even part-time, but I couldn't make enough salary to cover babysitting expenses. It was much more economical for me to be home, and I'm happy I was home with the children.

As Eric and Elise grew we realized we were outgrowing our house. It had only two bedrooms and one bath. There was so much to love about the house, but it was too small, and not conducive to meeting other families. It was not a neighborhood setting. I would be home all day and not see anyone. The privacy that we enjoyed as a couple with no children did not serve us well after Eric and Elise were born. This house was on a corner of two very busy roads so taking a walk with the strollers was not an option. Every outing required that I put the kids in the car and drive to a park. It was very lonely for me and the children there so Claude and I decided we needed not only a larger house but more of a family-friendly neighborhood.

25

OUR SECOND HOME

Our dream at the time, in 1979, was to live closer to the water in Huntington. Our first house was in South Huntington which is about a 15-minute drive to Huntington Harbor. When I wanted to take the kids on an outing, it was to Hecksher Park in Huntington to walk around the pond, see the ducks, and play on the playground. Other times I would take them to the "Village" as we referred to the town of Huntington. They loved the health food store where they would choose their favorite healthy snack. Also, Claude's family lived in the hamlet of Halesite which is one block from the water and the town boat ramp and marina.

We drove around Huntington with the realtors every weekend for six months. They knew our preferred location, but it became clear to us that homes became more expensive the closer we were to Huntington village and the harbor. The same home 15 minutes south of Huntington village would cost substantially less. We did see a few we could have purchased, but there were too many things wrong with each one. Some had ceilings that had suffered a leak and had not been repaired, kitchen counters with holes in them, no yard, or on a very busy main street. We finally had to accept the reality that we would have to look closer to our present neighborhood, which is a 15-minute drive to Huntington Village.

Happy that we finally came to this realization, the realtor took us to Evans Court which is a cul de sac with only ten homes on it. They were all the same model, but because they were built in 1956 the owners had them landscaped and personalized so it was not the first thing we noticed.

When we pulled off the intersecting road onto the cul de sac, there was a canopy of beautiful, stately maple trees lining the street all the way to the end. Turning onto the street we immediately felt the downhill slope of the road. It was a warm summer day, and it was like entering into a cool, shady forest with those maple trees welcoming us.

The owner let us in and we felt her sense of pride in her home. She left the house and the realtor began the tour with us. It was obvious that the homeowner cared for this house. Some rooms had been updated and renovated. Not everything was to our taste, but we considered it "move-in ready." It was certainly the best house we had seen so far. The property was beautiful, and because we were coming from a house with property like a park, we were very impressed and excited to see the large half acre with beautiful trees and shrubs. Another big plus was that Eric and Elise would be able to ride their bikes on this quiet, safe cul de sac. Eric was three years old and Elise was one and the house was in a good school district with the elementary school located on the next block; they would not have to take a bus. The hesitation we initially had about this house was that it was a split level. I lived in a split level for seven years of my life, and we both agreed we would like to have a one-floor ranch-style house. We went home, and that evening we realized that after all our searching for a home, even though it was a split level, this one felt right.

One of the reasons we wanted to move from our first home was to be in a neighborhood and have other families nearby with children for Eric and Elise to play with. Two months after we moved in, new neighbors moved in across the street. They had a boy and a girl about our children's ages, and we all became good friends. It was just what we were looking for in this move.

As we became friends we learned that their oldest child, John was adopted. Then we discovered that John and I had the same birthday so I said to him,

"Not only do we have the same birthday, we are both adopted. Isn't that cool?" He agreed and that was the last we spoke of it.

His mother told me how they came to adopt him. She was told by her doctor that she could not have children so she and her husband immediately began the application process to adopt a baby. After adopting John, she became pregnant and went on to have four more children. Needless to say, she found a new doctor.

John is the oldest of his siblings and they all live close to each other and their parents. We were fortunate enough to go to John's wedding and now he has two sons. The only thing he ever said to me about adoption was when he and his wife were due to deliver their firstborn. He was imagining what it will be like to have someone who may look like him. I know that feeling and I think most adoptees miss looking at a family member and seeing a little of themselves looking back. When my daughter was young many would tell me that she looked like me. At first, I didn't know what to say; it was a new experience.

In 1980 when we moved in, we discovered that we were

part of the Haldale Civic Association. It was made up of the ten houses on our block. We would go to meetings and parties, taking turns in each of our houses, and it was wonderful to be part of this community. At one of our first meetings, Claude was nominated president and I was nominated secretary. The joke was that Claude went to the bathroom and he came back to,

"Congratulations on being the new president."

There was also a treasurer who collected dues to offset some of the cost of parties. There weren't any particular responsibilities, and through the years the recordkeeping and dues faded away. The parties did not. Even today with many of the houses sold and purchased by new owners, the association continues. Every new owner has embraced our twice-a-year parties. One at Christmas/Holiday dinners, and a Memorial Day block party in the cul de sac. Now we also have a group email and use it to communicate news that we may need to share with our neighbors.

There was a very important original purpose of the block association though. When the original owners moved into these homes, they found that the builder had taken serious shortcuts. The cesspools, which should have been dug at least 30 feet deep in order to reach the sand were only 12 feet deep. Every one of the original owners had a sewage issue shortly after moving in with their families. Also, the windows in the back of the houses weren't straight or aligned properly. So the owners banded together and formed the association to take the builder to court. They won and the builder came back to bring the houses up to code. Even after the initial problems were solved everyone on the block agreed to continue holding meetings and parties. Together with our neighbors, we have successfully worked with the Town of Huntington officials whenever we needed a problem solved on our block.

We still have two original owners living on the block. One lives in an apartment in the house with their daughter who bought the house from them, and another house was also bought by the daughter who grew up here. Our other neighbors Doris and Carl live diagonally across the street. They know our children well, and it was their yard that my children walked through to get to their elementary school. Their route to school without this access would have been longer. I would have had to drive them every day or else they would have had to walk a very busy road with no sidewalk.

One time I was out doing errands while Eric and Elise were in school. Elise was in first grade and she was supposed to go to an after-school activity that day. That meant that I had an extra hour to complete my errands before I had to be home to get her at school. She forgot about going to the after-school program and started to walk home. Unfortunately, no one at the school reminded her to stay after school or even noticed that she went home. Luckily, my neighbor Doris was home when Elise came walking through her yard. Elise was very independent at an early age, and although I was always at the school to pick her up, instead of going back into the school to wait for me that day, she decided to walk home the way we did every day. Doris saw that I wasn't home yet so when I drove down my street to come home, there was Elise sitting with her on her front stoop enjoying cookies and milk and having a nice chat. Lucky for us Doris was there. No one wants to leave this block; it is truly a neighborhood where you can count on your neighbors.

We are still living in this house on this street and we love recalling our memories of the past 40 years with each other and our children. Eric's street hockey games, Elise's bike races, and now our grandchildren are recalling their memories. Periodically during our years here, we've thought of moving, again thinking of being closer to the water, but we find that we are very happy here. And as my friend Marilyn once said,

"Don't mess with happy."

My mother visited us from Florida twice a year on my birthday in June and my anniversary in September. Paddy often joined her on these visits. In 1987, at the age of 83, Paddy passed away after a year-long illness. My mother made all the arrangements for his wake and burial held in New York and my family and Paddy's children and grandchildren were with us for all the services.

Claude and I traveled to Florida with Eric and Elise during Thanksgiving week until I could no longer take them out of school for the three days prior to Thanksgiving. Also, I started working as a Teacher Assistant and had the same schedule. After that, we had to change our travel schedule and went to Florida during spring break or summer vacation. Our visits to Florida with the children became less and less frequent as they grew and their weekend extracurricular activities increased. We spoke every week but I knew she was missing so many of the milestones in her grandchildren's life. Still, we kept the relationship going well with letters, pictures, and many phone calls. When "Nana" visited they knew her and loved her. She was fun and joined in on whatever we were doing.

There was excitement in the house when we were anticipating a visit from Nana. When we first had a computer and printer that would print out banners, the kids would print a huge welcome sign to hang on the front of the house to greet her.

The airport was not too far from where Claude worked so my mother would time her flights to arrive and depart at the end and beginning of his workday. Around 5:30 pm we would be waiting at the door for her arrival, dinner simmering on the stove, her room ready and all of us anticipating her latest story. She always had a good one. We would watch as she exited the car and marvel at her latest style of hat. She loved hats and wouldn't travel without one.

This was a custom from her youth when she was a young working woman living with her mother and sister. She was walking home from work when she was approached by an agent who presented his card and told her to contact the agency. They would be interested in hiring her as a hat model. She was flattered and excited but her mother would not approve of such an occupation for her daughter.

We had twelve years of Nana's visits as she enjoyed watching Eric and Elise grow, and meeting their wonderful friends who came over to eat with us and play in our yard and on our quiet street. My mother really enjoyed people and as she got to know Eric and Elise's friends she remembered every conversation she had with them and would pick up where she left off each time she visited. She would make predictions (only to me) about their future occupations: this one a doctor, this one an engineer, this one a carpenter, this one in sales; she had high hopes for them all as she recognized and appreciated their intelligence and talents.

During those twelve years, she watched me evolve from a stay-at-home mom, to part-time worker, to college student, and finally to teacher. When I decided to pursue a college degree she didn't understand until I explained that I was anticipating going back to work full time and I wanted the work to be fulfilling. As I progressed through my school and work years she saw how happy I was and told me she was proud of me. It always means a lot to hear that from a parent.

❧ 26 ☙

SCHOOL AT 37

When I graduated high school in 1966, all I wanted to do was learn a skill, get a job, and be "independent." In 1967, after one year of secretarial school, I was able to begin my work career.

In 1980 when we moved from the house on Beverly Road to Evans Court, I was a full-time stay-at-home mom.

I always enjoyed working so when Elise was two and a half and Eric was in pre-school, I took a part-time job at a bowling alley nursery taking care of babies and preschoolers while their mothers bowled. I was able to bring Elise with me so it was nice for both of us.

My next part-time work was as a telemarketer for Katherine Gibbs Business School. You would think that tele-marketing has to be one of the worst jobs because most tele-marketers have to make "cold calls." This telemarking job was different. Potential students for this school filled out cards at job fairs asking for more information about the programs at the school. My job was to call them to follow up and arrange for them to come in for an interview. The school paid for a phone line in my home and I was working "remote" in 1981.

Once a week I went to the Katherine Gibbs school office to meet with a young and friendly supervisor to review my week's work in person. I was able to bring Elise with me. She was 2 and a half at the time, and the people in the office loved her. Other than going once a week to the school, I worked exclusively from home Monday through Thursday from 4:30-9 p.m. Claude would come home from work and the dinner prep would be done. It was too early to eat so around 6 p.m. he would heat it up, and I would leave the phone for ten minutes to eat with them. Then back up to the office to work. Claude would get the children ready for bed and I was able to come down and kiss them goodnight. It was a great job.

There was one more part-time job before I decided to go back to school. It was in sales, again on the phone, but in an office for a company nearby. It was another job that enabled me to work but be home for my kids before and after school. It was my last part-time job and I realized that I didn't want to go back to full-time office work again. The children were in fourth and second grades, and it was time to think about my future. It was time for me to find a career that I could love. What could that be? Teaching was my choice but the amount of school it would require was daunting.

With only one year of undergraduate credits, looking ahead to complete a four-year degree and then a graduate degree seemed like an impossible goal. Still, I always loved school so I took the leap and began a ten-year journey. Had I known how arduous it would be I may not have had the courage to start. I was 37 years old.

"How long will it take you to complete your degree?"

"How will you get your work done and still take care of your family?"

"How old will you be when you finish?"

"Will you even be able to get a teaching job?"

These were all thought-provoking questions that not only were asked of me but that I asked myself. Questions that might have made me reconsider my goal.

At the time, I heard a woman on the radio who wanted to go back to school to be an attorney. She doubted herself and exclaimed to her friend,

"It will take me five years to become an attorney and then I'll be 50 years old." And her wise friend said,

"And how old will you be in five years if you don't go to school to be an attorney?"

That made sense to me.

Immediately, things began to fall into place.

One Sunday afternoon we invited Elise's friend, her parents, and siblings, to join us at a barbeque at my brother-in-law's restaurant. Although we knew Jim and Mary from school events at our daughters' school, this would be the first time we would have a conversation and get to know each other.

During the barbeque, Jim asked me,

"What are you studying in school?"

"Elementary and Literacy Education," I replied.

Prompted by Jim, we discussed what school I was attending, how I would manage the hours required, and what my goals were. He was also curious about what made me choose this course of study. I later learned that Jim was a Director of Pupil Personnel Services in a nearby school district. That afternoon at the barbeque it seemed to be a very casual conversation, but soon I would realize it was an interview.

The next morning after I walked Eric and Elise to school, I was talking with a friend on the phone at my house for a while. This was not only before cell phones and texting, but before any kind of call waiting or the technology to leave a message on a home phone. If someone was trying to call you and the line was busy, they would have to call back. You wouldn't even know that someone was trying to reach you. Shortly after I hung up there was a knock at my door and there was Jim.

He had been trying to get through to me on the phone to tell me there was an opening for a teacher assistant in a primary school in his district, and could I go on an interview in an hour. Thanks to Jim's persistence that day, I made it to the interview on time and was hired as a primary school teacher assistant in 1988.

School alone had seemed like a daunting task and now I had a job on top of it. But family support and encouragement kept me going. Somehow the family's schedules aligned and accommodated my work and school hours. Organization for our family was key, no time to think about what had to be done in any area of our lives, just jump in and do it. Cooking, cleaning, driving to after-school activities, it was a whirlwind. Working in the school was a great motivation because it cemented my desire to work with children in the school environment. I was perpetually tired but happy.

Claude's mother and father were often my cheerleaders and would help us in so many ways. When I couldn't be home, Claude and the kids would go there for dinner. Not only was there support from them in a practical sense, but their encouragement and joy for what I was working to accomplish never wavered and often kept me going.

In 1991 when my undergraduate degree was completed, I immediately began the graduate program in Literacy Studies which would qualify me to teach K through 12 and first-year college as a Reading Specialist.

During my first year of graduate studies, I was still

working as a teacher assistant. As a teacher assistant, I had been in one school for two years and then was reassigned to two other schools over the next two years. After I had my teaching degree, but before my master's degree was complete, I applied for teaching positions in the same school district. The first principal I worked for as a teacher assistant saw my name on the hired list and contacted the Personnel Office to let them know he knew me and would like me to fill a first-grade position in his school. It was my dream come true. First grade was when students learned to read, and I would soon have my reading degree. I am forever indebted to that principal for giving me this opportunity. It was the beginning of the career I had always dreamed of. It was 1993 and I was 44 years old.

In 1996, after ten years of undergraduate and then graduate studies, my course work, practicum, and the three-year path to tenure was completed. Ten years working on a lifelong dream of becoming a teacher.

It was the completion of my formal course of studies, but rather than an end, it was only the beginning of the joy that this realization of my career goal would give me for so many years.

After seven years as a first-grade teacher, my new principal made me aware of a Reading Teacher position that would be available in our school. I was fortunate to have two supportive, caring principals. As much as I loved the classroom, I was excited about this new chance to concentrate on language arts which is what I loved most about teaching first grade.

We remained friends with Jim and his family and I saw him when he visited my school for his administrative visits and at the Administration building. If it wasn't for him, I don't think I would have had the career that I enjoyed and loved for 22 years.

Elise, Eileen, Claude, and Eric – Graduation Master Degree Literacy Studies

✦   27   ✦

"ONE OF THESE DAYS"

On October 19, 1992, while working as a teacher assistant in a Fifth Grade Special Education classroom, my education degree and teacher certification were complete and I was continuing my education for a master's degree in Literacy Education.

We had just enjoyed a visit from my mother three weeks before and I was scheduled to go to Florida to visit her in November. Since 1980 she had many serious health issues, but heart disease was the number one cause of her most recent failing health. When she visited in September we could see how even the slightest activity caused her physical distress. We asked her to please stay for a while; the weather was good and we would enjoy her company. She wouldn't consider it though because her sister Catherine was in Florida awaiting her return. Her team of doctors was there too and I know that was an important consideration. I reluctantly let her go, both of us content in knowing that I had my plane tickets to visit her in November.

As Claude was driving my mother to the airport after that visit, he noticed she was unusually quiet and as he looked over at her he asked,

"Mom, are you ok?"

He saw that she was flushed; short of breath and leaning her head back against the headrest.

"Yes, I'll be fine. I always get these spells. It will pass."

They were about halfway to the airport and he later told me he was not comfortable with continuing on especially considering she was traveling alone.

"Mom, I think I should take you back home with me. You seem too weak to travel."

She would not hear of it. She assured him she would be fine. She had the wheelchair arranged at the airport so she wouldn't have to walk at all. She would take it easy and call as soon as she got home. My brother Brian was picking her up at the airport.

My mother was always the boss. If she decided something there was no way anyone could persuade her to change her mind and once plane tickets were bought and paid for there was no going back.

I heard the click of the classroom intercom.

"Mrs. Resta?"

"Yes?"

"Would you please come to the office?"

"The classroom teacher stepped out for a minute so I can't leave the students."

"Ok, thank you."

I had a bad feeling. Within seconds my friend Penny, the classroom teacher, returned. I could see she was composing herself but I wasn't certain until she said,

"Come with me and bring your things."

As we walked out of the classroom I searched her face and asked,

"What's happened?"

With that, she took me in her arms and said,

"I'm so sorry. Your mother has passed away."

"Oh no," I said, "please, not yet."

Overwhelming feelings of disbelief, loss, and sadness rushed in. I knew she was frail but I still didn't anticipate this day would happen so soon. She had recovered well from so many serious illnesses in the last ten years that recovery became my expectation. It's what I wanted to believe. We had just spoken on Saturday and we didn't know it would be the last time. It was a happy conversation with talk of plans for my November visit. How did we say goodbye that day?

"I love you. See you soon."

Penny held my arm as we went down the stairs and I saw Claude standing in the hallway just outside the glass-walled office reception area. As we approached Claude, I saw compassionate, caring faces looking back at me from inside the reception area. Penny gave me one more hug and passed me into Claude's arms where we cried together. I barely remember leaving the building.

With that, he guided me to his car, settled me in, and took me home. I had many questions but he didn't have answers yet. I had to wait for more information from Brian and my aunt. As we left the school I just wanted to know if her death was peaceful. My aunt later shared the following account.

On Sunday, October 18, 1992, my mother and my aunt spent Sunday evening together at my mother's place. They lived in the same complex and their condos had an outdoor catwalk, a walkway to every resident's door. My mother and aunt could stand out on their catwalks and see each other's condos from their front doors. Sunday they had dinner together and then watched a movie. My aunt left around 11 p.m. and my mother stood on her catwalk watching her as she walked home. They waved to each other as my aunt went in her door. That was the last time they would see each other, however, as was their nightly habit, they would talk on the phone until one or the other would say they were ready to go to sleep.

The next morning on Monday, October 19, my aunt called my mother's phone several times, first thinking she slept late but after a short time knowing something was wrong. She had a key and asked a friend to go with her to my mother's place. There they found her stretched out on her den couch. I find it so hard to imagine my poor aunt finding her sister, her friend, and confidant for life, gone from her.

During the most recent visits to Huntington from my mother, I noticed that after she had her tea and breakfast in the morning, she would appear flushed and short of breath. She would get up from the dining room table and slowly make her way into the living room holding onto pieces of furniture on her way. She would then "throw herself" on the couch as she used to say, collapsing onto it as she tried to catch her breath. My living room, dining room, and kitchen are connected so we would talk as I cleaned up after breakfast. More than once she said,

"You know, one of these days one of these spells is going to take me."

I wish I could remember how I responded to that but I can't. Did I go to the couch and comfort her? Deny the possibility of what she was saying? Just ask her if I can do anything to help her? I have no idea. Memory is a tricky thing. I do remember that as she placed a pill under her tongue she reassured me her medication would revive her and she would be fine again. I know she minimized her problems so I wouldn't be worried. And I just wanted to believe that yes, everything would be fine, forever.

When my aunt came to my house for the funeral I asked her for more details. I wanted to be assured they didn't find my mother had fallen and couldn't get help. She reassured me that she was peacefully lying on the couch. My mother had correctly predicted how she would die. My aunt kindly described the scene when she arrived at my mother's place that morning.

"On the kitchen table was the newspaper, her empty teacup, a dish with remnants of her breakfast, and her daily medication container. She had taken her pills that morning."

From that description, I knew what followed because I had experienced this scene with her many times. Peaceful yes but I hope so quick that she had no time to be afraid.

In later years she talked about her death whenever we were together. Although I didn't want to hear it I knew it comforted her for me to know that she had made plans. Plans to make her death easier for ME: arrangements with the funeral home here in Huntington, instructions about the dress she wanted to be dressed in (showing me where it was in her closet whenever I visited), and appeals to me to watch over and visit my aunt which Claude and I did for the twelve years my aunt survived my mother. My mother was 79 when she passed and my aunt lived until she was 89. We honored all of my mother's final wishes; The wake at her chosen funeral home, burial in the cemetery with my father Owen, and a lunch at my house which we were able to have outside on my deck because it was an especially beautiful October day. The priest joined us at the house as we all shared memories of Mary Agnes Margaret Clancy Coyne Martin. There was sadness but laughter too because it was hard to share a memory of her without that bit of humor to it.

I have two favorites which I shared that day and they both relate to her faith.

On one of her flights to or from Florida to my home, she was reported by a fellow passenger to a flight attendant, who asked my mother,

"Excuse me Ma'am, were you sprinkling something around your seat?"

"Oh yes!" my mother answered, "It's holy water from Lourdes I sprinkle it for a safe flight."

She chuckled when she told us this story, as she realized how other passengers may have been alarmed.

Another incident occurred when she was shopping in the large Publix supermarket one afternoon and a fellow shopper approached the store manager to say,

"Excuse me Sir, but there's a woman in aisle 4 and she's ticking!"

The manager quickly followed the woman as she pointed my mother out.

"Ma'am, do I hear something ticking?"

"Oh yes," she happily replied. "It's my alarm clock. I'm doing a nine-hour novena to St. Jude and I don't want to miss the hour for the prayer while I'm here. It's hour 7."

I wish I knew what the manager said to that.

Shortly after the funeral, my aunt returned to Florida and it was hard to imagine her adjusting to life without her sister. My mother was the social sister and the one who made the plans, made the friends, and drove everywhere. My aunt didn't drive. She and I would talk frequently and she would share with me how she was coping. Many times Claude and I tried to get her to consider moving to an adult community near us but she wouldn't leave Florida.

The funeral was in October and Claude and I made plans to go to Florida early in December to empty my mother's condo. The plan was for Claude to fly to Florida during the week and rent a U-Haul there to bring certain things home. I had to work until Friday so I was going to fly down on Friday afternoon, two days after him, and together with my brother, my aunt, my niece and her husband, and some close friends, we would empty the condo. We knew it would be a hard and emotional task.

Well, on that Friday there was a blizzard and all flights were canceled. Rescheduling for Saturday was not an option since they were so delayed I would have arrived in Florida on Saturday night only to have to fly home on Sunday for work on Monday. I was devastated.

Claude was already there and everyone was helping. He would be able to complete everything and start the drive back on Sunday. There were many phone calls between Claude and me on Friday and Saturday before I finally accepted the reality that I had to surrender any thoughts of getting there. Claude said,

"She's still looking out for you."

I was spared the heartbreaking job of going through and disseminating her precious things. She loved her home and certain things were designated for Brian and me. It was all previously discussed and we always assured her we would respect her wishes.

Claude took two days to drive home from Florida, not an easy trip to make alone. When we started planning how we would empty the condo, we explored other options since I was worried about him driving back alone. He reassured me that the drive would not be a problem. Then he said,

"I want to do this. I want to be the one to bring your mother's things home to you."

It was a loving gesture and exemplifies the generous person he is.

My mother Mary was strong but vulnerable, raised old school but open-minded, often stressed in life but always ready for a laugh. We did not always agree on things but as I became an adult and a parent, what I know for sure is she was always there for me. I miss the comfort of calling her and receiving her encouragement and approval.

28

THREE YEARS LATER

Only three years later in 1995, Claude's mother, Simone, passed away. In 1990 she had been diagnosed with a fatal disease; one which would give us only five more years with her. We were all shocked and overcome with grief. She bravely fought this disease with Dad by her side. She needed special treatment, equipment, and trips to Maryland for an experimental program. Dad was her caretaker and was devoted to helping her through all the stages of her illness. He was dedicated to her daily care which included preparing the medication, sterilizing the many tubes through which it was delivered through a port which also required attention, and keeping the oxygen machine up and running without fail. He was her driver to the many doctor appointments and trips to Maryland. At her passing, we comforted Dad by recognizing his years of steadfast, loving care. As we held him he said,

"I wish I could do it forever."

After she passed he stayed in their house for two years, comforted by his memories of more than forty years of life there with his family. Eventually, the family knew it was time for dad to move and Corinne found a house nearby for her family, one with an attached apartment. She approached Dad with the idea that maybe it was time to sell the house and move into the apartment. Dad agreed and it was an ideal arrangement. He loved being there, once again involved in the hustle and bustle of family life, and Corinne and her children loved having him.

Still, we all felt he could use the companionship of someone his age. A family friend told Corinne about a widow who she knew very well named Jean who lived around the block from Dad. She was just a few years younger and they had a lot in common. They both grew up in big families in the city, her family was from Queens, NY, and his from Brooklyn, NY. We knew Dad would not make plans on his own so Corinne arranged to go to lunch with Dad, her friend, and Jean. After that Jean joined our family dinners and celebrations and she invited us to join her for occasions and dinner, but it took a while before Dad would make plans to go out with Jean alone. Finally, when he did, they had many adventures together. They each had their own homes but would often vacation together at Jean's condo on Cape Cod. They loved to take drives and explore new places. Jean became part of the family and joined us for vacations, weddings, births, baptisms, and holidays. She didn't have children and she loved spending time with ours. She and Dad spent time with her family also, traveling to Massachusetts and California to visit Jean's brothers and sister. She confided in me one day during the search for my birth family,

"You know, I considered adoption when I learned I couldn't have children, but I didn't have family support and decided against it."

Jean was a teacher for 35 years and her students became her children. We love her stories. On one of her vacations, she went to Holland and brought back wooden shoes for her entire class. The day she gave them to her students, she walked them to one of their other classes and the noise in the school halls of clopping clogs was deafening. Teachers and students ran to their classroom doorways to see what the racket was. Jean traveled extensively every summer and used her adventures to create excitement in her teaching.

29

"WHAT'S IT LIKE TO BE ADOPTED?"

This is a question that was posed to me many times, and I welcomed these questions because being adopted made me feel special. It was my closest friends who would ask me questions about my feelings, and since I had positive feelings about my adoption, I was happy to answer any and all questions they had. My brother Brian and I always knew we were adopted and we had an attitude of being in this reality together from the beginning. When we were very young my mother and father would tell us sweet and detailed stories that taught us about adoption in the most subtle way. I remember loving these stories but I wonder at what age I realized they were about Brian and me.

The message of these stories was the same: that a mother was unable to provide for her new baby and loved that baby so much, she gave it to a couple who would provide for and love the baby as their own.

My mother told me that in the early fifties when we lived in Bayside, NY she experienced discrimination against adopted children. One time when my brother wasn't invited to a birthday party, my mother asked why he was excluded.

"We don't want our child to play with him because he is adopted."

My mother would never tolerate such an insult especially against her child, and I'm sure there was quite a blowup. She wondered how many others felt that way but were keeping it to themselves.

I didn't experience discrimination firsthand as a child, but as I grew older I realized that many people just didn't understand what it means to adopt a child or be an adopted child; to understand that the love is strong even though the mother did not bear the child. Questions such as, "Wouldn't you want to know your "real" mother?" were confusing to me. In my mind, Mary was my real mother and Owen was my real father.

One comment that really surprised and disappointed me as an adult was,

"If I was adopted I would be afraid to have children, not knowing what may be in the genes."

I was happy that I already had my two children and that thought had never occurred to me. Also, who really knows what's in their genes?

Was I curious about my birth mother? Absolutely.

Did I think about her through the years? Yes, always on my birthday in particular.

These were passing thoughts though and I didn't dwell on them. They were pushed away and even denied.

My mother would tell me that often a birth mother would not tell anyone that she had had a baby. If I was able to find her and contact her, it may force her to divulge a secret to her family about a difficult time in her life. That was too much for me to imagine and I didn't want the responsibility of that possible upheaval. However, I also realize that it was in my mother's interest to scare me about this particular scenario since she did not want to lose me and be replaced by a mother who didn't even know me. Considering the length to which an adopted child's birth information is locked away in legally "sealed" files, this was a big fear for adoptive parents.

Occasionally, I would ask my mother to tell me again what she knew about my birth mother. I think I hoped she would remember a new detail to feed my imagination. She recounted what the nuns in the orphanage told her; my birth mother was young, unmarried, and without the support or resources needed to raise me. There were no government social services then and her family did not have the means to help.

In all those discussions, my birth father never came up. When I reflect on this it is yet another reminder of how society was different then. Men weren't expected to be responsible for the child they helped conceive.

My mother would sometimes ask me what I thought or felt about my birth mother. I knew I could be honest and told her that it must have been a difficult and frightening circumstance to be pregnant and unmarried in 1949. I would wonder what she looked like and if I looked like her. More importantly, I felt love towards her. My mother appreciated knowing my thoughts. I know she felt gratitude toward my birth mother from the beginning so she was not jealous of my love, as long as I did not pursue a reunion. She didn't have to tell me that; I just knew it.

Back in the '40s, '50s, and '60s mostly pat answers were given to adopted children in response to questions about their birth.

My brother and I were told,

"She was alone and couldn't afford to keep you."

"She was disgraced and you would have grown up in the shadow of that shame."

"She did what she thought would be best for you."

"You have a better life here with us."

Medical and genetic information was not something that was shared nor was it considered important. At that time, we adopted children were thought to be a clean slate in terms of identity, medical or genetic. Now we know the importance of each person's biological and genetic connection to their ancestors. Still, it was a blessing that so many babies were saved from a childhood in an institution because of people who wanted a child and could offer a good home. Most adoptees that I know, including me, are grateful and love the families who raised and loved them.

Young children for the most part want to please their parents. They are keenly aware of when their parents are comfortable with their questions and when they may be uncomfortable. As an adopted child, even with parents who are open to questions and seem to have the answers, a child senses their parents' emotions as they explain as best they can the circumstances of their birth and arrival into the family.

In, *You Don't Look Adopted*, Anne Heffron writes,

"If you think your voice is dangerous in its ability to hurt the ones you love, you learn to keep it quiet."

I grew up believing that we were all better off; the birth mother able to move on with her life without the shame of an "out of wedlock" pregnancy, the baby being given a chance at a better life with a stable family, and the adoptive parents feeling happy that they could have the baby they dreamed of and be responsible for saving that child from a life in an institution.

In retrospect, as an adult, an adoptee may realize it wasn't quite that simple.

Historically birth mothers were shamed and offered no other solutions than to give up their babies. The Catholic Church for one example offered housing and care to pregnant young women. However, the contingency was that they must give up their babies. This was not just the Catholic Church's demand but society's as well. Many adoptees are led to believe that their birth mother was happy for this way out of her dilemma, and maybe some were, but learning that they had no choice but to leave their baby behind puts another light on it.

As my brother and I were brought up to believe, when adoptees consider contacting their birth mother, they are usually told that they would be disrupting their lives, that they probably moved on after the birth, and have families that never knew a birth occurred. That certainly would discourage an adoptee to pursue a reunion. They disrupted this person's life at birth and now they would do it again? It's easier to go on with the family life you were brought into and leave well enough alone.

Today 95% of adoptions in the United States include some kind of contact between birth parents and children. That is remarkable and it is a step forward but not without challenges. Organizations such as "First Mother Forum," Parents for Ethical Adoption Reform, and Concerned United Birthparents work tirelessly to change and improve adoption laws.

In January of 2020, Governor of New York, Andrew Cuomo signed a law giving every adoptee born in New York the right to have a copy of their original birth certificate. This is a great milestone for so many adopted adults. I shared this information about the new law with my niece and nephew, and I think they may start the process of obtaining my brother Brian's original birth certificate.

Over the years my "leave well enough alone" viewpoint

has changed. It didn't change while my parents were alive, but much later when I decided to seek out medical information about my birth family. I have come to realize that more needs to be done to help the adult adoptee who wants birth information and/or a reunion and to help them prepare for all the possible outcomes a reunion may bring.

PART II

30

THE CHRONOLOGICAL ACCOUNT

AUGUST 3, 2010

When we were leaving Sister Jeannette in Montreal in July, she suggested two phone numbers I could call to begin my search in earnest. To begin, I called the Centre Jeunesse de Montreal for biological information and left a message asking for someone to call back. Next, I called Adoption Services, and as per Sister Jeannette, asked for Nancy. That message said to press 1162 and request a form for reunion information, if interested. I left a message asking Nancy to return my call.

AUGUST 4, 2010

Louise called from Adoption Services to say they will look for my information and send me a consent form to return. It will take about two weeks.

AUGUST 5, 2010

Nancy, also from Adoption Services called to tell me that we "are on the right path."

AUGUST 25, 2010

I sent the information request forms to Centre Jeunesse requesting biological information and possibly the opportunity to write to my birth mother.

SEPTEMBER 7, 2010

The application for birth information arrived and I filled it out and sent it to Centre Jeunesse the next day. It required that I include a copy of the Surrogate's Court, Queens County adoption papers, a copy of my baptismal certificate, and a copy of several identification cards with my photo and/or signature on them. The significance of the date of the arrival of the application for birth information has not escaped me. It is the date I was brought to Society de la rehabilitation, Crèche de la Miséricorde (the orphanage) from where I was adopted by my parents on September 9, 1949.

JANUARY 18, 2011

Nadia, the social worker assigned to my case, called from Post-Adoption Services to say they have received my application and are working on my case.

FEBRUARY 22, 2011

Nadia called with the happy news that my birth mother has tried to locate me many times. She will call the phone numbers in my file with the hope that my birth mother is still alive and we can contact her.

My family was informed of every bit of news to date, but it was after this last phone call that I decided to share the news of my search with my friends at work. Before this no one at work knew I was adopted, so after giving them some background, I answered their questions about how and why I decided to pursue this after all these years. They were so happy and hopeful for me.

Whenever Nadia called and gave me new information about the search, I was able to share it with my friends at work. They were a blessing to me and I will never forget their support as I ran an emotional gamut from joy to despair after every phone call from Nadia.

FEBRUARY 24, 2011

Only two days later Nadia called. I love the way she is keeping me up to date with any new developments in her search.

"Hello, Mrs. Resta. I have called the phone numbers I found in your file, but unfortunately they are no longer in service."

"Does that mean you will not be able to find her?" I asked.

"No, next I will contact the agency in charge of the government health cards that every Canadian citizen must have. They will be able to tell me if she is alive, and if she is not they will know the date of her death and cause."

"Thank you, Nadia. I will wait anxiously for your next call. I pray for the best news."

The application I sent in September stated that finding birth information and your birth family can take as long as 15 months. However, in consideration of the ages of my birth mother and me, Nadia is allowed and encouraged to prioritize my case and work as quickly as possible to find my birth mother.

"Yesterday I mailed your socio-biological information and a copy of the letter that your birth mother wrote to the agency asking them to help her find you. I think it will be nice for you to read and to see your mother's handwriting."

MARCH 3, 2011

The mail took a week from Canada, what a long week of waiting to read my birth mother's message. I received the information and the letter she wrote in 1986. It is so overwhelming to see my mother's beautiful handwriting, but the message hit me hard. She spoke so sweetly of her feelings for me and said she prayed that she could know that I was safe and happy. She hoped for a reunion with me. She asked if I would like to know my biological mother. Often, over the last ten years, I would say to Claude:

"If only I could write to my birth mother. I would thank her for giving me life and let her know that I've had a very good life."

It saddened me to now realize that if I had been able to do that many years ago I could have given her the peace that would come from knowing her baby is safe and happy.

I hoped that she would still be alive so I could give her that peace.

MARCH 8, 2011

It has been five days since I received my socio-biological information and the letter, and two weeks since I spoke with Nadia. I am so anxious to hear if she has any news, so at 11 a.m. I called Nadia and hoped to reach her before my next class.

"Hello, this is Nadia." What a relief to hear her voice again.

"Hello, Nadia this is Eileen Resta. Thank you for sending the letter and socio-biological information to me. I already feel closer to my birth mother and hope for good news today."

My cell phone is always with me throughout my workday as I wait for Nadia's phone calls and the possibility of locating my birth mother. Usually, I leave my phone at my desk as I go from classroom to classroom, meeting with my small reading groups. Since I heard from Nadia of the possibility of finding my birth mother, I have continued to work, of course. I am so thankful for the young children with whom I work every day. They keep me focused and engaged while I wait for news from Nadia.

Nadia continued,

"I have found another address for your birth mother from 2009. There are a few more phone numbers for me to call, and I will call you back as soon as I know if any of them are current."

My daughter Elise's baby girl is only six weeks old. Her brothers are five and three years old. A few times a week I drive directly to their house from work, visiting them and helping in any way I can.

They live about 40 minutes from my work and most of the trip is highway driving.

It was 4 p.m. when my phone rang. It was in my purse. Luckily I wasn't on the highway yet, but on a local road where I could pull over to answer. All I could think was,

"Please let it be Nadia!"

I quickly answered as I pulled off the road,

"Hello?"

"Hello, Mrs. Resta. I have very good news. Your Mother is alive!"

Barely able to find my voice, I asked,

"Where is she? Is she well?"

Nadia quickly replied.

"She is living in a home for the elderly."

She was 81 at the time and I was 61. Nadia doesn't know her physical or mental condition, but she spoke with the social worker at the home who was going to visit her and begin to assess her physical and mental state. Then he will call Nadia to let her know details of my birth mother's condition. Perhaps at that time, Nadia will be able to proceed with a plan for a reunion. We're getting close.

MARCH 9, 2011

Only one day later Nadia called. She continues to work as quickly as possible because of my birth mother's age. Today she is calling to tell me she spoke with the social worker from the home.

"He doesn't think she is physically well enough to withstand the shock, or cognitively be able to remember or comprehend." As my heart sank Nadia reassured me,

"Don't worry," she said, "the social worker has just started working at the home and is familiarizing himself with all the patients and their histories. I will speak to him again and get more detailed information."

It is so hard to think that she is alive, but I may be too late for a meaningful reunion. We will find a way to each other, and I know Nadia is fighting for me.

MARCH 12, 2011

It was March 12, 2011, Claude's birthday, and we were celebrating at Sfoglia, our nephew and niece's restaurant in New York City. March is a very busy birthday month in our family so there were six of us at the dinner: Claude and I, Claude's sister Corinne, his sister Martine and her husband Anthony, and my childhood friend, Clare. Martine's birthday is March 10, Clare's birthday is March 11, and Claude's birthday is March 12. We were having a very special dinner with champagne toasts to my birth mother and the possibility of a reunion. We all knew that my birth mother had been found, but we didn't know if her health and mental state would allow me to have the reunion I was hoping for. Claude's toast brought us all to tears.

"I would like to propose a toast to Eileen's birth mother to thank her for selflessly giving up her baby girl. Because of that decision, Eileen and I were able to be together all these years. I hope that we meet her soon so we can tell her we love her and thank her for her sacrifice."

Just before Claude's toast, we were served appetizers and our nephew Johan described the wine he chose for us as he poured it into our glasses and left the table. Five minutes later he came back to our table and not realizing a toast had taken place, saw that all six of us were crying.

"Is it the food?" he asked.

Then we burst into laughter. Johan delivered the comic relief we needed. It had been a very emotional six months of uncertainty and everyone at that table was anxiously waiting and anticipating a happy outcome to our search for my birth mother.

MARCH 15, 2011

Six days of waiting since I heard from Nadia but every day feels like three. I don't know how I get through each day waiting for news but somehow I do.

Since there has been no news from Nadia since March 9, I called her today around 9 a.m. I was prepared to leave a message but much to my relief, she answered the phone and told me she was going to call the social worker at the home as soon as we hung up and get back to me as soon as she was able to reach him.

Just a little while later my phone rang and it was Nadia.

"Mrs. Resta, I have some information about your birth mother. I am sorry to tell you that she has dementia and a reunion is unlikely. She has a son who visits her daily and I will try to contact him."

"I have a brother?!?"

Having siblings or half-siblings was something I had not considered. All my thoughts and wishes were for finding my birth mother and putting her at ease. I wonder if her son knows about me or will Nadia's inquiries come as a shock.

My birth mother has a nurse who, according to Nadia, has a "good relationship" with her. We are hoping that the nurse may be able to advocate for me to see my birth mother. Nadia said she would be working on getting more medical information, and try to get a picture of my mother to send me.

I was so saddened by this news—to think that she is alive but I cannot see her? And that I am too late to bring her the peace she needed? It's unimaginable. I don't want to accept that, and hopefully, the professionals there will advocate for me to find a way.

MARCH 18, 2011

Three more days of waiting; I'm growing impatient. When I called Nadia this morning I left a message asking her to please call me next week knowing the office is closed on the weekends.

MARCH 22, 2011

Four more days of waiting; it was 8 a.m. on Tuesday when Nadia called. I was still at home and preparing to leave for work.

"Mrs. Resta, your mother remembers you!"

Those words took my breath away and brought tears of relief and joy as Nadia expressed her happiness for me.

"What did she say?" I asked.

Nadia told me that my mother's doctor, who has been caring for her long before she was in this home, visited her to assess her memory and comprehension. When he asked her about having a daughter who she had to give up for adoption, he said she had tears in her eyes as she told him,

"I remember everything and I want to meet her. Meeting her would be very good for me. I have been looking for her for many years."

The doctor told Nadia he believed she would be strong enough to have a reunion.

Then Nadia added,

"Your brother would like to meet you also."

What a dream come true. Soon I will be meeting my birth family. People that I come from, and maybe even look like.

My emotions were intense and ever-changing. They were fluctuating between excitement, joy, disbelief, a little fear, and even a feeling of betrayal of my parents, my brother Brian, and all my relatives from my life since I was three months old. In my heart, I knew that finding the family I came from would not change the love I have for the family who raised me. Repeatedly during my life, I denied ever wanting or needing to know more than the little information I was given while growing up about the relatives I must have in Canada. From very young I learned to quell my questions. So now I had to put aside my fears and understand there is no one to hurt. I am at peace with that and feel grateful to have this opportunity.

MARCH 30, 2011

Eight more days of waiting. After Nadia's last phone call I had one foot out the door to leave for Montreal.

I called Nadia and left a message asking if she has any news.

APRIL 1, 2011

After two more days of waiting, I called Nadia at 9 a.m. and left a message.

At 12 p.m. Nadia called.

"I just spoke to your oldest brother."

"Excuse me? The oldest? How many do I have?"

"Your birth mother has three sons."

I grew up with one brother and now I have three more.

"Nadia, when can I go to Montreal and meet them?"

The meeting was set for April 14, 2011, at 10 a.m. at the Foyer home in Chateauguay.

Now there will be two more weeks of waiting and anticipating but this waiting is different because I know my search is over.

We will meet in a meeting room at the Foyer. The social worker from the Foyer, and my social worker Nadia will be there. After Claude and I are brought into the room, my brothers will come in to meet me. They want to meet me before they bring our mother to the meeting room. When you think of it they know nothing about me. I'm sure they wonder about my motivation and want to be sure to protect her.

Nadia told me that my three brothers have known about me since 1994 and have helped our mother search for me. My oldest brother told Nadia that all the brothers are happy that I have found them. He said they recently talked about trying to find me again, but this time when they asked her she said no. They helped her many times in the past to find me, and they understood why she said no. The disappointment would have been too great if it was another unsuccessful search.

"Nadia, can you tell me now my birth mother's name?"

"Yes, I'm happy to. It's Mireille."

What a beautiful French name. I can't wait to meet her.

Later I found out that although my brothers and their wives knew about me, their children did not. So on April 1, April Fool's Day, they were told I was coming to meet their grandmother, my birth mother, on April 14. Angela and Yves' daughter Sabrina, who was 16 years old at the time, thought it was an April fool's day joke.

We leave on Wednesday, April 13, 2011, for Montreal for our meeting on April 14, 2011, at 10 a.m.

SOCIO-BIOLOGICAL
INFORMATION

On March 3, Nadia told me she would send the socio-biological information (which I have included at the end of this chapter) that was in my file. I received it about a week later.

The information dates back to the time of my birth.

N/A means that the information is not available.

Not Applicable means that an item does not apply to my situation.

On the first page, under General Information, is my file number, then my name given to me when I was adopted, Eileen Mary Coyne, followed by my given name at birth, Marie Monique (No last name was given on this form because when Nadia sent this to me, she had not yet secured permission from my birth family.) This page also lists my place of birth as L'Aide a la Femme, the date, June 6, 1949, and time of birth, 15 h 15. It also indicated that I was baptized on June 7, 1949, the day after my birth.

The second page gives a very basic medical history. I weighed 6.1 pounds and was 25 inches long. That is really long and makes me wonder if it is a typo. My condition is listed as good, the pregnancy lasted 40 weeks, but there is no information about the duration of labor or type of delivery. It states that I had dark blue eyes and brown hair, but my eyes are brown. On August 26, 1949, I was immunized against diphtheria and whooping cough.

The third page states that the adoption consent was given by my birth mother on 5/7/49 so I wonder if she had to go to the clinic the month before her delivery date to register and fill out paperwork.

My official placement with my parents was on 9/9/49. Initially, I thought that I spent my first three months at L'Aide a la Femme, but in 2018 my birth family learned a different story from their Aunt about my first three months. My legal adoption was on April 19, 1950, when I was ten months old.

The fourth page outlines the requests by my birth mother for information about me in 1957, 1986, and 2002. According to my brothers and extended family, she tried to locate me several other times in addition to these years.

The fifth-page states I left L'Aide a la Femme on 9/7/49 and was placed under the care of The Societe de Rehabilitation Inc. of Sherbrooke. That agency placed me in the Crèche de la Miséricorde which was the orphanage where my family found me and adopted me on 9/9/49. On page 6 there is personal information about my birth mother that she must have provided when she entered L'Aide a la Femme to deliver me. She was 20 years old and weighed 92 pounds and was 5'1" tall. At 20 years old, I was 98 lbs. and 5'4" tall. She listed her eyes as brown and her hair as black. My eyes are brown and my hair was more dark brown than black. Her nationality was French Canadian and she was Catholic. When she was 13 years old she completed 7th grade and then she lists her occupation as dressmaker. In later conversations with my brothers, they told me they never knew she was a dressmaker.

On page 7 she is reported to be in good health. Some characteristics listed are that she liked dancing, going to the theatre, bicycling, and cleaning the house. Also that she was a nice person.

She lived with her mom and siblings, her father passed away when she was seventeen, three years prior to her giving birth to me.

On pages 8, 9, and 10 there is information about my birth father provided by my birth mother.

My birth father was 20 years old, weighed 160 lbs., and was 5' 9" tall. He had "chestnut brown" hair and blue eyes. He was also French Canadian and Catholic. Regarding "schooling" is N/A which means not available. His occupation is listed as working in a "cement works," and he was in good health. His characteristics are listed as swimming, going to the theatre and bicycling. They apparently shared the same interests. Mireille stated that he "could have a drink sometimes," he was cute, serious and a fine-looking young man. Regarding his relationship with his family, it simply states, "They were getting along." There is no indication in the file that my birth father was either informed of the pregnancy or the birth. Mireille said they saw each other for about four months and that she broke up with him when she found out she was pregnant.

On pages 11 and 12 is information concerning the extended families of Mireille and my biological father. Mireille's mother was 45 when I was born and her health is listed as good. (She was a young grandmother and I was her first grandchild but I wonder if she ever saw me.) Her father died when Mireille was 17 from angina. His occupation is listed as "commercial traveler" which my family told me is a salesman.

She had two brothers and one sister. Her older brother, Yvon had a 12th-grade education and was working in an office at the time of my birth. He worked for the railroad in technology during his career. Her sister is listed as having a 6th-grade education and unemployed at the time. Her youngest brother was still in school when I was born.

Concerning the extended family of my biological father, only information about his siblings is listed and it is quite an unbelievable account. He had 8 brothers and 10 sisters and does not indicate his rank in the 18 children. Perhaps two families joined together? The health status information raises even more curiosity. Four brothers and five sisters "were dead" but the cause of death is unknown to Mireille. One brother and two sisters were married. Two of the sisters were working as dressmakers and the others were still at school. The brothers, along with my birth father and his father, were working in the "cement works." Mireille said she was working as a dressmaker and according to this information; my birth father's sisters were also working as dressmakers. Perhaps working with his sisters was the link to her meeting my birth father.

The most helpful information from this report is the medical history that reveals my birth grandfather died from Angina.

<table>
<tr><td colspan="6">B. Medical History</td></tr>
<tr><td rowspan="2">At birth :</td><td colspan="2">Weight :

6,1 pounds</td><td colspan="2">Length :

25 inches</td><td>Blood group :

N/A</td></tr>
<tr><td colspan="2">Cranial circumférence :

N/A</td><td colspan="2">Thorax perimeter :

N/A</td><td>APGAR :

N/A</td></tr>
<tr><td colspan="6">Conditions of childbirth :

Good condition</td></tr>
<tr><td colspan="6">Weeks of gestation :

40</td></tr>
<tr><td colspan="6">Duration of labour :

N/A</td></tr>
<tr><td colspan="6">Type of delivery :

N/A</td></tr>
<tr><td colspan="6">Other information on birth of the child :

You had dark blue eyes and brown hair.</td></tr>
<tr><td colspan="6">Medical information :

You received immunisation against diphtheria and whooping cough on August 26th 1949</td></tr>
</table>

C. Adoption

Date of adoption consent :	Mother :	1949-05-07
		Year / Month / Day
	Father :	N/A
		Year / Month / Day
	Child :	N/A
		Year / Month / Day

Date of tacit abandonment ☐ Date of declaration of eligibility for adoption ☐	N/A Year / Month / Day
Date of placement with adoptive family :	1949-09-09 Year / Month / Day
Date of legal adoption :	1950-04-19 Year / Month / Day
Judicial district of legal adoption :	District of Saint Francis
Place of residence of adoptive parents at the time of adoption : (Parish and place of registration chosen by the adoptive parent)	Brooklyn, New York, USA

Conditions leading to adoption : N/A

Requests for information post-adoption :

On March 13th 1957, you biological mother called at the Aide à la Femme. She asked if it was possible to take you back with her because she was now able to provide for you. Unfortunatly, it was already to late because you were already adopted.

April 10th 1986, your mother wrote to our services asking for the possibility to find you. After researches, she received an answer in January 1987 saying that we weren't able to find you because you were adopted in the US and we didn't have access to information in that country to find you.

April 1st 2002, your mother called us again and asked if we can do something to help her find you. Unfortunately, she received the same answer from our services.

D. Placement History (if applicable) :

Date and type of placements :

September 7th 1949, you left L'Aide à la Femme and you were place under the care of La société de Réhabilitation inc. of Sherbrooke. Two days later, your adoptive parents take you home with them.

E. Development of child

N/A

II. INFORMATION CONCERNING BIOLOGICAL MOTHER AT THE TIME OF YOUR BIRTH

A. Description

Age : 20	Weight : 92 pounds	Height : 5 feet 1 inche
Colour of hair : black	Colour of eyes : brown	Complexion : N/A
Nationality : French Canadian	Ethnic background : N/A	Race : white

Region of origin of mother : Montreal

Civil status :   Single

Religion :   Catholic

B. Schooling

7th grade at 13 years old

C. Occupation

She was a dressmaker

D. Health of mother : Specific problems

She was in good health

E. Characteristics concerning your biological mother : description, personality, tastes, abilities

She liked to clean up the house. She like dancing, go to theatre and do some bicycling. She was a nice person.

F. Relationship of your mother with her family and description of the family

She lived with her mom. Her father died few years before your birth.

G. Was the family informed of the pregnancy ?

Yes

Mars 2010

III. INFORMATION CONCERNING YOUR BIOLOGICAL FATHER AT THE TIME OF YOUR BIRTH

The information contained herein was provided by :

☑ Your mother   ☐ Your father   ☐ Not indicated in file

☐ Others (identify) :

Your biological father is identified in the file :   ☑ Yes   ☐ No

A. Description

Age :	Weight :	Height :
20	160 pounds	5 feet 9 inches
Colour of hair :	Colour of eyes :	Complexion :
Chestnut brown	blue	N/A
Nationality :	Ethnic background :	Race :
French Canadian	N/A	white

Region of origin of father :   Montreal

Civil status :   single

Religion :   Catholic

B. Schooling

N/A

C. Occupation

He was working in a cement works.

D. Health of father : specific problems

Good health

E. Characteristics concerning your biological father : description, personality, tastes, abilities,

He liked swimming, go to theatre and bicycling. He could have a drink sometimes. According to your mother, he was cute and he was a fine looking young man. He was also described has a serious man.

F. Relationship of your father with his family and description of the family

They were getting along.

G. Was your biological father informed of the pregnancy ?

☐ Yes   ☐ No   ■ Not indicated in file

H. Was your biological father informed of the birth ?

☐ Yes   ☐ No   ■ Not indicated in file

I. Relationship between birth parents (duration and type of relationship)

They saw each other for 4 months. Your biological mother broke up with your biological father when she found out she was pregnant.

IV. INFORMATION CONCERNING THE EXTENDED FAMILIES OF YOUR BIOLOGICAL PARENTS

A. Parents of your biological mother

1. Age of her father : Not applicable	Age of her mother : 45
2. Occupation of her father : He was a commercial traveller	Occupation of her mother : N/A
3. Health of her father : Not applicable	Health of her mother : good
If deceased : Age : 45 Cause of death, if known : angina	If deceased : Age : Not applicable Cause of death, if known : Not applicable

---

B. Siblings of your biological mother

Brothers : 2	Sisters : 1	Rank in the family : N/A	Family of 4 children

Health status of siblings (presence of hereditary diseases or other) : good health
One brother had a 12th grade and was working in an office. Her sister had a 6th grade and was unemployed.

Cause and age of death of siblings if necessary : not applicable

Twins :

☐ Yes   ☐ No   ■ Not indicated in file

C. Parents of your biological father

1. Age of his father : N/A	Age of his mother : N/A
2. Occupation of his father : Cement works	Occupation of his mother : N/A
3. Health of his father : Good	Health of his mother : Good
If deceased : Age : Not applicable Cause of death, if known : Not applicable	If deceased : Age : Not applicable Cause of death, if know : Not applicable

D. Siblings of your biological father

Brothers : 8	Sisters : 10	Rank in the family : N/A	Family of 18 children

Health status of siblings (presence of hereditary diseases or other) :

4 brothers was dead and 5 sisters was dead too, but we don't know the cause of death. One brother was married and 2 sisters were married. 2 of the sisters were working as dressmaker and the others were stillat school. Brothers were working in the cement works.

Cause and age of death of siblings if necessary : N/A

Twins :

☐ Yes   ☐ No   ■ Not indicated in file

Copies of appended documents :   ■ Yes   ☐ No

____

Nadia Quévillon, social worker

____

Date 2001-02-22

❈ 32 ❈

MONTREAL

APRIL 13, 2011

It has been almost impossible to bear the wait until this day when we could finally leave for Montreal. For the past two weeks I have told everyone that I have to be very careful, nothing can happen to me. This is one appointment that cannot be missed.

Our emotions were high as Claude and I left our house in Huntington at 6 a.m. for Montreal. My thoughts were uncontrollable. I couldn't concentrate on any one thought for long.

I kept repeating to myself,

"Tomorrow you're going to be with your mother who gave birth to you."

Then marveling at what has transpired in such a short time.

"How did this happen?" This was never a conscious part of my life plan.

"Will I be accepted by my brothers? Did our mother share her feelings about me with them?"

Then back to a practical thought,

"Did I remember to pack the album I made for Mireille?"

My mind would not stop going over and over the events of the last nine months leading to tomorrow's unimaginable reunion with my birth mother. I had no thoughts or expectations for the future beyond the 10 a.m. meeting.

As we rode along on our way to Canada I was thinking about the emotional journey so far and how she and I could look forward to our reunion without fear. Many adoptees or their birth families would not be able to say that. She knew that I searched for her and I knew she searched for me. It is like being pre-approved by both families before the actual reunion. This comforting fact allowed me to feel happiness and joy that we would both finally be able to have peace. Without the fear, I was able to experience the excitement and nervous anticipation of the next day.

The trip takes between seven and eight hours including a few stops along the way. We have a brand new SUV so the ride will be a pleasure. The route we take is the same as when we drive to Lake Placid, but we will pass that exit on the Northway and continue on for about two more hours to the Canadian border. I've packed a cooler with a couple of bagels and bottled waters, and as we usually do on our way to Lake Placid, we will stop at the New Baltimore rest stop on the New York State Thruway. It is a good stopping point, about 2 and a half hours from home, where we can use the facilities and stretch our legs. We've already eaten the bagels on the way and now treat ourselves to a Café Mocha from Starbucks.

Back on the road again and the next planned stop is in Plattsburgh, NY which is another 2 and a half hours on the Northway. Plattsburgh is a busy town and we have nice lunch options. We chose a little French café named Quiche et Crepe. Why not begin our French weekend a little early? It was authentic French cuisine and we enjoyed hearing some of the patrons around us speaking French. Canadian citizens from the Montreal area visit Plattsburgh to shop and enjoy lunch or dinner before driving home.

After lunch, we continued our journey to Douanes au Canada which is the French name for Customs at the Canadian border, an hour's drive from Plattsburgh. The Northway ends at the Canadian border but the highway continues past the Champlain-St. Bernard de Lacolle Border Crossing into Quebec as A-15 toward Montreal.

As we approached we saw a short line of cars waiting to pass through Customs to enter Canada, so the wait will not be too long. There are five questions that customs officers typically ask when you are crossing into Canada.

"What is the purpose of your trip?"

Claude could not hold back. He said,

"Tomorrow my wife will be reunited with her birth mother for the first time in 61 years. She was adopted in 1949 from Montreal and brought to the United States by her adoptive parents."

The customs officer was visibly moved by this pronouncement, but she had to do her job so she asked the following questions as quickly as possible.

"How long do you intend to stay?" she asked.

"We don't know yet, depending on how our meeting goes."

"Where will you be staying?"

"We will be at the Hyatt in Montreal."

"Do you have anything to declare?"

"No, nothing to declare."

Smiling, but with tears in her eyes, she wished us good luck and waved us on.

Over the last four months with all the emotional ups and

downs of my search, I have cried at one time or another with my family and friends; tears of sadness, relief, fear, and finally, tears of joy.

As we drove through customs into Canada we saw the road signs all in French. We enjoyed listening to the voice of our GPS pronounce the French names with an American accent. We proceeded over the Champlain Bridge and were treated to a stunning view of the city of Montreal. My parents would have taken a completely different route on their drive to Montreal in 1949. There was no New York State Thruway (1954), The Adirondack Northway (1957), or Champlain Bridge (1957). We think their route must have included Rt. 9, and the bridge they must have taken is the Honore Mercier Bridge built in 1932.

We arrived at the Hyatt around 3 p.m. At check-in, we were given specific information about the hotel, its amenities, and the surrounding sights of the city of Montreal. One feature is a mall below the hotel, and after we checked into our room we decided to go to the lower level and walk through the mall to pass the time and find a restaurant for dinner. It is a very large and beautiful mall with shops and restaurants for everything you could need or want. After riding in the car for eight hours, it was very therapeutic to be able to walk for an hour. Unfortunately, it was too cold and rainy to walk outside that day.

The Baton Rouge Restaurant looked inviting and we had an excellent dinner accompanied by a glass of wine, but our thoughts and attention were on what tomorrow would bring. Claude was practicing his French at the restaurant, ordering in French and making a few comments. The server was very kind and would correct us when we misspoke. We wondered if my brothers would be able to speak English, and hoped they would. Claude and I kept looking at each other and kept up some conversation, but it all came back to the same question.

"Is this really happening?"

We could not wait to go to sleep, so we could begin the next day when, after 61 years, I would be reunited with my birth mother. Sometimes I and others would say "meet" your birth mother, but I finally realized that I have already met her and looked upon her face at the time of my birth. This will be a true reunion. When she carried me for nine months I heard her voice and was part of her. French was my first language in the womb and for three months after birth. Sometimes I think about how, as a three-month-old infant, I experienced the abrupt and radical change in language and surrounding sounds the day I was adopted. French was the language I was already accustomed to and at three months old I would have been cooing and beginning to babble with French vowels. Can a three-month-old feel fear when suddenly everything she hears and sees is unfamiliar? She will have to learn to recognize the faces of her new loved ones. She will have to learn to coo and babble in her new language. A disruption in her development, but one she is able to overcome.

APRIL 14, 2011

We left the hotel at 9 a.m. for our 10 a.m. meeting. On this special day, I thought,

"What do you wear to see your mother for the first time in 61 years?"

It may sound inconsequential, but it was that calming detail that kept me moving forward that morning as I prepared to reunite with my birth mother.

Claude went ahead from our room to get our car and wait for me in the driveway of the hotel entrance. As I exited the revolving door and looked ahead, there he was standing by the car smiling at me. In September of this year (2011) we will be married 40 years. My heart still leaps at the sight of him even during very ordinary occasions so this morning my heart was bursting with gratitude and love for him and his never-ending support of me throughout our lives.

"What would I do without him?" is my recurring thought.

This is an impossible dream come true. All the months of waiting and hoping for this day still have not prepared me for the emotions I am feeling: nervousness, fear, joy, love, and hope. Arriving at the Foyer, the name for the French-Canadian nursing home, I was able to ignore the pain in my stomach and some lightheadedness as we walked slowly from the car through the sliding front doors.

There was a small reception desk, and they were expecting us so no introduction was necessary. From the room near the entrance, I could hear the voice of my social worker Nadia.

Nadia was my link to my birth family. Month after month her welcomed calls came through apprising us of the progress, the starts and stops, of the search for my birth mother. Every phone call came with the possibility that my search was over. Barely saying hello I would listen for Nadia's voice and hope she had good news. She followed every lead beginning with a phone number from nine years prior only to call and say that my mother was no longer at that address. Finally, the insurance card that every Canadian has was the way that Nadia was able to determine if my mother was still alive.

The bouquet of flowers we brought for Nadia was shaking in my hand as I presented them to her. I am filled with joy to be meeting her. It is as if we know each other already. She is responsible for reuniting my family. We share a heartfelt hug and then, filled with anticipation, proceed to the reserved meeting room.

IMPORTANT TIMES

THURSDAY, APRIL 14, 2011

The room seems vast and impersonal with stark white walls illuminated by unforgiving fluorescent overhead lights. The room had file cabinets and a coffee/water station in the corner. The large conference tables were set up in a "U" formation with the center-left empty. We were at the Foyer in Chateauguay, Canada, where my birth mother Mireille lives. Seated at the end of one of the tables in clear view of the doorway was the Foyer's social worker, a serious-looking man ready to witness and steer this meeting.

Nadia, who found Mireille and brought us together, left my side as we entered the room and proceeded to walk around the tables and sit at the furthermost table in the corner. During the reunion, I would catch a glimpse of Nadia crying while she witnessed our momentous day. She has three young daughters, and later told me she was imagining the grief of being separated from them.

Claude was at my side, as always, protective and steady.

There was a chair for me, but I was too anxious to sit down. The Foyer's social worker said,

"First you will meet your brothers before they bring your mother here."

By this time I knew I had three brothers and I understood why the brothers wanted to meet me first. It must have been incredible for them to learn that after 61 years I was looking to reunite with my birth mother especially since they had tried to find me for so many years. Why now, they must have been thinking. Why didn't I pursue the reunion years ago? I wish I had a clear answer to give them. Even though the thought of it was nagging at me for years, my fear always overcame my thoughts until I was visiting Montreal. Montreal had a magical influence on me and little by little I found my courage.

The Foyer social worker called the receptionist to let her know that we were ready for my brothers to join us in the meeting room.

When the three of them appeared in the doorway, it seemed as if they moved as a single unit. They inched their way into the room with Guy the eldest in the middle and just slightly forward, flanked by Pierre and Yves, Mireille's second and third sons. As they all focused their eyes on me, I thought I saw them all together take a step back with their mouths open and eyes wide.

Later, they told me they were literally taken aback when they saw that I looked exactly like our mother twenty years earlier, and as they walked to her room after meeting me they said to each other,

"We certainly can't deny her."

When they saw me they knew I belonged to them. The thought of that takes my breath away.

When I'm nervous I either can't think of a thing to say, or

I can't stop talking. Shortly after I began to talk, my husband gently stopped me and asked my brothers if they could understand me. He didn't want them to miss anything I said, and they all speak French as their primary language. They all nodded enthusiastically and said,

"Oui, yes!"

I don't think I missed a beat before getting back to my monologue. What did I say? I don't know, my emotions took over, but it must have made sense because they kept smiling and nodding. Mostly, I wanted them to know that I was sorry I didn't find them sooner so I could have given our mother the peace of knowing that I am happy and safe.

My brother Guy said,

"We are so happy you have found us. We have been helping our mother try to find you since she told us about you in 1994."

All those years I wondered and thought about my birth mother, she was wondering and thinking about me. Now we would be reunited.

Claude came over to stand with me while we waited for my mother to arrive. She had been waiting for us in her room for about a half-hour, and now I was waiting for only five or ten minutes and it seemed so long. Maybe it was just me, but I felt as if we were all holding our breath.

Then she arrived, pushed in her wheelchair by my sister-in-law Angela, my youngest brother Yves' wife. I saw my birth mother, Mireille, scanning the large room, straining to find me. It pained me to cause her even this brief, one more minute of anticipation. I quickly walked toward her so she would find me, and our eyes locked.

I bent over to give her our long-awaited hugs and kisses and then pulled back to look and take each other in; finally reunited. It is like looking in a mirror for us; Mireille looking at her younger self, and me looking at my future self. Our eyes are the same shape and color; our noses long and distinctive, our hands and protruding wrist bones identical. As we looked at each other it felt as if we were the only two people in the room. After 61 years, we cannot look long enough at each other to make up for all the lost time.

The family is looking on, my new family. Each person's face reveals their thoughts. They look on anxiously, cautiously, and with apparent compassion and love. They are very protective of their mother, and maybe wary of their newfound sister, but appreciate my importance to their mother. They are satisfied that finally; their mother's wish to know her daughter before she dies has been fulfilled.

I felt a chair positioned under me as Claude gently guided me to sit. She and I were now at eye level. Her English was limited, most likely due to lack of use and maybe her increasing dementia. But I know a little French and all we needed was, "Je t'aime" and our hugs. We were both in tears as we realized that this day was one we never thought would happen.

"Je t'aime!"she told me.

"Je t'aime!"I said. "I'm so happy to finally be with you again!"

"Me, too!" she answered.

These are the words that made up this first conversation as we took each other in with hugs, kisses, and holding hands.

Before our reunion, I thought about my childhood, my parents and my brother Brian, my children, and what questions she may have. I also wondered what I should bring with me for our reunion. I decided on a book of photographs depicting my life. Not to overwhelm her, I chose just a few. My brothers repeated to her, in French, my comments on the photographs. She was interested, but more interested in looking at me as I was more interested in looking at her. Our time went so quickly, and we could see her exhaustion setting in, so she went back to her room with my promise to see her again in a few hours.

When Angela first wheeled Mireille into the reunion room, she was accompanied by my brothers and our Uncle Yvon, Mireille's older brother. He and Mireille are the two oldest in their family and were very close growing up. I was so happy that he could be part of this day. It was after Mireille was taken back to her room that I looked around to see who was in the room with us. Mireille and I had been in a bubble and we only had eyes for each other.

Nadia came over to us as we were preparing to leave.

"Is this typical of most reunions you have witnessed?" I asked.

"Not at all," she replied, "this reunion is a very rare and satisfying one."

She wished us good luck and I told her I would keep in touch.

My brothers and I exchanged phone numbers so we could communicate and see each other soon. It was very soon because as soon as we left the Foyer together, we all decided to have lunch while our mother rested in her room.

The Foyer social worker, in the interest of formally closing the meeting, asked us,

"Are you satisfied with the outcome of this reunion?"

There is no experience for me to compare this to, but it was more than satisfying to me. It feels so natural to be with this family, my family, even though I've been absent from Mireille for 61 years and from my brothers' entire lives.

THE REUNION

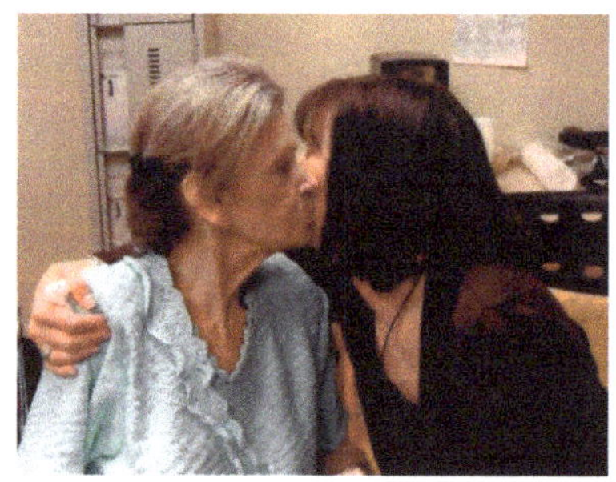

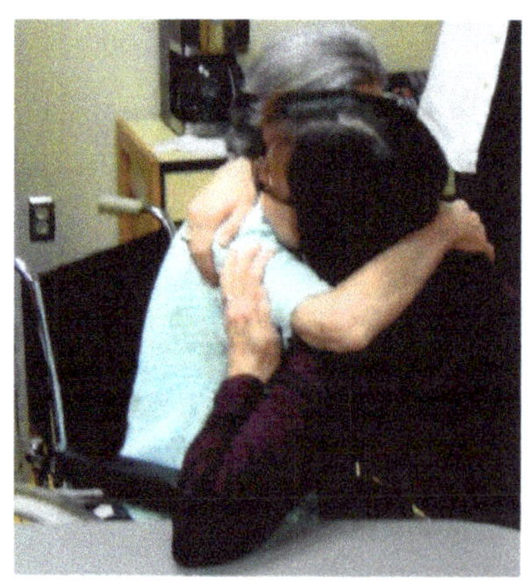

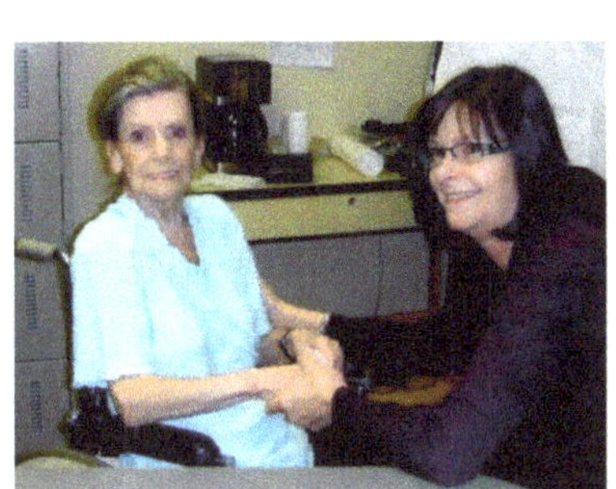

Front – Guy, Mireille, Eileen, Yvon Back – Pierre, Angela,
Yves, Claude

Unknown to me at the time, 70% of those who searched for a birth parent or birth child, and 89% of those who did not search but were found, did not experience an immediate bond with their birth parent or child. This was reported in a British Study, <u>The Adoption, Search, and Reunion Study,</u> published in The Guardian. Nadia was correct in calling my reunion rare.

I later learned that she almost passed away in February of 2011 just when Nadia called me to say she was following leads to find her. I believe her love and determination was so strong that her thoughts and wishes to find me were getting through to me in an inexplicable way. I finally listened to that little voice that took me to Montreal and started me on the search. It is tempting to lament the loss of time and opportunities, but instead, I will try to make the most of the time we will have.

We left the home with Guy, Yves and Angela, and Pierre. They asked if we would join them for lunch. We were delighted although I had no appetite. I was very happy to extend our time together. As we were leaving the Foyer, Claude thought to take a picture of me with my three brothers. That has become an important memento for all of us.

Siblings together at last - Pierre, Yves, Eileen, and Guy

❃ 34 ❃

THE AFTERNOON

After our lunch with my three brothers and Angela, Claude and I went back to the Foyer to visit Mireille. Our first visit this morning was in the reception room, but this time we will go directly to her room for the first time.

Mireille is on the third floor which houses patients with Alzheimer's and Dementia. The elevator is locked to prevent the residents from wandering off the floor, so we were given the passcode. The old Otis elevator was slow and noisy as it took us to the third floor. When we stepped off the elevator to go to Mireille's room, the nurses' station was in front of us behind a large glass window. There were three nurses and aides that I remember looking out from behind the glass directly at us when we walked off the elevator. When they saw me they put their hands to their faces and started to exclaim in French about how I look like my birth mother. Although I remember basic phrases such as bonjour, cava, and merci from my high school and college days, I didn't need to know the language to understand what they were saying. The story of the reunion of Mireille and her daughter was circulating around the home well before I arrived, even before Nadia was able to arrange our reunion. They all knew the story and were curious to see me for the first time.

After a few nods and smiles, we were directed to her room down the hall. As we turned the corner, away from the elevators, we looked ahead to a long hallway of doors, painted green walls, and polished tile floors. The overhead lights were bright fluorescent. On the wall outside every room, as a means of introduction, was a laminated, decorative 8 and a half by 11 page with a small photo and details of the person residing in that room. It was heartening to see how this made sure that every person was recognized for whom they are, for the lives they have lived, and for the important place they hold among their family members. These introductions are written in the first person. On her page, Mireille introduces herself and tells us she was born in Montreal and moved to Chateauguay in 1960 where she lived before coming to the Foyer. Included are the names of her siblings, Yvon, Lise, and Guy; her late husband, Jean Gilles, and her children, Guy, Pierre, and Yves; grandchildren and great-grandchildren. From this, we learned that she loves music, camping, traveling, and going to restaurants.

My name was not included in this list, as expected, but a pleasant surprise was in store for me on a subsequent visit when we met Line, my brother Guy's wife, for the first time at the Foyer two days later.

Since 1994 I was not a secret to my brothers, and they had tried to help her find me through online adoption websites and even a French television show that reunited families. These efforts helped them accept the idea of an older sister long before meeting me. If I had been adopted by a Canadian family, they would have been able to find me. United States adoption records are closed and cannot be unsealed.

We entered her room and she was very happy to see us again. Our eyes lit up whenever we saw each other. The room was a little homier than a hospital room, mostly because the family decorated it with personal touches for her comfort and enjoyment. On her nightstand were framed photos of the family and across from her bed were pictures drawn by her grandchildren and displayed there for her to see. On her bed was her favorite blue and white lightweight comforter.

The large window overlooked a branch of the St. Lawrence River and the curtains were wide open for us to see the sparkling water and hear the whooshing sound of the river rushing by. Next to the window was a comfortable, high-backed chair to sit and enjoy the outside view.

She was already sitting in her wheelchair and waiting for us. She looked refreshed and I hoped she wasn't waiting long for our return. We sat with her there in her room, taking a few pictures of us together, and looking at some of the framed photos she had of the family.

"Are you happy?" she asked me.

"I'm very happy, and especially happy that I have found you," I told her.

She asked,

"How long have you and Claude been married?"

"40 years," I told her.

This was the opportunity for me to tell her about my children and grandchildren. I showed her pictures of them all and told her a little about each one. She just listened and smiled.

We talked about our shared interests but there were no deep conversations, and she didn't ask me any more questions.

Did she want to know more about how I felt growing up

as an adopted child and how I thought of her through the years? I would have liked to know about what life was like for her as a young woman before she was pregnant with me. Did she have fun with her friends and her siblings? Did she go dancing and bike riding as a teenager?

My brothers told me she was engaged to a soldier but she broke it off when he was leaving for active duty. We don't know who my birth father was and through the years she never revealed his identity, but we know that it wasn't the soldier because he left long before she was pregnant. It is natural to think that I would have asked many questions of my birth mother, however, there was no discussion about the circumstances of my beginning and birth. My instincts were holding me back from those questions. I wasn't sure her memory would serve her, and I didn't want to cause her any discomfort. To me, she seemed too fragile, not just physically but emotionally as well. I put myself in her place and thought how overwhelming this reunion must be. She seemed happy to just be in the moment with Claude and me and that's what we did. As much as I wanted to know, I contented myself with just being together after all these years of wondering and imagining. I was there to bring her peace. We were both at peace together.

It was time for her dinner and she asked if we would take her in the wheelchair to the lobby dining room. We were happy to take her out of her room to another location. In the dining room, there were other residents, but we stayed to ourselves. Claude and I didn't eat; it was just for the residents unless a reservation was made for family to join her. Although there were servers helping the residents, we helped Mireille with any requests she had. On the menu, that night was hamburger which she enjoyed along with some fruit and potatoes. It was a day of huge activity, physically and emotionally challenging for all of us, and her appetite was a true illustration of that.

Eileen, Mireille, and Claude – Foyer Lobby Dining Room

When she asked to return to her room, we knew she was tired. Her face and body were showing the effects of an incredibly trying day. The elevator door slowly opened up and one of the nurses, seeing that we were back from dinner, followed us to her room. She saw her fatigue and was prepared to begin her bedtime ritual. Once she was comfortably settled in her bed, we kissed and hugged and told her we would be back the next day in time for her lunch. As I looked back at her from the doorway her eyes were already closed, and I was hoping her dreams would be as sweet as I expected mine to be that night.

While we were ending our visit, Claude's cell phone began to ring and he walked into the hall outside Mireille's room to answer. It was my brother Yves asking if we would come to their house for dinner. We were happy to say yes to this thoughtful invitation.

Their house is only a few minutes from the Foyer. When we arrived, Yves and Angela were taking groceries from their car into the house. They have a house similar to ours with multi-levels and an open concept living room, dining room, and kitchen. At home on Long Island, NY, April is when we look for the beginning signs of Spring; the buds on the trees and bushes and the grass trying to come alive after a long, cold winter. So when we walked into the backyard with Yves, the promise of sunnier, warmer days were the bulk of our conversation. We learned that Yves loves planting and nurturing the trees. The pool was still covered from the winter, but we could imagine the fun they have in their yard during the warm weather, swimming in the pool, grilling dinner, and sitting by the fire pit in the evenings. We were introduced and greeted by their children, Sabrina, 17, and Joey 14. They are beautiful, loving children and we were all excited to meet each other. They have a sweet dog, Rosie, and a cat, Luna who didn't hide but came to check out the newcomers.

Angela is a master in the kitchen and along with Yves, they made a delicious dinner for the six of us. Hearing us speak of our love of chocolate mousse earlier, there was a chocolate mousse cake for dessert.

Pierre, Angela, Yves, Eileen, Claude, Guy, and Line

Yves and Angela and their children are all fluent in French and English. Angela also speaks Italian. Her parents came to Canada with their families from Italy, met in Montreal, married, and started a nursery business selling trees, shrubs, and flowers. It is a good amount of land and her parents and Angela's grandmother live in the house where Angela and her sisters and brother grew up. On one of our later visits to Chateauguay Angela and Yves took us to meet her parents and grandmother who have known and loved Mireille for many years. They were very excited and happy to meet her daughter.

There was so much for Claude and me to digest and talk about on our drive back to the Hyatt in Montreal. We marveled at how we were the recipients of more love and acceptance today than we could have ever imagined. We were physically and emotionally exhausted and collapsed into bed for a deep sleep. I'm sure I slept with a smile on my face all night.

35

SPECIAL WEEKEND

FRIDAY, APRIL 15, 2011

When we arrived at the Foyer at 11 a.m., we went to her room first, and not finding her there, we went to the dining room on the same floor. She had just been served lunch. There were many other residents from her floor there, but as soon as she saw us she wanted to go back to her room and eat her lunch there. We were happy to do that because the other residents were a big distraction. Some of them would shout loudly or break out in song. In the quiet of her room, she ate some and then wanted to rest in bed. I sat with her, holding her hand while she slept. She would open her eyes once in a while and smile at me.

She was concerned for my comfort at one time asking if I was tired. Then another time she said I was quiet. I asked her about when she was a dressmaker before I was born. She just smiled as if in confirmation but didn't elaborate. My brothers said they knew her best working at home taking very good care of them and cooking large meals. There was always extra for anyone who stopped by during meal time and she was happy for their company. We talked about travel and how much she liked to go to Hollywood Beach, Florida.

Although it was clear that she knew where she was and who we were, her dementia had taken a toll. Claude and I would tell her about our children and grandchildren, and she would smile. We knew that she liked traveling to Florida, dogs, cooking, and anything to do with the family so we were able to keep the conversation going. It seemed she understood everything but did not initiate conversation. To be fair that may have been due to our language differences. My brothers told us that she spoke English in the past, but didn't have the need to for many years. She spoke French to all her family and friends and I wonder if I spoke French she may have had more to say to me. She also tired easily. In spite of these things, she was smiling and beautiful.

By midafternoon we left the Foyer and went back to Montreal. While Claude did some work in the room, I found a place in the mall to develop and buy frames for the picture of me with my three brothers. I framed five, one for Mireille to have at her bedside, one for me, and one for each of my three brothers. The four siblings, finally together.

As I shopped, my mind was going over the miraculous events of the past two days. My first meeting with Mireille was spent mostly looking at each other and expressing our love. At subsequent meetings, we would discuss our likes and dislikes in general. Cooking and dancing were two of her favorite pastimes, and they are two of mine also. Every summer she enjoyed camping with the family in a community of cottages, and every summer I enjoyed boating with my family.

My brother Guy has talked with Uncle Yvon about who my birth father may have been. He had some photographs of

Mireille when she was young with a man to whom she was engaged. There are no specific dates as to when the engagement broke off but she dated other men after that break-up. We all believe that Uncle Yvon may know who my birth father is but when Guy asked him he said he can't remember because it was too long ago. As much as I would like to know more about my heritage and biological information, I am content to have found Mireille and my brothers and their families.

In 2002 my brothers and sisters-in-law tried to find information about me through the internet and through a French television show, Claire Lamarche. Mireille was hoping that with new technology there would be a way to trace me in the United States, however, they soon learned that because I was adopted by an American family and brought to the United States, where adoption records are sealed, that there was no way of finding me. Although my French Canadian name is on my birth papers, my American name was a well-protected secret. I thought,

"How could they just leave my real name on the papers?"

I could just look up the names in the phone book, or later on the internet, and start calling people.

If I had known how easy it would be to locate my birth family and more importantly, known that Mireille was looking for me, I would have sought them out long ago.

"Why don't we call your family and ask them to meet us in Montreal for dinner?" Claude suggested when we returned to the Hyatt Hotel in Montreal.

My brothers and their families all live in Chateauguay, a suburb of Montreal but work in the city of Montreal. We suggested that they meet us for dinner in the city before they went home, but they told us they would have to go home first and then return to the city. We didn't want to inconvenience them and said we could see them in Chateauguay the next day when we come to visit Mireille. We knew the trip from their houses to Montreal would be time-consuming since it involved going over the Mercier Bridge which is always under construction and fraught with delays. Even so, they made the trip to see us. Guy and Line weren't able to come, but Angela, Yves, and Pierre met us at the Hyatt.

When they arrived, they guided us to a Tapas restaurant where we all had a martini along with our tasty tapas. For dessert, Angela suggested we walk to Juliette et Chocolat, a restaurant specializing in desserts. There we had crepe suzettes and café au lait. We are in French food heaven. We can't believe we only met them yesterday and we are so at ease. We enjoy the same things.

My birth mother, Mireille, must have been an exceptional mother. Her three loving sons are a testimonial to this. I know from their accounts that their father was exceptional as well. I cannot put into words how much I already love my family. They are so thoughtful, sweet, kind, and generous with me. To think I would have lived without ever knowing them and now my life is so much richer for knowing them. I couldn't wait for all my loved ones in the United States to meet my French Canadian family and love them as I do.

I have marveled at how accepted and welcomed I have felt from the very first meeting. After sharing this feeling with my friend Marilyn, she commented that because they all knew about me and helped her try to find me; I lived in their minds before they met me. It strikes me also that I had two mothers who were very open. My mother shared my adoption story from before I can remember, and my birth mother shared her story with her sons.

SATURDAY, APRIL 16, 2011

Yesterday when Angela and I were in the lobby of the nursing home, I read a sign "Trefle D'Or." She told me this means "gold four-leaf clover." This was very meaningful to me because many years ago, my mother, Mary Clancy Coyne, gave me one from Ireland to hang over the front door of my home. We are beginning to see many parallels between my birth mother Mireille and my mother Mary. After my father and then my mother passed away, I noticed what I interpret as signs from them. I often say,

"Oh, there's my mother or my father saying hello." This was another one from my mother, and I'm sure it was to give her blessing.

When we arrived at the home at 11:30 a.m., Mireille was sitting and looking out the front windows near the door of the Foyer with my brother and sister-in-law, Guy and Line. This is our first meeting with Line. She gave us a very big hug, and we were happy to meet her. Mireille was smiling and waving as we came in.

Daughter and Mother Reunited!

The family made a reservation for all of us to eat in the dining room of the Foyer with Mireille. We were seated at a long table in the middle of the room. There were other smaller tables throughout the large room with families eating, but we were not distracted by them. Claude and I and my brothers and their families were all seated at the table. How incredible that I would be sharing a meal with my birth mother and closest biological family members. Even though we were in a nursing home, I was so enraptured with everyone at the table that the surroundings and the meal itself were unimportant.

What I remember about this dinner was the warmth and love I felt as I sat there among my family. We only met 48 hours ago but I felt as if I've known them all my life. I try to remember what we talked about or what we ate and I am at a loss. Instead of remembering those details, I remember feeling awestruck and as if I was having an "out of body" experience. I was observing everything and everyone without consciously taking in the significance of this occasion. Although in the short time since we met I had already shared meals with my brothers and their families, it occurred to me that it was the first meal I was having with all my siblings and our mother together.

In our family, as with my Canadian family, we are fortunate to live close to each other and share many meals together. Not only for holidays or special occasions but also for no reason other than to see each other. In the winter we may share a hearty stew; in the summer we have the grill going in the yard and everyone brings something to share.

On this day I was imagining a time when Mireille was well, and we could have shared this dinner experience at one of our homes. I see her mingling and talking with everyone in the family, enjoying the grandchildren, playing with the pets, and helping to prepare one of the dishes. It is easy to imagine because these family dinners are when I am happiest.

Our families are so similar that I am able to allow myself

these imaginings. In many of the adoption memoirs that I have read, the birth family and the adoptive family are very different and the adoptee has trouble relating to their birth family after being assimilated into their adoptive family.

After this special meal, we all proceeded back to Mireille's room; walking through the lobby, waiting for the elevator, experiencing the slow ascent, and then arriving at the door to her room. I was ready to walk directly into the room, but Line gently stopped me and pointed to the introductory sign on the wall next to the doorway. I thought it was the one I had seen on my first visit to the Foyer, and perhaps Line didn't know I saw it on my first visit. But the sign was revised. My name was now listed as one of Mireille's children, and my two children and my four grandchildren were now included in the total number of Mireille's children and grandchildren. I was so surprised and touched to see my name was included in this important history of Mireille. Line smiled at me, and I learned that Line recreated the poster, adding my name as Mireille's daughter and my children's and grandchildren's names. This thoughtful act by Line was a memorable, loving gesture and was a tangible illustration of my acceptance into the family.

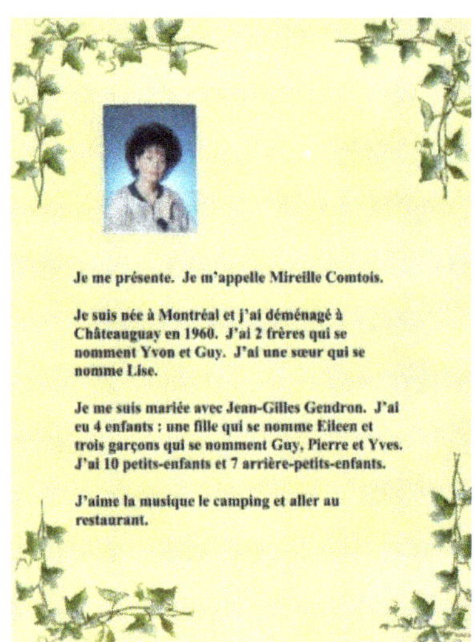

After Mireille fell asleep, Guy and Line took us to their house which is also a few minutes from the Foyer. Line's mother Diane lives with them and it was the first time for us to meet. She is so gracious and sweet. The house is divided into two separate living spaces so they each have their own apartment.

Their children Michael, 20, and Melissa, 22 live with them. Guy's daughter Josee lives in another town with her daughter Joelle. All my brothers and their families were there for dinner that day except for Pierre's son, Pierre Charles, who lives in Toronto.

Guy loves to cook for family and friends as did our mother, and his dishes include special sauces and accompaniments worthy of a fine restaurant.

To start we enjoyed prosciutto and melon, cheese and crackers, and homemade bruschetta.

The menu was marinated steak with oven-roasted potatoes. In addition, Angela made couscous with almonds, cranberries, currants, and a salad with a special vinaigrette dressing using Canadian maple syrup.

To begin the celebration dinner, the champagne was popped and poured into glasses containing a strawberry as we toasted Mother and our good fortune to find each other.

To end the dinner, Guy and the family brought out a bottle of 250-year-old cognac that Mother would share with the family on special occasions. As we gave a toast of thanks to her, everyone agreed that she would want us to celebrate with her cognac. It was another perfect day and a dream come true, but one that I never imagined possible.

SUNDAY, APRIL 17, 2011 (PALM SUNDAY)

During the weeks that Nadia was searching for Mireille, I was keeping Sister Jeannette up to date on the events by letter. When I knew that I would be in Montreal for my reunion with my birth mother, I let her know and asked if we could visit her while we were there. She was able to make time for us and on this Palm Sunday, we went to the convent of the Soeurs de la Miséricorde.

We shared all of our good news and pictures and she was happy to hear that we had such a positive reunion. I remember when we first met her and she said reunions did not always turn out well. She wanted us to be prepared.

We had a sweet visit with Sister Jeannette who is an especially loving, caring person working very hard caring for the elderly sisters who are ill. Her life's mission has been to care for others. Even though my birth mother Mireille was not in the care of the Soeurs de la Miséricorde, Sister Jeannette provided the inspiration I needed to go forward in my search for information. She gave me the courage I needed to take that first step. I was so surprised when she told us during our first visit that there were records on all the babies that were born at that time. Although I had my name, Marie Monique

Comtois on my adoption papers, I always doubted it really was my birth name. My friends who were adopted in the United States never had their birth name since all adoptees at that time only had a baptismal certificate with their adopted family name. I was happy and secure in who I was, and I never thought that my birth mother was looking for me.

After our visit with Sister Jeannette, we went to visit Mireille. My three brothers and their wives, Claude and I were all there. This was the end of a weekend of a lifetime. We were all in her room and she was listening to everyone and smiling with a look of joy and contentment as she followed along with the conversation. According to my family, my arrival has re-energized her.

After her lunch and visit with all her children, the nurses prepared her for bed. Claude and I were going to leave for our home on Long Island, New York. My brothers and sisters-in-law left before us. Mireille and I kissed and hugged. We told each other "Je t'aime," and she said she would miss me. I said I'll be back as soon as possible. I was sorry I had to leave to go back to work.

She said,

"I'll wait for you."

She has been waiting for me for almost 62 years and now she has to wait for me again.

36

MONTH 1 - MAY 2011

On April 17, 2011, we returned to our home on Long Island. The reunion weekend was more perfect than we could have imagined. I now had a new family and we left them with promises to see each other soon. When Mireille told me "I'll wait for you" as we left, the thought of her waiting there at the Foyer doesn't leave my mind.

The Sunday after we came home was Easter Sunday and it is one of the holidays Claude and I host at our house for our family. There are 25 of us so it is a big party filled with fun as the children hunt for the Easter eggs carefully placed all over the yard by the older cousins while our brother-in-law Anthony plays the banjo. On the following Monday, I sent pictures of that day to my Canadian family. We want to get to know each other and what our family traditions and occasions look like.

My Canadian family and my American family share so many similarities. Most of our family lives in the same town here in New York and most of my Canadian family lives in the same town in Canada. We grew up in the town where we now live, and they grew up in the town where they now live,

Consequently, as it is with us, their children and grandchildren know their aunts, uncles, and cousins well.

We all enjoy having family over for dinner and we enjoy the same types of foods, meals based mostly on the Mediterranean diet.

After spending the weekend in Canada, we started planning our next visit in May.

A few days after Claude and I returned from Canada, my brother Guy called me and told me to expect a package from him. He said the mail from Canada is slow, but as soon as I receive it to please let him know. What could it be?

It took more than a week to arrive. Just as Guy mailed it, they had a postal work slowdown in Canada. Finally, it arrived and I opened it to find Mireille's black onyx ring. It was the first time I saw the ring. The family told me it was her favorite piece of jewelry, and I can see it on her finger in all the pictures my family has shared with me. They wanted me to have it since she was not able to wear it in the Foyer where she is living. Again, their thoughtfulness told me in actions rather than words that I mattered to our mother and therefore I would matter to them. It was another way they were illustrating their acceptance of me. It means so much to me and I am so happy to wear it. It is something I treasure.

FRIDAY, MAY 13, 2011

Claude and I left for Lake Placid from my school in Commack, New York. We arrived at the Whiteface Lodge that evening and we were excited about the next day when we would see Mireille again. It had been a month, and my brothers told me she was very happy we were coming. I couldn't wait to see her again. There is a good reason why we make The Whiteface Lodge in Lake Placid, New York our stopover on our way to see my family in Chateauguay.

In 2005 Claude and I received a phone call from Claude's sister Martine and her husband Anthony excited to tell us about an opportunity they just found. We knew they were away on a road trip and were curious to hear the news from them.

"We were driving through Lake Placid on a sightseeing vacation and we happened upon an exceptional new condo development that we think our family should invest in."

Claude and I were not looking for a second home of any kind, but we were very interested in what they had to say and we trusted their intuition. We knew that Claude's Dad would be interested as well since anything that brought the family together was of utmost priority to him.

Martine and Anthony shared how they came to find and investigate this property.

"We were walking around the town when, without warning, the skies opened up and a curtain of rain began to fall."

They took shelter under a storefront awning, hoping for the storm to pass quickly, but the wind blew the rain sideways and the awning was not keeping them dry. They turned to look in the storefront window and saw the logo for The Whiteface Lodge. This was a new property in the process of being built and this was the sales office. Martine and Anthony went in to stay dry, get information, and make waiting out this storm much more interesting. That afternoon was the prelude to a new and important chapter in our family's future.

"Welcome, may we help you?" asked the animated sales staff almost in unison.

Looking around the office, Martine and Anthony saw the pictures of the Lodge in many stages of its development.

They accepted the invitation to sit down with one of the sales representatives who proceeded to tell the story of the development of the Lodge, built according to the vision of its owner and developer, a local resident of Lake Placid.

The storm passed, and the sales person offered to take them on a tour of the property which is located just five minutes from the sales office. They were very impressed with the presentation and tour and now all they had to do was sell the family on the idea of purchasing a vacation condo.

It was helpful that The Whiteface Lodge offered us all a complimentary weekend to stay at the Lodge and experience everything it had to offer. After that visit, we were all excited to think that we could be part of this growing community. The paperwork was completed that weekend, and we purchased a third-floor, three-bedroom, three-bath unit with a porch that overlooked the mountains. We would be able to enjoy sunsets and stunning views of the mountains through every season. Martine and Anthony chose this unit on their very first visit to the Lodge. They considered the size of the porch and its westerly view as important considerations for our future enjoyment there.

"That was a very fortuitous rainstorm," we all say.

That storm and the curiosity of Martine and Anthony feels like a result of divine intervention.

We purchased this condo in October 2005. I met my birth family in 2011. Lake Placid is only two and a half hours from my family's town in Chateauguay, Canada. When we go to our condo, my brothers and their families join us when possible and enjoy everything Lake Placid has to offer. We knew the Whiteface Lodge would bring our New York family closer together, but it was six years before we realized that it would bring our Canadian family closer as well.

SATURDAY, MAY 14, 2011

We left the Lodge after breakfast which will give us time to arrive at the home to see Mireille by 11 a.m., in time for her lunch.

We went directly to her room. She was sitting up on the edge of her bed, her wheelchair parked near her feet.

"Bonjour Maman," we said as we approached her.

She looked up and we bent to embrace her. As I gently put my arms around her, I felt the frailty of her body. When I pulled away to look at her, her eyes only landed on my face for a few seconds before looking around the room, then down to her lap and to the wheelchair. She appeared anxious and distracted as if she didn't know what to do next.

Her lunch arrived and we sat with her, using the food as our topic of conversation. Although she picked at some of her lunch, overall she was disinterested. Her furrowed brow, darting eyes, and melancholic expression was giving us a window into her mind as she seemed to struggle with staying in the moment.

We called the nurse to help her into the wheelchair so we could take her around the Foyer. The weather was not good that day, so we pushed her up and down the halls, past all the rooms and many of the residents who were walking on their own. She became impatient if we had to stop to let someone pass as the halls were narrow. The route around the halls of the Foyer was short so we walked the same path over and over for much of our visit that morning. The movement seemed to have a calming effect on her. We stopped a few times in a small lounge that had a large window overlooking the water, but she quickly tired of the stillness and asked to continue walking. Yves and Angela met us in the lounge. Mireille's fatigue became apparent to all of us, and she asked to go back to her room to her bed. On our way back to the room we asked the nurses if they would help her into bed. After she was comfortably resting, we left to go to Angela and Yves's house where we will spend the night.

Angela prepared a delicious lunch of endive salad with blue cheese, cucumbers, and lettuce. It was the perfect lunch. Forgive me if I share the menus of meals that my family prepares for us; it is because these occasions remind us again and again that we are family and share the same tastes and customs. How much is in the genes?

Claude and I returned to the Foyer in time for Mireille's dinner. Again she wasn't hungry and wanted to leave her room and explore the halls of the 3rd floor. A few times during our walk, she asked to go back to her room, but once at the doorway, she would shake her head "no" and wave us to continue back into the hall. We were willing to walk with her for however long she wished if it would help her feel better.

Before Mireille's bedtime, Guy and Line, Pierre, Angela, and Yves met us in the room. We all visited her together while the nurse prepared her bed. We knew by her smiles that she was very content to see us all together even though she was not feeling very well, and did not speak much. I loved listening to all the French and was able to understand some. This is the day that I learned that she loves candy, especially chocolate-covered cherries. Chocolate-covered cherries were my father's favorite and my gift to him on many occasions.

Again it was time to leave her once she was settled comfortably in her bed. I lean over to give her a hug then wave and blow kisses as I leave the room. It doesn't get easier to leave her, but sleep is what she needs. Prior to now, I had no experience with visiting any loved one in a nursing home and feeling the sadness of leaving them at the end of the visit.

The family arranged for us to go to a favorite restaurant of theirs for dinner. Pierre joined us there with his daughter Lydia. His other daughter Anyssa was working and could not join us. The restaurant allowed us to bring our own wine, so we brought a bottle of our La Bonne Vie. We brought this bottle from home which we made at the wine school where we've been making our own wine since 2006. When we started this wine-making adventure, we had only one grandchild. Now we have four. Each of the first four vintages we made was named after one of our grandchildren: Jackson Estates, Cash Reserve, Le Petit Owen, and Evelyn. The fifth bottle we named after Claude's dad, Francesco. It's called Oompah's Vineyards. When our children and his other six grandchildren were young they could not say "Grandpa" so they named him "Oompah" and they still call him by that name. The last bottle we made is La Bonne Vie, the good life. This is the wine we brought with us to Canada, and we think the name is quite appropriate.

Throughout the dinner, with my brothers in the restaurant, my mind was wandering to thoughts of Mireille. She would have loved to be with us at the restaurant to enjoy the food, wine, and conversation and to again see her four children together. At least we did have the other day when we were able to be with her in the dining room in the Foyer.

After dinner, we went to Guy and Line's house to talk and look at old photographs again. Everyone was sharing stories about their life with our mother. Even though we began as strangers only a month before, because of their love for their mother and their never-ending desire for her to find and be reunited with her daughter, they are open and generous with their time. That makes it easy for me to feel I am part of the family and belong with them.

SUNDAY, MAY 15, 2011

Yves and Angela made us feel very comfortable in their home. They shared stories about Mireille and vacations they shared with her to Lake Placid and Cuba while they made a delicious breakfast of crepes with strawberries; eggs, bacon, ham, and watermelon.

Yves and Angela told us they took a weekend trip to Lake Placid in the 1980s with Mireille and her boyfriend at the time. They recounted stories of eating in fine restaurants, swimming in the lake, and seeing the sights in and around the town. These are all things that we also enjoy during our visits to Lake Placid. Some landmarks including the hotel where they stayed are still there, and I marvel at the fact that Mireille may have been at an exact spot where I have been, enjoying the same view and sights 25 years earlier.

In Mireille's letter asking for help in finding me, she says "...every time I see a girl who is about her age, I am wondering if she could be my little Monique..."

The Hollywood boardwalk was filled with the sounds of French Canadians escaping the cold of Canada for Florida. While visiting my mother in Ft. Lauderdale in the 1970s and '80s our family would walk along the boardwalk by the ocean. Listening carefully to all the French chatter around me and looking at women around a certain age, I would imagine passing by my birth mother. So it seems we were both going through our lives wondering and dreaming that our paths would intersect.

"Please take me for a walk outside."

This was my birth mother Mireille's request every time we visited her at the Foyer, the nursing home where she lived. On one particularly sunny and mild day, we arrived for our visit just after she had her lunch, and her smile when she saw us revealed not just happiness to see us but also relief. Relief because she knew she would be able to get out and away from the confines of the Foyer even if just for an hour or so.

We were always more than happy to get out with her, escaping the stale, heavy smell that permeates throughout any airless institution that is part residence and part medical facility.

She was already in her wheel chair and anxious to get going so she flipped up the footrests, put her feet on the floor and started, to "walk" herself forward in the wheelchair. I was helping her put on her sweater but not getting her coopera-tion so Claude started pushing the wheelchair down the hall to the elevator while I shuffled alongside helping her get her arms into the sleeves.

We arrived at the elevator doors and waited for it to reach our floor. We could hear it slowly approaching our third floor, humming and creaking all the way. Finally, it was there, on the other side of the doors and we could hear it, but it was a few more minutes before the doors opened. We got on the elevator and took the slow ride down to the lobby. What I have learned about Mireille since we have been reunited is that she was never a person to "dilly-dally." Once she decided to do something she forged forward. I could see her impa-tience with this entire process to just leave the building and I felt for her.

As soon as we arrived in the lobby, we wheeled her as quickly as possible toward and through the double sliding doors as we flashed our permission pass to the attendant at the front desk with barely a sideward glance. It felt as if we burst out into the sights, sounds, and smells of the outdoors where we all took a deep, calming breath.

The location of the Foyer is next to the St. Lawrence River and its landscape and plantings stretch for acres around the building and adjacent to the river. On our walks even on a sunny, relatively warm day the winds off the river cause a chill in the air. There were signs of spring emerging all around us throughout the property, and I loved seeing how happy she was to be outside. She is very frail though and it is difficult for her to concentrate on conversation. Fortunately, the language of nature is universal, and she seemed content to just sit with us looking over the river, taking in the combined scents of the mossy riverbank and the early spring flowers and budding trees while listening to the sounds of the water and the wildlife. It was a peaceful time and words were not necessary as we each contemplated our own "in the moment" experience not needing to do anything or be anywhere.

Nature can be a true healer of the spirit.

After we brought her back inside, we stayed with her in her room while she had her dinner. She knows who we are and smiles and tells us she loves us. The time outside seemed to energize her and she asked to look at family pictures, while we talked about cooking and her travels. Claude and I did most of the talking, in English, but using the pictures for context, she and I were able to share some experiences. She was in good spirits and seemed to enjoy the day with us. After she was ready for bed we left her to sleep and went to Yves and Angela's for the night.

The next day, it was time for us to leave for New York again. We held hands and looked into each other's eyes. She knew I would be back in one month. She was so frail and I thought of how long a month must seem to her. It was my last month of work, and then I would be retired.

37

MONTH 2 – JUNE 2011

FRIDAY, JUNE 24, 2011

My retirement day has come!

It is a bittersweet day, the end of a career that I loved. It was 22 years of going to work happy and energized. The first seven years as a first grade classroom teacher and the following 15 years as a reading specialist in the same school. My friends and colleagues planned a very special retirement party earlier in June. Everything was perfect, from the venue on the water, the boating theme with poems and photos in nautical frames, to the DJ and the food. It was an amazing party. I will miss the challenges and joys of teaching young children, and miss the camaraderie of the team of friends who made going to work especially wonderful.

We leave from my school for the last time and drive directly to The Whiteface Lodge in Lake Placid, NY. Saturday morning we will leave early for Chateauguay and The Foyer to see Mireille and my family.

SATURDAY, JUNE 25, 2011

When we arrive to see Mireille at the Foyer we are greeted with her biggest smile and have the most wonderful hugs and kisses.

Our visit proceeded as they have in our previous visits; she had lunch and we took her outside for a walk down by the river. It was another beautiful afternoon but breezy as usual. When she was inside she complained about being too warm so she enjoyed the breeze very much.

On this day, a relative of one of the residents brought a cute, small white dog to visit. Mireille was very excited to pet the dog. My brothers told us,

"Mother loves dogs and we had many dogs when we were growing up."

Then Yves and Angela told us about Mother and their dog Zach, a Yorkshire terrier.

"When Mireille was living alone in her apartment, she would come to our house while we were at work or school and she would spend the day with Zach."

Everyone knew that Zach loved the company as much as Mireille did.

Now Yves and Angela have their terrier Rosie and they told us,

"Mireille loves it when we bring Rosie to the Foyer to visit her."

When I was growing up I was so happy when my parents said yes when I asked for a dog. The parents of many of my friends at the time would not allow pets in their homes, but my mother really loved dogs too. We had several "mutts" as they were called then; rescue dogs today. When we first moved to Greenlawn, I opened the sliding door of our play-room one day and our little dog got out and ran away. The new development of houses was on half-acre lots, with newly planted trees. Every yard looked the same. We had only been in the house a very short time and we think he must have gotten lost. Every day and night we would call for him and slowly drive our car around the neighborhood looking between the houses and into the yards, but we never found him. We finally decided that he was so cute someone must have taken him in. Imagining that was a good way to ease my sadness and guilt.

It was about two years before we thought about getting another puppy. My mother loved French Poodles and had a friend who knew a breeder. I remember going to the breeder's home to pick our puppy from a litter. There were three puppies to choose from and I can't remember why we picked our Gigi but she was the one. She was only eight weeks old with curly black fur, black eyes, and a Pink nose peeking out from all the fur. She was a toy poodle so would only grow to be about 12 pounds.

The breeder told us that Gigi would be a good dog for breeding when she was old enough. My mother agreed and when Gigi was three she had a litter of four puppies.

They became my playmates and every day after school I would care for them; give them water, feed them and change the newspaper in their large box which was their home with Gigi. When they were old enough to start running around I would take them out of the box and run back and forth in our long, narrow playroom with them following me as fast as their little legs would take them. Then I would turn back in the other direction as they turned and slid and then regained traction on the linoleum floor. After two runs back and forth, I would collapse on the floor laughing as they jumped all over me.

We were able to sell three to good homes and when we

were down to only one puppy, I begged to keep her. My mother and father agreed so then we had Gigi and Missy and I always had playmates.

When my children were growing up, they wanted a dog. Claude did not grow up with dogs and he wasn't a fan of the idea. I told him,

"It would be very good for the kids to have a dog."

"Ok," he conceded, "but I won't be involved in the care of it."

I knew he meant it too but I was prepared to take on a puppy with the kids. In spite of his reluctance, he and I found a breeder and went to pick out our Westie to surprise the kids at Christmas. Westie's are independent and feisty; very different from the "how can I please you" poodles that I was used to. Still, she was a lively and fun playmate for us all and we enjoyed 18 years with her. And who took her along with him when he went to get bagels on Sunday morning? Yes, Claude did.

We no longer have a dog and have no need for one since Elise has four rescues and Eric has one. They live nearby and when I visit, which is often, I get my dog fix. Mireille enjoyed visiting Rosie when Yves, Angela, and their children were at work and school, and I can relate to that. When I am asked to go over to let the dogs out when no one is home, I stay and play with them awhile. Being around them makes me feel like a kid again.

We also learned that Mireille loved cars. On one of our walks, she noticed the New York license plates on our car as we walked by. She liked the car and said she wanted to get in the car and take a ride with us. The brothers have several pictures of her posing with various cars throughout the years and she had her favorites.

My brother Pierre had four Chevy II Novas. One was a

1969 which was his race car, two 1972 SS, and one 1966. My first car was a 1963 blue Chevy II Nova. One of his Nova's was the same Chevy Nova blue as mine. Of all the cars I could have had as a first car, that coincidence amazes us.

Part of Guy's work as a police officer in Chateauguay was protecting the safety of those on the road. In order to catch speeding motorists, he and his sergeant would sit in the patrol car on the side of the road waiting for them to pass by. It was usually in the morning, just the time people would be on their way to work.

Guy said they would hear the roaring engine in the distance and a car fast approaching their post. Guy's sergeant would comment,

"Is that your brother again?"

With that Pierre would flash by in his fast car on his way to work.

"Talk to your brother. We'll have to give him a ticket eventually."

After leaving Mireille this day, Yves and Angela arranged for us to have dinner with the family and to meet Angela's sisters and husbands at Le Cactus, an authentic Mexican restaurant. During our May visit, we met Angela's parents, Giuseppina (Josephine) and Giuseppe (Joseph), and her grandmother, Angelina at Angela's childhood home.

The warm welcome and the love in the house that I felt when we visited Angela's childhood home reminded me of the first time I visited Claude's childhood home and met his parents and sisters. I felt immediately at home. Mireille loved Angela's family and especially loved spending time with Angela's grandmother, Angelina. Mireille spoke only French and English and Angelina spoke Italian but they were able to communicate through their love of music, dancing, and being with friends and family. Angela was never far from them at their parties so she was often relied on for a translation.

At 61 years old, I was the same age as Mireille when Angela's family met her. At dinner, as her family looked at me, I knew that for them it was like seeing Mireille all over again. Each new family member I meet has the same reaction and it is a new experience for me. Some adoptees may look similar to their adoptive family, as my brother Brian did, but for me, there was no resemblance to any family member. Since the reunion, during every visit to my family in Canada, I experience a new sense of belonging I didn't know I was missing. Although the most obvious indication of belonging is my physical appearance, I wonder how much of Mireille my family may see in me beyond that.

Although I didn't share any physical characteristics with my adoptive family, I know that when I was younger I took on many of the temperamental and emotional behaviors of my parents. As I matured I took on some of the behaviors that felt right to me and rejected those that didn't. Perhaps that's true whether a person is adopted or not. I didn't miss a sense of belonging, because I did belong to a family, my adopted clan, and we all blended together to form our family.

We will stay at Yves and Angela's again and we are grateful that my Canadian family has welcomed us into their homes because there are no hotels in Chateauguay. We have stayed with Pierre, Guy and Line, and Yves and Angela. If we had to stay in Montreal, as we did on the first visit, there would be a lot of wasted time traveling to and from Montreal instead of visiting. Angela was so wise when she pointed out that we want to get to know each other and staying in their homes is the best way. She is kind and giving of herself.

SUNDAY, JUNE 26, 2011

When we arrived at the Foyer this morning, Line was already there walking Mireille outside in the wheelchair. We did that for about an hour and then brought her inside for lunch and rest.

After our lunch with Guy and Line, Claude and I went back to the Foyer for another visit. We spent the afternoon walking and talking with her.

She enjoyed Claude's company. He was able to joke with her and she got all his jokes. She was very quick and loved having fun. I was sitting next to her and she said to me,

"I can tell he's a good man."

That meant a lot to me because he is the BEST man, and I was pleased that she could see that.

Then she tells me she loves Claude, and he makes her laugh.

As always we stay with her until she gets tired. Then the nurses prepare her for bed, and when she is settled we leave her. Again it is very hard to leave her, but there is nothing more to do, and we know that she will fall asleep quickly, and sleep can help her keep her strength.

Visiting a loved one in a nursing home is challenging. There are so many distractions from the other patients, and there is limited space or places to go that would simulate a visit in a person's private home. All of our visits were similar because of the nature of the home but also because of the limitations that our mother had. She was not able to communicate with me in a way that would have led to a deep conversation, especially since I am not fluent in French, but when my brothers and their wives were there she would join in on some of their conversations in French.

MONDAY, JUNE 27, 2011

After seeing Mireille again this morning, Claude and I left Chateauguay for The Whiteface Lodge. Claude's dad, Corinne, Martine, and Anthony were there and anxious to hear how Mireille is doing and details about our visit with her. They welcomed me as family since I was twenty years old, and their love and support now and through the years have been a constant in my life. I wish Claude's mother Simone was alive to share this with me. She was a big part of my life, always giving me confidence and encouragement through every milestone. I loved her and miss her.

❧ 38 ❧

MONTH 3 – JULY 2011

SUNDAY, JULY 31, 2011

A few weeks ago, Line and Guy called to ask Claude and me to join them on a family vacation to a Lake House and Hotel in Canada from August 1 to 5. This trip was planned long before they received the phone call about me that would upend their lives. They had already secured the rental house which would accommodate their families. When they considered asking us to join them, they knew there was a hotel on the property, and that we would be able to reserve a room. I was thrilled to be included in their trip. Sharing this time together would be an opportunity to enjoy and learn more about each other. We told them we would love to go.

"Let's go up to Plattsburgh the day before we leave on vacation with my brothers," I suggested to Claude.

We will stay overnight at the Holiday Inn and get an early start to Chateauguay and the Foyer the next day. I wanted to have a leisurely visit with Mireille that morning before we left from Chateauguay on vacation.

MONDAY, AUGUST 1, 2011

We left Plattsburgh and when we arrived at the nursing home Mireille was having lunch in the common room on her floor. She was very happy to see us and I was happy to sit with her while she ate. There were others having lunch also, but instead of everyone eating together at a large table, each person was in their wheelchair with a tray of food in front of them. I didn't see any interaction between the residents. Some are more handicapped than others, and it was sad and unsettling to hear loud calling out and other disturbing noises from some of the patients. Mireille was seated away from those more needy patients. The seating appeared to be planned that way and when a resident who was sitting closest to Mireille would look at us and smile, I thought it possible that if I wasn't there she may have tried to engage with Mireille.

It was another beautiful day, although hot, to take her outside. She asked us to go to her room first so she could get her sweater. We didn't discourage her from taking her sweater because during our walks, even though it was warm, we would see her shiver when the wind picked up. We also wanted to protect her from the strong rays of the sun so in addition to her wearing her sweater, we found some shady paths.

Although we chatted a little about anything we saw on our walk, during the quiet moments my mind was free to think a little about the days ahead with my brothers and family. The significance of the upcoming vacation with them was on my mind. Mixed in with the excitement and anticipation of spending quality time with them was my hope that the ease we have felt with each other to this point will continue and form a solid base for our family bond.

When the reunion was scheduled for April 14, 2011, I had

no thoughts or expectations of what would come after. I couldn't imagine what I would experience during the minutes or hour of the reunion, never mind how it might change my life. Whenever I think back from the reunion onward I am astonished by my inclusion into the family so quickly and completely. We sat by the river and the wind was blowing Mireille's hair. I could see she wanted to fix it so I fastened it a little tighter, and told her I would style it in any way she would like when we went back inside. Styling hair was something I enjoyed when I was young, and after I had my daughter Elise, and her hair grew long, she was very patient and happy to let me style her hair. We would collaborate and experiment with two braids, one braid, French braids, or any other style we decided to try. Now my daughter is 32 and after all these years I am out of practice, but even so, I offered to French braid Mireille's hair. Angela was there and as I braided my birth mother's hair, Angela and I locked eyes and without words, we felt the poignancy of this moment.

Sabrina and Joey were there with Yves and Angela and they brought their cute dog Rosie who Mireille loved. Rosie always cheered her up and she smiled as she petted her.

Yves explained to Mireille that we were all going on vacation to the mountains together and we would be back on Friday. I could see she loved the idea of us all being together, but as she looked at each one of us as if for confirmation, I saw a sadness there too when she realized she couldn't come with us.

Initially, I felt happy about spending time on vacation with the family, but now that we were leaving her, a feeling of unease was replacing the excitement of the trip. I was thinking,

"Please wait for me."

PART III

VACATION

MONDAY, AUGUST 1, 2011

The scenic drive from Chateauguay to our vacation at the Lake House, Manoir des Pins in St. Lucie on Lake Sarrazin in Quebec, gave us a preview of the natural beauty of the pine trees and mountains we would enjoy over the next few days. My brothers' rental house/chalet, on one section of the property, had five bedrooms, while our room in the hotel portion of the resort was reminiscent of staying in a historic and inviting home of a family member.

After checking in, we pulled into the luggage drop-off area closest to where our room was, and Guy, Pierre, and Yves were there to help us if needed. Everyone was excited to settle in and start their vacation. Our room was on the second floor of the hotel and we were responsible for bringing the luggage up to the room. There was no elevator.

We had two very large, heavy suitcases, a laptop for Claude's work, and a backpack. In our defense, after this vacation, we were returning to see Mireille, and then going on to

The Whiteface Lodge for a week. We would be away from our home in Huntington for two weeks. Claude was having back problems at the time so my poor brothers had to bring our luggage up to our room. I was embarrassed and wondered why we hadn't packed a separate smaller bag for the short four-day stay at the Chalet.

We left our unpacked suitcases as soon as they were deposited in the room and we all took the short walk across the beach by the lake to the family's rental chalet. There we were greeted by Line, Guy's daughter Josee and her family, Pierre's daughters, Anyssa and Lydia, and Angela with their children Sabrina and Joey. It was a full and happy house.

The afternoon passed quickly in the backyard of the chalet. We were all tired from the day and the drive and were content to sit, relax and plan for the upcoming few days. The family is cooking at the chalet and Claude and I are eating in the hotel dining room since dinner was included in our hotel rate. After dinner, we returned to the chalet and visited with the family for a short while. We were all fading, and ready to call it a night, so we left our French family saying,

"Bonne Nuit!"

"A demain!"

As Claude and I walked back to the hotel, we marveled at the full day we just had and couldn't wait for the next day.

TUESDAY, AUGUST 2, 2011

Our first morning at the vacation lake house started with breakfast, which consisted of pancakes, Canadian maple syrup, breakfast meats and eggs, and a variety of breads and pastries. Following this feast, we went on an exploratory walk around the property with the family. In addition to the full-service hotel, there are many rentals on the lake ranging from one-room cabins to five-bedroom chalets. Most of them have wood fireplaces and Jacuzzi tubs. Some of them are near the beach on the lake and others are nestled away in the pines overlooking the lake. Manoir des Pins is a charming country getaway in the Laurentian Mountains, a mountain range in southern Quebec, Canada which is north of the St. Lawrence and Ottawa Rivers. The sparkling, clean mountain lake provides the breathtaking backdrop for the property.

It was a beautiful day and everyone was anxious to get outside and start our day of playing and relaxing on the beach. There was horseshoes and badminton, kayaking and swimming, and lounge chairs for relaxing and chatting as we watched all the activity. It was the perfect environment for getting to know my new family and for them to know me.

There was a kayak for two that Claude and I chose. As we started paddling, we could see a beautiful house with a turret at the far end of the lake. We decided to paddle the entire length of the lake to see it up close. There was a dock right in front of their house and from a distance it looked like there were two little children, a boy and a girl, sitting on the dock. We went closer and saw that they are statues.

Although dinner (supper) was included in our room charge, today we stayed with the family for a barbeque. It was a night of games. They taught us a game called "golf" which was fun and easy to learn, and we brought a game called left-center-right which is also very easy to learn. The children really enjoyed it and since there is no limit on how many can play at once, it was perfect for a big crowd. However, if you're looking for a game with strategy, this is not it.

WEDNESDAY, AUGUST 3, 2011

Today Guy was going to the nearby town, Saint Agathe-des-Monts on Lac des Sables, to buy a few things for dinner and he asked if I would like to go with him. He knew I wanted to buy a few bottles of wine and some appetizers for a cocktail hour that Claude and I would be hosting on the terrace off our room on Thursday, our last night.

As we pulled into the town I told Guy,

"This town looks like a picture from a travel magazine."

The buildings were impressive, European styled, and colorful. Guy told me,

"This town dates back to 1869 and has a population of 10,000. When Angela's parents married, they had their honeymoon here."

It has been a popular vacation destination for a long time.

Guy is very easy to talk to so there were no awkward moments of silence. This is true of all my brothers and their families. I've been at ease with them from the beginning.

Once inside the market Guy and I went our separate ways looking for what we needed. We met at the checkout, and we discussed the wines and appetizers I chose for our cocktail hour the next evening.

On the way back to the Chalet, we passed a hot dog stand and Guy commented,

"When we are on vacation, if we see a hot dog stand that we haven't tried yet, we make it a point to have lunch there during the vacation."

He said he noticed that this one is always busy which was a good sign, and we would have lunch there on the way home on Friday.

After another evening of games, Claude and I walked back to the hotel. Every evening, while we still had the light of day, we walked from the hotel to the Chalet to visit the family. We navigated the irregular stone steps and then a steep and winding grassy path to get to the open flat beach on our way to the Chalet.

After spending the evening, it would be very dark on our way home around 11 p.m. The first night we didn't think about how dark it would be and how difficult to return to our room using the path and the stone steps. We learned quickly though and had a flashlight for the rest of our nightly visits.

THURSDAY, AUGUST 4, 2011

Today I'm thinking of my Aunt Catherine, my mother Mary's sister. It would have been her 96th birthday.

It was another beautiful day at the beach; another day of swimming, kayaking, playing horseshoes, and badminton. Since the first day, the weather has been perfect for the beach, warm and sunny with occasional clouds.

Tonight is the night when the family will join us before dinner for wine and appetizers. Claude and I planned this specifically to pay tribute to Mireille on the last evening of our vacation together. The terrace is across the hall from our room at the hotel and overlooks Lake Sarrazin. It is rustic and charming and perfect for this mountain retreat. It isn't too large, but large enough to hold the family comfortably with a table set up for our food and drinks and a few comfortable chairs. When we all stepped onto the terrace there was a young couple relaxing in the sunshine, enjoying a cocktail and a cigarette.

We began sharing stories about Mireille and how incredible it was that we have been reunited. Our stories continued and the young couple, undoubtedly noticing the seriousness of our party, left the terrace.

Claude uncorked the wine and everyone held out their glass for him to pour. Then Claude held up his glass and proposed a toast,

"This is a toast to Mireille. I am so happy that she and Eileen have been reunited after all these years, and I am sorry it wasn't sooner. I am grateful and thank her for her sacrifice of placing Eileen with the Sisters of the orphanage and that I could have her all these years. And to Eileen's brothers and their families, I say thank you for your generosity in sharing your time, your families, and your homes. This is why we have been able to know and love you in such a short time and to feel confident that our connection will grow stronger with each year."

We all embraced and each family member, in turn, shared what our reunion means to them, and especially what it means to our mother who is finally able to be comforted knowing that her baby girl is no longer lost to her.

This unforgettable evening was not over and we could feel each other's contentment as we left the terrace and took the staircase to the lobby. This is a historic, stately hotel with many of the original wood details still apparent in the wide, curving, and dramatic staircase leading to and from the second floor. Once at the front desk we were led to our large reserved table in the dining room near a beautifully decorated huge stone fireplace. It was too hot for a fire but it was a stately backdrop to our table. All 17 of us were there at a long table with enough elbow room for us to be spread out. We were a happy, boisterous family enjoying each other and the many appetizers, entrees, and wine to accompany it all. A perfect ending to a perfect vacation.

FRIDAY, AUGUST 5, 2011

This is our last morning and I was feeling anxious to get back to Chateauguay and see Mireille. We saw her before we left for vacation on Monday, and I will see her when we return to Chateauguay later today. I missed seeing her on Tuesday, Wednesday, and Thursday but the time with my brothers has been important and I hoped she felt that way too.

As promised, we stopped on the way home at the hot dog stand following Guy's tradition. We all agreed they were very good but Guy said maybe not the best he's had.

After lunch, Claude and I left in our own car to go directly to the Foyer to visit Mireille. The rest of the family went back to their homes in Chateauguay first. They are thoughtful and give me some time alone with Mireille. When we arrived at the Foyer, Mireille was in her bed and she didn't look well. I was alarmed to see the oxygen tank and the tubes to her nose.

I quickly left the room to find a nurse and ask about her condition. The nurse didn't speak English but she was able to tell me that she has pneumonia. Soon Line and Guy, Angela and Yves and Pierre arrived. We all stayed with Mireille, and the nurses said she was stable, responding to the antibiotics and her fever was down. She appeared to be resting comfortably, and after a couple of hours, we could see that she continued to be sleeping peacefully.

We proceeded with our original plan to leave for Lake Placid that evening, understanding that the family would call if there was a change in her condition. On the way to Lake Placid, Claude and I decided we would drive back to Chateauguay on Sunday or Monday.

❧ 40 ☙

OPPORTUNITY

SATURDAY, AUGUST 6, 2011

We spoke to Guy and Line and Yves and Angela on Saturday morning to check on Mireille's progress. At that time, she was still stable and they assured me they would call immediately if there was a change.

SUNDAY, AUGUST 7, 2011

When Claude and I arrived back in our room after breakfast, I found that we had two missed calls from Angela. I called back and she said that Mother was not doing well and the doctor said she would not live through the night.

Claude and I quickly got ready and left for Chateauguay.

We arrived at about 1 p.m. and joined my brothers, Line and Angela at Mireille's bedside. Uncle Yvon, Mireille's older brother, was also there.

None of us spoke as we all congregated in a circle around

our mother. Even though her eyes were open, she was no longer responsive. Her breathing was difficult and we could see she was relying on the oxygen.

The nurse came in and gave her medications through an IV tube. Line suggested I speak to her alone and everyone left the room except Claude and me. We knew the end was very near. It was thoughtful of Line to suggest I have time alone because I never would have presumed to have them leave the room so I could say my last words to our Mother. Everyone stepped outside the room. Claude and I stayed and I was able to say my last words to her.

"I am so happy that we found each other, and I hope you are at peace," I whispered to her. "You were with me as I came into this world, and I'm with you as you leave. Now I know my three wonderful brothers and their families and we will have a beautiful future together, because of you. I love you."

Then each of the others took their turn. Guy and Line were the last to go in and they were by her side when she passed.

My overwhelming feelings were loss, gratitude, and disbelief.

Loss of more time as mother and daughter;

Gratitude for the four months we had; and

Disbelief that she was gone.

When I received the copy of the letter she had written asking for help in finding me, I wished aloud,

"If I could just find her before she dies and give her the peace of knowing that I am well and have had a good life."

My wish was granted and I am very grateful, but I can't help feeling heavy-hearted that we did not have more time.

I think most people have some regret when a loved one dies. I was on vacation with my brothers when I could have been by her side for those last few days. When we returned from the vacation, I could have stayed with her for the last day, but not knowing it was the last day I left her side.

From the poem, The Last Time
The thing is, you won't even know it's
the last time
Until there are no more times.
And even then, it will take you a while
To realize.
So while you are living in these times,
Remember there are only so many of
Them
And when they are gone, you will
Yearn for just one more day of them.
For one last time.
-Author Unknown-

I hope that in her final thoughts she knew that her children were together and happy and because of her faith and love we were reunited.

Outside her room we were all together hugging, crying, and comforting each other. This was their mother who raised and nurtured them. I had been absent all those years from her life. My grief was not from memories of growing up with her that I would reflect back upon, but only the short memories of a reunion that was never expected, but very beautiful. It is a life experience that will always be with me. How was it that I decided to seek out the circumstances of my birth after 61 years? Mireille was calling for me, and in doing so brought me peace that I didn't know I needed.

The nurse came and confirmed her passing, and we sat with her in the room, each with our own thoughts.

We left the Foyer and went to Guy and Line's house. There I was with my newly found family looking through old photographs and sharing their grief over the loss of our mother; the mother they knew so well, but for me the mother who gave me life and loved me from afar. Our grief was different--theirs for the loss of someone so much a part of their lives—mine for the loss of opportunity to have known her as a daughter should know her mother. But then the gratitude takes over and I am thankful for what we had.

Yes, we wondered about and missed each other throughout our lives. She wished she could know I was safe and happy; I wished I could tell her I was safe and happy.

We didn't know each other as mother and daughter but we were able to find happiness because...

Mireille was not lacking the experience of being a loving and loved mother.

I was not lacking the experience of being a loving and loved daughter.

These were comforting facts of our lives.

I can't believe what has happened between July 2010 and August 2011. When I read the letter that she wrote in 1986 wishing she could meet me before she died, I felt a great urgency to find her and hopefully give her the peace of mind she needed. According to my family, she was very ill with pneumonia in February around the time that Nadia found her. They expected her to die at that time, but she recovered. That was within days of the time when Nadia called me to say she had phone numbers to try to find my birth mother.

During the years just leading up to the reunion, I could not put her out of mind as easily as I did when I was younger. Was she calling me? I feel as if I was led through all the events to finally be with her after 61 years. I sometimes felt like a spectator in my own adoption search.

Although we did not have much time together, it was rich and comforting for both of us. Of course, after her passing, as whenever you lose a loved one, I started wishing I had found her sooner, stayed longer, or spent more time. Sometimes I imagine I got there 10 years ago. What would we have done together? Cooked, shopped, and visited with family? She would have come to visit me at my home and I would have spent time with her in her home. Whenever these thoughts come, I stop and remember my gratitude for having the time we did have together. How lucky I am to have been able to grant her the wish she made in that letter of 1986,

"to know if she is happy before I die and to see her because every time I see a girl who is about her age, I wonder if it could be her, my little Monique..."

MONDAY, AUGUST 8, 2011

After waking, we went with Guy to meet Pierre and Yves at the Funeral Home. We met with a representative who explained everything in French to my brothers. It was mostly pre-arranged from 2009, but there were additional arrangements to be made.

On Sunday, August 14, 2011, there would be a wake/service/reception at the funeral home.

After the meeting, we left Chateauguay and arrived at The Whiteface Lodge in Lake Placid around 4 p.m. Dad, Corinne, Claire, Martine, and Anthony were there to greet us and express their condolences. I am saddened and shocked that she passed away so quickly. It takes my breath away when I think four months and I could have missed her completely. When I saw her on August 1 she did seem frail but not sick. The onset of pneumonia was on August 4 and she passed away on August 7.

Tuesday through Friday we were at the Lodge. Claude was working quite a bit. I spent my time walking, reading, and writing. It was a very quiet time as I contemplated the loss of my birth mother and counted my blessings for having found her just in time.

❦ 41 ❦

INSIDE GATHERING

Six months ago we didn't even know that Eric and Elise's biological grandmother was alive and now they will be attending her funeral. They have only seen pictures from my reunion with her, and they were looking forward to September 2, 2011, when they and their families would meet her. We are all disappointed and sad that they missed that opportunity by only one month. I ask myself why I didn't realize how weak she was and rush my family there earlier. There is no answer, no excuses, just regret.

Early on Sunday, August 14, 2011, the four of us drove directly from the hotel in Plattsburgh, New York to the Funeral Home in Chateauguay and arrived at 9:15 a.m.

As we pulled into the parking lot of the funeral home, my brothers were there to greet us. Eric and Elise would meet their uncles for the first time. After introductions, there were hugs and words of condolence as we made our way into the funeral home.

My brothers led us from the hot parking lot into the cool air of the funeral home. We step into a large circular lobby with several doors and three large openings to the right, center, and left leading to the reception room, the chapel, and the dining room. Where we live in New York our custom is to have the wake (reception) and funeral prayer service at the funeral home, a funeral mass at the church (optional and usually the following morning), graveside prayers at the cemetery after the church or funeral home service and then a gathering with food and drink at a restaurant. The Canadian custom of having everyone together at one location for all three parts of our farewell was very calming and comforting.

We hear hushed voices to our right coming from the reception room where the entrance to the room, although large, is crowded with friends and family coming to pay their respects. My brothers stay by our side as they introduce us to our previously unknown family members. We hadn't met Mireille's sister Lise and brother Guy yet. Only they and my sisters-in-law, their children, and Uncle Yvon will know who we are. Or so I thought.

Before my brothers could introduce me, Mireille's sister, my Aunt Lise, approached me. She took my face in her hands and looked very intently at me while smiling and exclaiming in French,

"Oh Mon Dieu! C'est Mireille!"

Mireille at 20 years old

Eileen at 20 years old

Everyone was curious and many were surprised, but they

knew who I was. They saw Mireille in me, and as we were introduced their eyes would linger on my face as they took in the strong resemblance of their Mireille who they knew well. They welcomed me, and I became part of a family I never knew.

As we went further into the room we saw the table surrounded with flowers and a beautiful photo of Mireille. Next to her photo, there was a pretty container with her remains. The room was filled with picture boards, and my family included pictures of me with them and Mireille from our visits during the four months that we were together. A video of pictures from Mireille's life was running in one corner of the room, and the family included pictures of me with Mireille, my brothers, and their families. Again I am touched by their inclusion of me; making me feel as if I've always been part of their lives. I owe this to Mireille and her openness about loving and missing me.

Many of her friends sought me out to tell me how much they loved Mireille. They approached me with big smiles and arms open wide for a hug as they reminisce about their fun-loving friend and their times together and how much she will be missed. It was a telling tribute to her friendships.

From this room, we continued on to the room next door, the Chapel. It had a center aisle with rows of pews along each side. First, the friends were instructed to enter the chapel and have a seat. Then the Priest led the immediate family into the room and guided us to the first row on the right in front of the podium from where he would speak. Claude and I were seated with my brothers; Elise and Eric were seated on the other side of the aisle, also in the first row. A table with Mireille's ashes, picture, and flowers was next to the podium in the front and center of the chapel for all to see.

The priest started the ceremony, speaking in French.

Claude and I, and Eric and Elise were the only non-French-speaking loved ones there and we listened carefully to understand as many words as possible. After his remarks concluded, he began to repeat his entire eulogy in English in consideration of us. This was an unexpected and thoughtful surprise. The priest also knew my mother Mary had already passed away and during part of the service he remarked directly to me,

"It has occurred to me Eileen that you have lost two mothers. The one who gave birth to you, and the one who raised and cared for you."

Through my tears, I smiled and nodded at the truth of that thought. It was a touching moment for me, and I felt recognized and understood.

Line and the family composed a tribute to our mother's life. It was read in French and then in English.

Mireille was a lovely woman who enjoyed life to its fullest

She was a people person and was happiest when surrounded by family and friends.

Mireille was known for her great taste in food and wine especially when entertaining large gatherings of friends and family

(Needless to say that the Gendron, Comtois and Resta families are just as hospitable when entertaining family and friends)

Maman was a determined woman who knew what she wanted in life, but nothing was more important to her than her children:

Guy, the portrait of his father and the love of her life

Pierre, has been called many times Maman's chou-chou

Yves, her darling baby (accepting the fact that the youngest one grows up is always difficult)

Mireille was very proud of her boys, but her biggest regret in life was having given up her precious baby daughter for adoption. She searched for her daughter all her life without being able to find her, yet she never lost hope.

Finally in the last year of her life, Maman was reunited with her darling daughter Eileen who searched and found her mother.

This was one of the most beautiful moments in Maman's life.

Unfortunately, Maman passed away on Sunday, August 8th at 3pm. She was granted a final precious wish, to be surrounded by all of her four loving children.

Rest in peace Maman, we love you.

The service was followed by a musical interlude in which they played two songs chosen by the family. One was a special French song, perhaps a favorite of Mireille's, and the other, Somewhere, sung by Barbra Streisand (from West Side Story) which promises a time and place for us somewhere even if only in our hearts.

As Line read the tribute to Mireille, I listened to the

poignant music and reflected on the circumstances of my two mothers.

On September 7, 1949, I was brought to the orphanage by my birth mother Mireille. It was three months and one day after my birth.

On September 9, 1949, I was adopted from the orphanage by my mother, Mary, and father, Owen. When my mother came to my crib with my father and brother by her side, she told me she knew that I was the one.

Only two days! I was given up but then chosen.

Two mothers at the beginning of my life —one experiencing heart-wrenching sadness and one experiencing joy and contentment.

One mother shunned by the public and family. In her letter, she wrote of the clinic where she gave birth.

"We were treated like criminals. It was a real nightmare."

One mother praised for saving a child from life in an orphanage. Many times I heard people tell my mother,

"You have a seat in heaven."

One mother desperately trying to keep her baby but knowing that she could not give her even the most basic of life's needs. Selfless and loving, she faced that reality and found the courage to relinquish her baby girl to the Soeurs de la Miséricorde at the orphanage in Montreal.

One mother who was ready with so much love and resources to give to the little girl she had hoped for. At the border, the United States Border Patrol didn't want to allow the baby to pass into the United States claiming a medical issue with her eyes. My mother replied,

"She just needs care and that is what I can give her."

The doctors were called, and they were mulling it over when she declared,

"I'm not going home without her!"

She was also desperate not to give her up.

Two mothers and one baby--a baby wanted by both but impossible to be shared.

After the funeral service, we were led through a door in the front of the chapel on the left side into an adjoining dining room. It was a large room with one long wall set up as a buffet with a wide variety of hot and cold food. As everyone began to help themselves to lunch, I saw my three brothers all together at the far end of the room. Guy motioned to me to come over and join them.

As I approached, I saw that Guy, Pierre, and Yves were all looking at something in Guy's hand. Guy spoke for them all when he said,

"Eileen, we would like you to have Mother's watch."

During one of my visits to Mireille I commented on a pretty watch she always wore and it sparked a conversation between us. She smiled when I noticed it, and told me she liked to wear a watch.

I put it on immediately and wear it in remembrance of her. I treasure it along with the beautiful, black onyx ring they gave me when we first met. In all of Mireille's pictures, we can see the beautiful black onyx ring which she wore on her index finger. It fits my middle finger perfectly.

In our will is a note that these two pieces of jewelry will be given back to my brothers when I pass away so they can have these very special mementos for their children to inherit.

In another room off the lobby of the funeral home is a wall of small, vault-like, locked boxes recessed into the wall. This is where the ashes of the deceased are stored until the family is able to make preparations for the burial. Claude and I will be returning to Chateauguay in October for the grave-side service and burial.

OUTSIDE GATHERING

It was a cloudy October day when we returned to Chateauguay to be with the family for Mireille's final service and burial at the well-kept town cemetery. The cemetery is within walking distance from Guy and Line's house but it began to drizzle as we left the house so we decided to drive. Claude and I sat in the back seat of Guy and Line's car with my brothers and their families following us. It was a somber, quiet ride, just the intermittent sound of the wipers.

The cemetery is situated on a rectangular piece of land surrounded by a chain-link fence. As I looked out the window I could see the entire cemetery with its variety of headstones, large and small. At the end is the old church where I went with my brothers when they made final arrangements. There are narrow roads, more like passageways, running through the cemetery. The parking is haphazard and our cars were stretched out alongside the road, half on the grass, next to where the headstones began. We were prepared for the drizzle with umbrellas and boots and we began to walk to the gravesite. The road was muddy with many holes so we all stepped carefully.

Small groups of family and friends approached, joining us and the priest by the grave in no particular order. Our mother's ashes will be buried next to her mother, Fedora Trudeau. We saw her mother's name, our grandmother, with her date of birth and death chiseled on the headstone.

My Grandparents Joseph Comtois and Fedora Trudeau

In 1925 Fedora Trudeau married Joseph Comtois, our grandfather, with whom she had four children. He passed away in 1946 when Mireille was 17 years old. At the time of Fedora's death in 1989, she was married to Lucien McDuff, her third husband, and this is his family plot.

There were about 20 of us at the gravesite as the priest began his prayers and gave his blessing. I remember standing there gazing down at the headstone with my hands crossed in front of my body listening to many relatives and friends speak about their love for Mireille. Suddenly there was no more speaking and I looked up to see all eyes on me. Oh my, I was expected to speak.

I didn't have any words prepared for this day but somehow I found my voice.

"Four months and I would have missed a very momentous day in my life and the life of my birth mother. How fortunate we are to have found each other just in time and to know that our love for each other never wavered. And now, thanks to Mireille, I belong to my new family."

Neither of us had any bitterness or disappointment in the other. She did not reproach me, nor did the family, about taking so long to find her. We were so grateful to finally be reunited that nothing else mattered.

As is usual after graveside funerals the family leaves the unfinished site and will come back when the grave marker is completed and installed on the grave. We will be back in Chateauguay for that day in the spring.

Many of our friends at home sent condolence cards and one friend sent money for us to use for a memorial of our choice. According to my brothers, Mireille's favorite flower was the rose, and they suggested we have a beautiful rose engraved on Mireille's headstone.

❧ 43 ❧

LOSS

In 1994 Mireille told my brothers that they had a sister. During one of my visits with my brothers after Mireille died, I asked Guy,

"What do you think made her tell you about me after so many years of silence?"

Guy told me that one day while he was with Mother; she was frustrated by something and said to him,

"If my daughter was here she would help me."

Guy said,

"What do you mean your daughter?"

"Yes, it's true I have a daughter."

Guy was shocked and wondered if it was true. My three brothers, Guy, Pierre, and Yves then went to their father Jean Gilles to confirm this news and he did. He explained that he and Mireille, our mother, were friends while she was pregnant with me.

Later, thanks to their Aunt Renee, Jean Gilles' sister, we all learned what a tremendous part he played in helping Mireille during her pregnancy and after my birth.

It was several years after Mireille passed away that Aunt Renee revealed new information about what happened immediately after my birth.

My adoption papers listed my name as Marie Monique Comtois. I have known that name since I was very young but never believed it could actually be a name that was given to me by my birth mother. According to what the sisters in the orphanage incorrectly told my mother, Mireille had not even seen me but was forced to relinquish me right after birth.

The true story is that after giving birth to me at L'Aide a la Femme, a clinic in Montreal, Mireille was determined to keep me, not give me up for adoption as she was being pressed to do. She described the nurses at the clinic as being cold and heartless. There was no one to turn to for help, or so it seemed.

Jean Gilles, who later became her husband and father of my three brothers, had been helping her cope during her pregnancy. Now, he again came to her aid by offering to find a room in Montreal for her and me. His father, Joseph Alexandre, owned a taxi and would drive Jean Gilles and his sister Renee to us every day bringing supplies and helping however they could. Renee said she held me often in the first week when Mireille was too weak to care for me. Mireille, with the help of Jean Gilles and his family, kept me for three months.

Jean Gilles Gendron and Mireille Comtois

Aunt Renee shared this information with my brother Guy as recently as 2018.

Guy asked Aunt Renee,

"Why didn't you tell us about this when we first reunited with Eileen?"

Aunt Renee replied,

"I wasn't sure it was the right thing to do."

Aunt Renee kept this part of their lives to herself from when she was a young girl. Those three months were a secret time for Mireille, Jean Gilles, Renee, and Joseph Alexander. I can understand her hesitation to reveal it after so many years of secrecy.

For those first three months of my life, which was during the summer, we lived in a single room with no heat or hot water. This arrangement lasted from my birth on June 6 until September 7 when they realized they had no choice but to bring me back to L'Aide a la Femme. The weather was turning cold in Montreal, and they did not have the means to keep me.

L'Aide a la Femme then released me to the care of La

Societe de Rehabilitation, Inc., and they placed me in the Crèche de la Miséricorde, the orphanage where my mother, father, and my brother Brian adopted me on September 9, 1949.

A few weeks after Mireille and Jean Gilles brought me to L'Aide a la Femme, they went back to reclaim me and bring me home. Jean Gilles reported that she would not stop crying in the weeks after bringing me to the orphanage, and he was determined to find a way for her to keep me. He loved her and did not want her to be unhappy.

How happy she must have been to think she was on her way to being reunited with her baby girl.

My imagination puts me with them on the steps leading into the building where just weeks before they reluctantly released me to the care of the sisters of the crèche. Anxious, happy, excited, and relieved are some of the feelings Mireille must have had as she ran up those steps.

As they entered that building, it is probable that they didn't expect to hear I was already gone. Taken to another country where I was already weeks into my new identity.

My imagination further allows me to enter the building, see two young twenty-year-olds anxiously looking left and right to find the person who would be able to help them. Maybe they were brought into an office and asked to have a seat and wait while that person looked up the record of my arrival several weeks before. Mireille and Jean Gilles were hopeful and believing that I was sleeping safely in one of the many cribs there and they would be able to reclaim me. They knew there were hundreds of babies available for adoption. Surely I was still there.

Was the person gentle and kind or matter of fact when they explained to Mireille that I had been adopted weeks before by a couple from the United States? I try to picture

Mireille and Jean Gilles being given the news that I was no longer at the orphanage but already taken to the United States and untraceable because of sealed adoption records.

It is inconceivable to think of the despair and grief she must have felt leaving that orphanage without her three-month-old baby girl whom she had nurtured from birth. A loss so devastating; to think your baby is out in the world somewhere with strangers, but you may never know where. How she had to find the strength to get up and walk out the doors of the crèche and continue on with her life. Jean Gilles was there for her to lean on.

My brothers have all told me what a wonderful man their father was, they loved him very much.

When I received the copy of the letter that Mireille wrote in April 1986 I learned that she had named me and wished to know that I was happy and safe. She wrote that letter with hope that the agencies could help her find her baby girl. It wasn't until January 1987 that she received a reply, and her hopes were dashed again when the letter confirmed that I was adopted into the United States and they didn't have access to those records.

In 2010, before my reunion with my birth family, I visited the orphanage from where I was adopted. I walked those same front steps imagining my adoptive mother and father walking up those steps hoping to find their daughter and then leaving by those same steps to bring me home to Brooklyn, NY.

Now I think of Mireille, my birth mother, leaving by those same steps without me, twice. First when she had to relinquish me to the clinic as the weather turned cold, and then a few weeks later, seeking to reclaim me but finding I was already adopted and taken to the United States. I cannot imagine the depth of the sadness and pain she must have felt as she descended those steps for the last time.

She was only 20 years old and her life had to go on, but not before a period of mourning for the daughter she lost.

Two years later, Jean Gilles and she married.

44

REFLECTIONS

What has this experience meant to me and to my loved ones? Specifically, people would ask,

"What do Eric and Elise think about you, their mother, being adopted?

That is a good question and somehow, as my mother Mary did, I was able to let them know about my adoption from when they were young. When I asked them if they remember being told, they say they just always knew.

I don't remember them asking me or talking about my adoption, and I think adoption, although accepted, may still be regarded as a secret and not to be openly questioned.

The only memory I have is of Eric when he was about 20 years old saying,

"You know, we could be descended from Aboriginals in Canada!"

The fact that I, their mother, was adopted rarely came up in discussions with Eric and Elise.

"You're right. We could be."

I reminded him that although I knew my birth mother was French Canadian, I had no information about my birth father's heritage.

We left it at that but comments such as these reignited my curiosity about my birth family, especially coming from one of my children. His thinking aloud reminded me that the mystery surrounding my adoption not only affected me but Eric and Elise as they became adults and contemplated having their own families someday. There would always be that unanswered question about their genetic history, that missing link.

Eric also said he didn't think too much about my being adopted and that he thought it was great that I had parents that I loved and who loved me.

We have enjoyed a very loving relationship with Brian and Kellianne, my brother Brian's children since they were born. Eric commented that although my brother Brian and I were not genetically related, we are family, and he and Elise, Kellianne and Brian are close cousins.

Elise told me that she was curious, but knew it was up to me to want to pursue my birth family information. She said she understood why I had been reluctant. It was a big leap of faith to go down that path and could lead to emotional pain or disappointment.

On the forms Mireille filled out at the clinic, she shared information about my birth father and his family. She did not give his name but revealed he was also French Canadian from Montreal, and that she broke up with him when she found out she was pregnant. I did not have this information when Eric speculated about our heritage.

Perhaps Jean Gilles, my brothers' father, knew who my birth father was but even after Mireille told my brothers that she had a daughter, and it was confirmed by Jean Gilles, no one revealed any information about my birth father. Jean Gilles passed away one year after confirming my birth to my brothers. It seems at no time after that and through the years of my brothers helping Mireille search for me, did anyone ask Mireille who my father was.

After I met my birth family, the question resurfaced of who my birth father could be. Mireille and I were so happy to be reunited; I didn't ask her for information about my birth father. Earlier I wrote that knowing the close bond Mireille had with her brother Yvon, he must have known. If so, he held that secret until his death. I suspect that regarding my birth father, Mireille swore the family to secrecy.

As I reflect on my life as an adopted child, and its part in my growing up, I remember wondering who my birth parents might have been but then quickly putting it out of my mind. Why dwell on what you cannot know and especially on something that could upset your parents. Adoptees often fantasize about who their birth parents are. I read that most adoptees think they are descended from either royalty or criminals.

Gratitude and a positive attitude are what I think of when I think of my mother Mary. She had so many trials in her life and I remember them all; some I experienced with her, and others I feel as if I lived through because of her dramatic storytelling talent. So that was why I was struck, during one of her visits from Florida to my house in Huntington Station when she told me one day over a cup of tea,

"I've had a good life and I'm very grateful."

All I could think of was her abusive childhood, the death of her father at nine years old, her rejection by her mother in favor of her sister, experiencing my father's near-death twice, and then finally his death at a young 54 years of age, and her own recent medical emergencies.

Her cup was always half full. Both my parents, Mary and Owen had positive, "can-do" attitudes. I believe that is why they were so confident about adopting children. They never made me or my brother feel as if we weren't theirs.

We were very different though.

We looked different.

She was an Irish beauty with strawberry blond hair and green eyes.

"I have the map of Ireland on my face." She would often say.

She was always battling her weight but enjoyed her cake with tea in the morning. She loved clothes and hats and she had beautiful taste. She could be flamboyant.

I have dark hair and brown eyes. I was always thin. I didn't look like anyone in my family. I also liked clothes but there was a time my style was more conservative, and she used to say I was a "tailored woman."

My brother Brian looked exactly like our very Irish mother. They both had fair skin with freckles, reddish-blonde hair, and light eyes. My brother, not well-adjusted about being adopted, would exclaim,

"I look exactly like you. Why can't I really be yours?"

That was hard for our mother to hear because to her he was hers. Brian's birthday was March 17, 1944, and he was adopted on April 9, 1945. Although we did celebrate his birthday on March 17, St. Patrick's Day, he also celebrated every year on April 9 by sending our parents a card telling them that to him the day he was adopted was the day he was born. After our parents had passed, Brian would call me every April 9 and say,

"Do you know what day this is?"

And I would answer,

"The day you were adopted and became Owen and Mary's son."

Our personalities were different.

She was so outgoing and often made friends while she was waiting in line at any store you can name. And when I say made friends, I mean exchanged phone numbers, and the next thing I knew there was a new friend at our kitchen table having tea.

She was spunky and would never back down from a fight. She was also a problem solver. If something wasn't right she would jump in and fix it. She didn't wait for someone else to make her happy or solve a problem. She was fearless.

As a very young girl, I was not outgoing and in fact, was very shy. When we moved to Huntington and I started fourth grade at St. Patrick's School, I was not making friends. I was lonely but didn't know how to begin to make friends. Since I skipped third grade, I was very aware of the maturity of the other girls in fourth grade and knew I didn't belong. Everything was too hard for me and the nuns had no patience for immaturity. In their defense, there were 30 or more students in every class. Also, the other students in fourth grade had been together in that school since Kindergarten. No one even noticed me, and I was too shy to ask any of the other kids if I could join in and play at recess.

During the first few weeks, my mother would ask,

"Eileen, have you made any friends yet?"

After hearing me answer no, she would suggest ways to make friends, but I just couldn't bring myself to follow her advice.

I was just walking around the playground during recess one afternoon when my mother showed up and introduced me to the girls in my grade.

"Hello, this is Eileen and she is new to this school. She would like to play with you at recess."

She must have instinctively picked the nicest girls because they started including me at recess, and I ended up being friends with one girl into our 20's.

It was during the teenage years that my mother and I experienced ups and downs in our relationship. My father's death illustrated how we relied on him as the buffer and peacemaker in the family. After he died I was very sad and angry. I took it out on my mother and we would clash every day. I wanted to be out of the house as much as possible to avoid the conflict, and she wanted me home because she was lonely. As I grew and matured and she was happier, we were able to find common ground for a good relationship.

Biological mothers and daughters can be very different also. Genetic history isn't always obvious in a person. Each person is unique and the product of a long line of genetic possibilities.

My birth mother Mireille and I look so much alike and yet I'm not sure how much our personalities were alike. I do know that she loved and valued her family over everything, and I feel that way too. She liked dancing and cooking, as I do, and we both loved cars.

Like my mother Mary, Mireille also could be flamboyant and she loved clothes. When I look at the many pictures my family has shared with me I can see Mireille dressed beautifully with well-chosen accessories for every outfit.

When we met, she had dementia, and although she knew who I was, we were not able to converse to the extent that we could really get to know each other. My brothers and their families have shared their stories and experiences to bring Mireille to life for me. Through these stories, I hear how

Mireille was also a strong mother with a "can-do", positive attitude.

There was a song written in 1944 that I remember my mother and father singing when I was growing up. It was "Ac-cent-Tchu-Ate the Positive" (Eliminate the Negative), written by Harold Arlen and Johnny Mercer. I think my parents took those lyrics to heart and through all their difficulties displayed hope and faith.

My two mothers both experienced many hardships during their lives but they still found joy and gratitude for all that was good. It's a powerful message they passed on to their children.

"I have enough family."

This was my response when the thought of pursuing my birth origins would surface. A cavalier attitude to be sure, but I realize now fear of the unknown was at the heart of that statement.

Now I know you can never have enough people to love. My life is so enriched by the beautiful family I have found. I never expected anything and I have received everything.

Since I met my birth family we talk about our similarities as families.

We love good food and wine and family dinners.

Claude has three sisters; I have three biological brothers and my first loving brother, Brian.

Claude is French and Italian, I am French Canadian.

We live in the same town as our children and two of Claude's sisters and their families.

My birth family all live in the same town in Canada.

When we met my brothers and sisters-in-law, we would talk about how incredible it is that I married a French man and have been so attracted to everything French. I explained that my mother Mary, who was Irish-American, loved everything French, from decorating her home to listening to the language. I took French in high school and as I walked in the door to my house after school, I would often hear my French dialogue records playing on our 1937 Magnavox record player. My mother would listen to them while she was working around the house. I would ask her why, I thought it was funny when I was 14, and she would say,

"I LOVE everything French!"

45

PEACE

When I share my story with people they are sometimes overcome with emotion.

"How did you feel as an adopted child?"

"Did you always want to find your birth mother?"

"Why did it take you so long to look for her?"

Since I have been reunited I really have to bring myself back to what it was like before I found them. I was always curious about my birth mother and her life after giving birth to me.

When my mother would say, "You are French Canadian," I felt proud.

There were times, my birthday and mother's day in particular when I would wonder about my birth mother. What kind of life she was having and if she had other children. All of the same things that I learned she was wondering about me. We both had happy lives, but there was always that missing, unresolved part. Still, life was good and we carried on.

61 years it took me to finally pursue my birth information and reunion. My insistent, inner voice had become louder and

louder and I could no longer sustain my lifelong denial of wanting to know. Little by little I found the courage, to be honest with myself and give up my long-held pretense that knowing my birth family didn't matter.

"I have no family history, I'm adopted." This was my response to every doctor's question about family history. When I was young, I didn't have that many doctor visits. As I've grown older, I see many doctors, and family history has become more and more important in light of discoveries of the link between genetics and the health of each new generation. I am used to not having a history to share with them, and I told my children that I am making the medical history for them. They have medical history from Claude's side of the family, and along with my short history, I felt that would be enough. However, when I was presented with the chance to have my family medical history, I realized that I would love to. So now I know that my birth mother enjoyed very good health throughout her life, but because she smoked, she suffered from emphysema and COPD. My doctor visits since I met my mother have often ended in joyful tears. I was able to tell them about my medical history but not without, as briefly as possible, telling them about finding my birth mother at 61 years of age.

Now that I have met my birth mother, I know that I can never regain what was lost, truly knowing her. We only had four months. Even when my brothers and their wives talk about her that is their experience. She and I have never known what it's like to be mother and daughter. There is so much for me to be grateful for that I cannot linger long on that thought. Four months and I may never have looked into her eyes or held her hands in mine. Now I have three brothers and sisters-in-law, nieces and nephews, and aunts and uncles. I am so happy to belong to this beautiful family, my birth family.

We were together every day of our reunion weekend from April 14 until April 17 when I had to leave and return home. When I told her I was sad to leave her but had to go, she asked, "why?" I explained about work and told her we would come back in three weeks. She said,

"I'll wait for you."

Three weeks was a big promise for her to keep and I prayed she would have the strength.

Often in the most important times of our lives, there are conflicting emotions we have to address and feel. I was sad for many things:

Lost opportunities to really know my birth mother,

Lost opportunities for her to know me and have peace through the years,

And lost opportunities to know my siblings.

But regret serves no purpose.

Instead, I think about the four months we did have. The peace that I was able to bring to her and the peace she gave to me.

So I will be grateful for the unforgettable memories of looking into my birth mother's eyes, telling her I love her, thanking her for giving me life, and her looking back at me, at peace, finally.

"I'll wait for you."

And she did.

"Do you still see your birth family?"

This is one of the first questions I am asked after people hear my story. They wonder if we have been able to maintain the family connection we experienced when we first met.

"Yes, we love spending time together, and have worked around work schedules and other family responsibilities to make sure we see each other."

In "Does Search Always Mean Reunion? The Answer is No," Kathleen Kelly Halverson reports three separate parts to adoption searches.

- Search
- Reunion
- Reconnection

Search does not always lead to reunion and reunion does not always lead to reconnection. The previously mentioned British study from The Guardian notes that some reunions cease after one or two letters or one face-to-face meeting.

Also, one of six new relationships fell apart after one year and 60% ended within eight years.

The American Adoption Congress published: <u>Search and Reunion Etiquette: The Guide Miss Manners Never Wrote</u> by Monica Byres. She writes, "It typically takes as long as five to eight years for the initial reunion to evolve into a natural rhythm." It may progress from normalizing to shared experiences and then to a more fluid back and forth that eases and solidifies with time.

During the ten years since my birth family and I were reunited, we progressed quickly from the reunion to the reconnection phase.

Since we met we have established a pattern of regular visits. Usually, Claude and I go to Chateauguay every year around the time of our April 14 reunion. My brothers and their families visit us on Long Island during the warm weather months when we enjoy the beaches and outdoor entertainment and also in Lake Placid when we are vacationing there. If they are not able to come and see us in Lake Placid, we sometimes drive to Chateauguay for a visit with them after our Lake Placid vacation.

In October 2011, just six months after meeting my Canadian family they came to Long Island to visit us. Guy and Line, Pierre and his daughters Anyssa and Lydia, Yves and Angela, and their children Sabrina and Joey drove from Canada to spend a weekend with us at our house. We were very excited for them to meet our New York family and friends but especially happy for them to spend time with our children Eric, Elise, and Mike, and our grandchildren.

There would be nine overnight guests so the linens and towels were prepared and ready, and we set up the air mattresses in the family room for the four teenagers.

Next, we considered our menus and what we could

prepare ahead so we would be able to enjoy their company and not spend too much time with meal preparation. The shopping was done two days before their arrival and enough meals were prepared the day before and stored in the refrigerator.

Dad's friend Jean loved a shopping challenge. When my family was coming from Canada for their first visit to my home in Huntington, I told Jean I was looking online and calling stores to find a Canadian flag. "Team Canada" was arriving in just a few days and even if I found one online, it would not arrive in time. (Shortly after Claude and I met my Canadian family, he started referring to them as "Team Canada" and we as "Team USA.") I wanted to fly the flag next to my mailbox for them to see as they approached our house for the first time. Also, I wanted my neighbors to know my family was coming.

Telling Jean was all I had to do and she was on the job. She made phone calls to stores all over Long Island, went online, and found Canadian flags but they would not arrive in time. She then researched the various online companies and their warehouse locations and found a warehouse about 45 minutes from where we live. She called them and they said they could not sell her a flag because they are not a retail store. Not willing to give up, she proceeded to tell my story about why we needed this flag. After hearing our touching reunion story, they agreed to sell her the flag. Jean and Dad wasted no time and immediately hopped in her hybrid Honda and set out to locate this warehouse. It was not easy to find, tucked away in the back of a building. They had to climb a full flight of stairs located on the outside of the building leading to a single door at the top. In they stepped into one large room filled with large tables piled high with fabrics of many colors, sizes, and patterns. Once in, she quickly explained who she was and they sold her the beautiful Canadian flag that we display for every visit from my family. Since then my Canadian family displays the American flag when we visit there.

The morning of their arrival we were so happy to put the Canadian flag out by the mailbox, did a little last-minute fussing around the house, and then waited for their arrival.

No one in my Canadian family had ever been to Long Island and we understood the nerves of steel you need to quickly navigate the bridges and parkways as you make your way onto Long Island. Cars and trucks driving above the speed limit careen past with no regard for someone unfamiliar with the route. It is easy to make a wrong turn and no easy way to right that wrong turn. No one had GPS at the time but they did have very explicit directions from us.

Close to their arrival time I was pacing back and forth in the living room and looking out our picture window at the driveway hoping they had arrived. Finally, I heard the engines of the cars as they pulled in, and Claude and I ran out to the driveway to greet them.

They were tired from the long drive so we helped them bring in their things and showed them where they would be staying. It was a beautiful October day so we took them outside to the deck where they could stretch their legs and relax with a cold beverage and some appetizers. We could see that it was going to be a beautiful autumn sunset so we asked them if they would like us to take them for a sunset cruise on our boat. It involved a short car ride to our marina at the Harbor Boating Club in Huntington Harbor where our boat is docked and everyone agreed to go. It was a perfect evening with calm waters and clear skies as we motored out of the harbor and into the Long Island Sound where we viewed a breathtaking sunset. Along the way, we pointed out some

Huntington landmarks and coves where Claude and I have enjoyed more than fifty summers of boating.

Nieces and Nephew – Anyssa, Sabrina, Lydia, and Joey

Nieces and Nephew – Anyssa, Sabrina, Lydia, and Joey

When we were planning for the family visit, we knew we wanted all our New York family and friends to meet my new Canadian family. Realizing our house couldn't hold fifty guests, we reserved our boat clubhouse in Huntington. Our family and friends who cheered us on and were with us through every twist and turn of the journey to find my birth mother were there. There were tables set up in the large open room off the kitchen of the clubhouse and more tables outside on the front porch which overlooked the marina and Huntington Harbor. It was another beautiful day and everyone could enjoy spending time outside. Throughout the afternoon I flitted from one group to the next, making sure introductions were made; witnessing the ease of the conversations, and listening to friends express their condolences to my brothers for the loss of our mother and relief that we had been reunited just in time. Everyone could feel the love and joy that day and when we left to go back to our house we still had plenty of time to relax and relive the events of the day. The following day they were leaving but we knew it would not be long before we were together again.

Claude and I, Martine and Anthony, and Corinne were going to The Whiteface Lodge in Lake Placid in December for a week; one of the eight weeks in a year that is available to us as fractional owners at the Lodge. We told my brothers and their families that we would be there and asked if they could come and enjoy some vacation time with us.

It wasn't their first time in Lake Placid, but it was the first time they visited the Lodge so we enjoyed taking them to some of our favorite places. You can see Mirror Lake in the background of our group picture. It is less than a two and a half hour drive from Chateauguay, Canada to Lake Placid and now my family meets us there as often as they can.

Front Row: Lydia, Anyssa, Joey, Sabrina Second Row: Anthony, Martine, Corinne, Eileen, Pierre, Angela Back Row: Claude, Guy, Line, Yves

On April 14, 2012, the one-year anniversary of meeting my birth mother Mireille, my brothers, and their families invited us to visit for the weekend in Chateauguay. We would stay with Yves and Angela, Sabrina who was 16, and Joey who was 14. Eric and his son Cash (4) drove with Claude and me in our car. Elise and Mike, Jackson (5), Owen (3) and Evelyn (14 months) drove in their van. Our grandchildren were too young to understand exactly who our new relatives are but when we arrived at Yves and Angela's house, they saw play-doh set out on the table for them to play with and cucumbers, a favorite of theirs, to eat. Sabrina and Joey were there and started playing with them right away. You could feel and see the excitement of the children as Sabrina and Joey drew them in with games and art projects. By the end of the weekend, they helped the children make and decorate little cardboard treasure boxes which they took home as a special memento.

A few hours later, Guy and Line, Pierre and his daughters, Anyssa and Lydia, Guy's daughter Josee and her daughter Joelle, who is 5, arrived. We had appetizers and a champagne toast to Mireille and our one-year anniversary. It was especially nice to spend time with Joey and Sabrina, Anyssa, and Lydia. They have grown up together and are close cousins. Together they kept all the young children happy.

The next day we woke early with the children and after breakfast, we left for Guy and Line's house to spend the day. Pierre was there with Anyssa and Lydia. The kids had fun playing with everyone outside on the deck, followed by a walk with them to a local park and playground.

Guy and Line prepared a delicious barbeque lunch accompanied by some of Angela's side dish specialties. After lunch, Guy, Pierre, Yves, Claude, and I took a walk from Guy and Line's house to the cemetery to see our mother's headstone. It was the first time I saw it completed. It is beautifully finished and engraved with a lovely delicate rose, her favorite flower.

It was a very special day with my Canadian family, my children, and their children, and as with most meaningful days, it went too quickly. It was time for us to go back to Yves and Angela's house, and there were many hugs and kisses and expressions of gratitude for the wonderful day we had together as a family.

We felt so close to them after such a special weekend, and on Monday, after many thanks and hugs for Angela and Yves, Sabrina, and Joey, we left for home.

What words should I choose to describe my feelings about a weekend when my children and grandchildren met my birth family, their blood relatives? Incredible, amazing, rewarding, and unforeseen just a year and a half ago, this introduction felt so natural. We love them and I am extremely proud to call them my family.

Growing up as an adoptee I didn't dwell long on the type of person and family I was born into. Even though the possibility of being descended from unsavory people would sometimes sneak into my thoughts, I would quiet those thoughts and believe they were good people. What I am overjoyed to say now is that if I had to pick a birth family, it would be them.

In July 2012, Claude's dad Francesco, who was a second father to me, turned 90 years old. We had a big party for him at the Whiteface Lodge in Lake Placid and some family members came down from Chateauguay to celebrate with us. Dad was so happy for me when I found my birth family, and they could feel the love from him and our family towards them. He and Jean were at the Lodge whenever any of my brothers and families would visit. Dad, having been fluent in French from his years in Paris, would sometimes speak French to them. We also had many visits from my Canadian family to our house in Huntington. Dad and Jean would join us whenever they visited.

Dad passed away in April 2013, just two years after I was reunited with my family. His funeral was in Huntington at St. Patrick's Church. None of us expected my brothers to be able to make the long trip to Huntington; however, Pierre called to say he would be coming. Since Guy and Yves were working and unable to take time from work, Pierre would be making the trip alone. Claude and I were very moved by his willingness to represent and express condolences from my brothers and their families.

Pierre and Diane have been together since they met in 2017. She has become part of the family and is loved by all. In 2017 Claude and I kept our boat out in Montauk on Long Island for the summer months. Montauk is about two and a half hours east from our home in Huntington Station. We met Diane when the family visited us in Lake Placid early in 2017 and Pierre and Diane told us they would like to take a road trip to visit us in July. We were thrilled to welcome them and appreciated their sense of adventure to make the long drive out to

Montauk for a sleepover on the boat. As we have learned they love to take road trips and after they left us in Montauk they went on to drive to many towns on the east coast.

Claude, Diane, and Pierre on our boat in Montauk, NY 2017

Claude and I kept in touch with Uncle Yvon and Aunt Pauline from 2011 until 2019 when we received notice that they had passed away within two weeks of each other. During one of our last visits with them, Uncle Yvon told us that when he turned ninety he suddenly lost his strength and was experiencing many medical problems.

Eileen, Aunt Pauline, and Uncle Yvon

"I don't know what happened. I was fine up until 90 and now I no longer have the good health I enjoyed all these years."

In one of his emails, he expressed his dismay at the aging he was experiencing. When he was 90 he was very active with bowling, ping pong, and swimming. When he turned 91 in September 2018 he fell and hurt his right knee. He said that after that,

"I became an old man of 91, hurt, tired, and trying to rest and recover."

This was sad for us to read because he was full of life and talking about his many interests during our visits. It was a blessing for him to have enjoyed a long healthy life but his mind was outlasting his body. Even with his physical problems we were able to communicate by email. His last email to us was in December 2018, and he wrote,

"Be well and enjoy life. Love and kisses, Old Uncle Yvon and Aunt Pauline."

Even though it was my last correspondence from him, we sent cards letting him know we were thinking of him and Aunt Pauline.

Aunt Pauline was not well for many years but was able to enjoy her family. She was an avid reader and whenever we visited I would ask her about her most recent book. She didn't speak English but she was able to let me know which ones were her favorites. Uncle Yvon would translate what we wanted to say.

In July 2019 we received an email from the family that Uncle Yvon had passed away and we asked them to let us know when the funeral would be. Then, within two weeks Aunt Pauline also passed away. Their children decided to have a funeral honoring both their parents on August 18, 2019, and we made plans to be there.

When we visited Uncle Yvon and Aunt Pauline they would proudly talk about their four children and share pictures, but we hadn't met them. During the funeral services, we had the opportunity to tell them how we loved our visits with their wonderful parents. Uncle Yvon was always clearly happy to see me and would smile as he told me how much I reminded him of his dearly loved sister, my mother Mireille. Now after the deaths of Uncle Yvon and my mother Mireille, there was only one sister and brother left of those siblings. All four siblings have children, my first cousins, and I met them all that day.

My first cousins - 2019

In particular, my Aunt Lise's daughter Monica was there and we spoke for a good part of the afternoon. (I met Aunt Lise at Mireille's funeral in August 2011. Sadly, Aunt Lise, Monica's mother, passed away in May 2020 from the Covid 19 virus.)

Monica told me how much she loved my mother from when she was a young girl. Then she told me,

"When I was born I was named Monique."

I replied,

"When I was born I was named Monique!"

Monica's mother Lise was the younger sister of my mother Mireille by two years, and some in the family agree that Lise grew up in the shadow of her older sister. They were very different. Mireille was outgoing and Lise was reserved. For many years, off and on, they were estranged.

Prior to meeting my cousin Monica, my brothers and family told me there was another Monique in the family, born to my mother's sister Lise about 10 years after I was born. It seemed curious to me that Mireille's sister would name her baby girl the same name as the baby girl her sister Mireille gave up for adoption. I asked Monica,

"Do you think your mother knew about me?"

"I don't think so," she said. "During the year that Mireille was pregnant with you, my mother Lise was living and working for another family as a companion. I think Mireille was living with an aunt during her pregnancy."

I imagine I was a well-kept secret, to most of the family. My reunion with Mireille may have been the first time many family members learned of my existence.

In all the stories and reminiscences of my brothers and other family members about my birth mother, I look for glimpses of myself, her daughter. Since the reunion, our physical resemblance to each other is obvious to family and friends who knew Mireille well.

Even though mothers and daughters can be alike or different in looks or personalities, we are family, and threads of commonality will bind us together. Although my adoptive mother Mary and I didn't share any physical resemblance, we had strong emotional ties and her carefully taught life lessons guide me to this day. Nature vs. nurture, the debate goes on.

It has been ten years since I was reunited with my birth mother and family. Up until early 2020, we saw each other four or five times a year. However, as I write this in January 2021, we are living through the Covid-19 pandemic and the United States/Canadian border will be closed indefinitely. Now we stay in touch and maintain our connection through zoom calls, emails, messenger, and WhatsApp texting. We can't wait until we can visit them in person again.

.

Jean Gilles and Mireille – June 1951

Eileen and Claude – September 1971

Eileen and Claude

Owen, Mike, Elise, Jackson, Eileen, Eric, Claude, Evelyn, Cash

ACKNOWLEDGMENTS

My biggest thanks and gratitude go to Claude with whom I shared my thoughts and plans while writing this memoir and who has consistently made time to listen and provide feedback. He is my first editor, advocate, and my very important I.T. person. I'm lucky to have him as my partner in life and all its adventures. I could not have realized this dream of writing my memoir without his support.

Thank you to our children Eric and Elise and son-in-law Mike for their encouragement and interest in this project and for being the loving people they are. They and their children are everything to us and make us proud to be parents.

Thanks to my entire American family and close friends, in particular Claude's father and Jean, his sisters and brother-in-law, and my brother Brian's children who were engaged with the progression of my search from the beginning, journeying with me through every twist and turn as the story unfolded. A special thanks to our dear friends Marilyn and Rich who generously took the time to read and respond to the manuscript.

My Canadian family has done everything possible to welcome me into the family over these past ten years and I am so proud to be included. They read the manuscript and shared important comments for accuracy. I can't wait to experience all the future has to hold as we continue our lives as a family together.

Nadia, our diligent and kind Canadian social worker, sensitive to my birth mother's advanced age and declining health, prioritized my case to assure the best possible outcome. She was the voice of hope through my emotional journey.

My friends and colleagues at the two primary schools where I taught were caring and generous with their hugs throughout the ups and downs of my search.

Our Whiteface Lodge friends in Lake Placid loved my story from the beginning, listening, cheering me on, and, at times, crying tears of joy and sadness as I shared new developments.

I also want to thank the incredible writers, and now friends, of my library writing group who have provided encouragement and inspiration from my first meeting with them. They have been invaluable to me.

And finally, thanks to the Long Island Writers Club where I met several authors whose books were published by Stephanie Larkin, owner of Red Penguin Books, and who made me believe I too could bring my story to publication.

ABOUT THE AUTHOR

Eileen Resta is a retired primary school Teacher and Reading Specialist with a Master's Degree in Literacy. Although reading and writing has been an integral part of her life for as long as she can remember, writing a memoir was unexpected. It was her experience as an adult adoptee seeking information about her biological background that led to unforeseen miraculous events and ultimately her decision to write this book.

Eileen lives on Long Island, New York with her husband, Claude. Their children and grandchildren live nearby and this book provides the missing link in their family history. She enjoys traveling, hiking, boating, and cooking, but mostly she loves any time spent with her American and Canadian families.